Hornswoggled

Also by Donis Casey
The Old Buzzard Had It Coming

To receive a free catalog of Poisoned Pen Press titles, please contact us in one of the following ways:

Phone: 1-800-421-3976
Facsimile: 1-480-949-1707
Email: info@poisonedpenpress.com
Website: www.poisonedpenpress.com

Poisoned Pen Press
6962 E. First Ave. Ste. 103
Scottsdale, AZ 85251

Hornswoggled

An Alafair Tucker Mystery

Donis Casey

Poisoned Pen Press

Poisoned
Pen
Press

Copyright © 2006 by Donis A. Casey

First Edition 2006

10 9 8 7 6 5 4 3 2 1

Library of Congress Catalog Card Number: 2006900733

ISBN: 1-59058-309-4   Hardcover

Poisoned Pen Press
6962 E. First Ave., Ste. 103
Scottsdale, AZ 85251
www.poisonedpenpress.com
info@poisonedpenpress.com

Printed in the United States of America

This book is dedicated to two pillars of the house:
My mother-in-law, Mabel Koozer, whom I never knew,
and my sister, Carol DeWelt, who lived it with me.

Her children arise up and call her blessed:
her husband also, and he praiseth her.
Prov. 31: 28

Acknowledgments

Many thanks to all the people at Poisoned Pen Press; Geetha and Jessica, the incomparable Monty, and my friend Nan, who traveled with me hand in hand. And of course a deep bow of gratitude to Robert Rosenwald and Barbara Peters, without whom none of this would have happened. You know you have a good editor when her suggestions make you slap your forehead and exclaim, "What was I thinking?"

So many people contributed to and helped me with my research that I can't possibly name them all here, but it would be remiss of me not to mention Rebecca Burke, who gave me her grandmother's bumblebee song, and my cousin Don Wagner, for the fascinating background on the Old Wire Road that passed through Lone Elm, Arkansas. My childish feet trod that ground a hundred times, yet little did I know.

Special thanks to Carolyn Hart, master author, for her warmhearted generosity and guidance to the lively Oklahoma literary scene. Don't be modest, now. I'd have been lost in my own country without you.

As always, my love and thanks to my beloved family and friends, my bedrock support crew. And to Max, who stands alone.

The Family Tree
March 1913

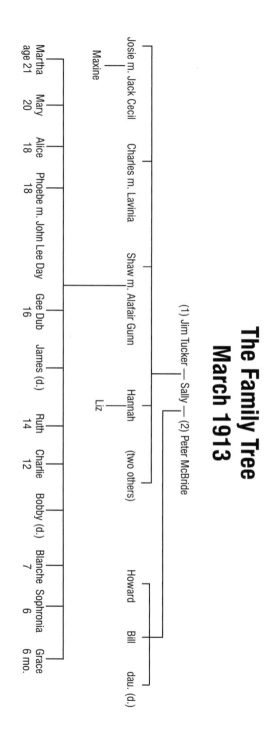

Chapter One

Something bad was bound to happen. It was just that kind of hot, humid, Oklahoma July day, with a gritty wind that blew everything awry. Fifteen-year-old George Washington Tucker, known as Gee Dub, hunkered on the grassy, overgrown banks of Cane Creek, grimly hanging on to his fishing pole, trying to ignore the sweltering heat and the clouds of gnats, mosquitos, and various other disgusting critters who were trying to fly up his nose and into his eyes and drink the salt off of his sweat-slick skin. The hot wind was maddening, the way it blew first out of the north, then out of the southwest, then died and dropped his damp, black curls into his eyes. At least when it picked up again, it blew the gnats away for a few seconds. And it wasn't even quite noon, that was the sad thing.

Normally Gee Dub loved fishing, since he was a contemplative boy. He loved thinking about what his mother was going to do with the little perch or crappie, or occasional catfish, that he would catch. Oh, how good they would taste, rolled in cornmeal and fried quickly in bacon grease until the tender white flesh was encased in a golden crust. Having to eat the fish slowly, so slowly, and chew so carefully to avoid swallowing one of the hundreds of tiny bones only enhanced the dining experience.

But today, the joy of fishing was ruined not just by the worrisome weather, but by Gee Dub's eleven-year-old brother, Charlie, and Charlie's ever-present canine companion, Charlie-dog.

Charlie-boy had insisted on going swimming. Gee Dub had sent him and his dog as far downstream as he could and still keep an eye on them, but it was no good. All his splashing and jumping and hollering had spooked the fish, and there would be no fried fish for dinner. Gee Dub was bereft.

He could hear Charlie yelling at him, "Look at me, Gee, look at me!" But Gee Dub didn't look. He didn't want to encourage the boy. Charlie was climbing up into a young cottonwood, crawling out onto a wayward branch that hung over the creek, and dropping himself off into the middle of the water with a whoop. He must have done it ten times, with the dog running up and down, barking the whole time, and Gee Dub had just about had enough. The weather was getting hotter, the fishing was bad, and Charlie was driving him right 'round the bend. He pulled in his line.

Suddenly there was a crack of noise as loud as a rifle shot, and a splash, and Gee Dub leaped where he sat. He looked downstream, wide eyed. Charlie was nowhere to be seen. The yellow shepherd was leaping and barking frantically on the bank. Gee Dub jumped to his feet and scanned the creek bank anxiously. No skinny, naked little boy. Just a fairly large cottonwood branch floating away from him in the middle of the water. Gee Dub's heart fell into his stomach, and he started running toward the broken tree, hollering for Charlie.

He was already barefoot, so he didn't have to worry about taking off his shoes when he dove headlong into the murky water near the last place he had seen his brother. The water wasn't very deep, but it was impossible to see anything, so he groped along the slimy bottom with his hands, until he couldn't stay under anymore and exploded to the surface with a gasp. He flung his dark hair out of his eyes with a toss of his head and scanned the bank again. No boy, but the dog had joined him in the water and was dog paddling around in a circle close to a tangle of cottonwood roots. Gee Dub struck out toward the dog.

"Charlie!" he yelled.

Out from under the cottonwood roots, next to the bank, a boy's voice responded, "Here, Gee Dub."

Gee Dub's arm paused in mid-stroke, and he grew faint with relief right there in the water. Just as he reached the undercut bank, Charlie's blond head popped up from under the root tangle, practically in Gee Dub's face. Gee Dub was so glad that the child was alive that, for a second, he forgot to be angry and reached out to hug him. When his hands touched Charlie's bare shoulders, he shook him instead.

"What in the turkey feet do you think you're doing…"

"Gee Dub," Charlie gasped, "there's somebody dead down there."

"You're lucky it ain't you, you punkin-head," Gee Dub spat, too angry to listen. He climbed onto the bank and tried to heave the boy up after him, but Charlie resisted.

"No, no," Charlie sputtered, as he crawled out of the water on his own. "Listen to me. I'm telling you there's a drowneded woman stuck up there under them branches. I was on the tree and the limb broke and I fell down there and I felt her long hair and her face!"

Gee Dub hesitated. By this time Charlie was out of the creek and dancing with excitement on the grass. Gee Dub, sitting on the ground with his feet still in the water, wiped his hair out of his face. "You're just imagining things."

"I ain't, I ain't, I ain't," Charlie exclaimed hysterically. "Go down and see! I swear it's true. Go down and see for yourself, Gee."

Charlie's manic certainty gave Gee Dub pause, and he grabbed the boy's arm to settle him down. "All right," he soothed. "I'll dive under there just to hush you up, even though it's probably just a old dead goat and I'll get the pox or something and it'll be all your fault."

"Gee Dub!" Charlie wailed.

"All right! Mercy! You stay right here and don't twitch a toe. I mean it, now." He looked back over his shoulder at the shepherd. "Dog," he ordered imperiously, "you watch this here boy."

Gee Dub slipped back into the water, took a deep breath, and ducked under the roof of cottonwood roots. He could see nothing, of course. The water was a grey-green swirl of dappled light and shade, cooler under the branches. The slimy mud squished between his bare toes. It was just the kind of sheltered place in which a big old catfish would love to lurk, or a nest of water moccasins, and Gee Dub shuddered in spite of himself. He swung his arms tentatively through the water a couple of times, hitting a branch or two and the muddy bank. Then his fingers passed through what he at first thought was floating vegetation. Fine floating weeds. He swung his hand back, and his fingers tangled. Hair. He resisted an urge to gasp, just releasing a couple of bubbles. He brought his fingers to his face, close enough to confirm that they were entangled in what looked like long, dark hair. Please, Jesus, let it be some old mule tail, he prayed, even though he knew it wasn't. Nervously, he let his hand follow the hair through the dark water, until it lighted on a smooth, cool dome. His heart was thumping so hard that it hurt. He felt a forehead, eyebrows, ears, a nose.

Gee Dub backed himself out from under the roots as fast as he could move and flung himself up to the surface. He took a couple of gulps of air to calm himself. "Charlie," he said evenly, "run home as fast as you can and get Daddy."

"I was right," Charlie declared. He was breathless with excitement.

"I think so," Gee Dub admitted. "Now, run! Run!"

But Charlie was already ten yards across the field, with the dog at his heels.

～～～～

An hour later, Gee Dub was standing in the creek up to his chest beside the cottonwood roots, waiting for his father and the sheriff to come to the surface and either confirm or deny his find. On the bank, Gee Dub could see Charlie, wrapped in such a big blanket that he was nothing but a tousled head and dirty splayed feet, watching eagerly. Standing close behind Charlie was their mother, Alafair. Gee Dub couldn't see her face well, since it was shaded by a blue poke bonnet, but she was standing stiffly with one hand on Charlie's shoulder and one hand on her hip. The front of her calico apron was bulging with Gee Dub's latest sibling.

The three watchers stirred when Shaw Tucker surfaced calmly, followed by his cousin, Sheriff Scott Tucker. Shaw wiped his hair back with both hands and used two fingers to flick the water out of his drooping black mustache. He turned toward the bank.

"Charlie, Martha is coming up the path now with a couple of mules. You run to meet her and ride back to the house and bring me a length of rope."

"Is it a body, Daddy?" Charlie said.

"Looks like it."

Charlie turned to run, but Alafair caught his arm. "Put your britches on first," she instructed. "I don't think the neighbor ladies would appreciate seeing the same naked little jay bird that come running up to the house just lately."

Charlie sputtered, then laughed a little with embarrassment and rushed off into the bushes to retrieve his overalls.

"Ain't Martha bringing rope?" Gee Dub asked his father.

"She is." Shaw kept his voice low. "But I want him away when we bring up the body."

"Is it bad?" Gee Dub wondered with dread.

"Don't know, Gee," the sheriff told him. "Bad enough."

After Charlie was off and Gee Dub's oldest sister, twenty-year-old Martha, had arrived riding on the extra mule with the equipment, the two men struggled for several minutes to free the tightly wedged body from its prison of roots. Finally, after hacking away some of the growth with an ax, the men managed to pull the poor soul free and manhandle her sodden form up onto the bank. Alafair, unwilling to expose her coming baby to a shock, turned her back and refused to look.

"Is it bad, like Gee Dub wondered?" she asked Martha, who was standing next to her mother and watching with an expression that was a mixture of interest and repulsion.

"Like Scott said, it's bad enough, Ma. Her hands... Well, it looks like the fish were beginning to nibble on her fingers a little bit, but her face is all of a piece, still. She's puffy-faced, real white skin, purple marks on her face. I can't tell if she's bruised or if the purpling is from the water. She's a big woman. Hard to say how old she is. She does have lots of long brown hair all loose around her shoulders. She's dressed kind of nice, in a blue shirtwaist with a dark pattern on the front, and some kind of big white button."

"Can you tell who she is?"

There was a moment's silence while Martha studied the bloated face. Then Alafair felt her straighten. "Why, Ma," Martha exclaimed, "it's Miz Kelley!"

In spite of herself, Alafair glanced back over her shoulder. "Miz Kelley? The barber's wife? Miz Kelley has drowned in Cane Creek?"

Scott and Shaw were bending over the body in a cursory examination, and Scott sat back on his heels when he overheard Alafair's question. "This woman didn't drown, Alafair," he observed. "This dark pattern Martha mentioned is a bloodstain, and the white button is a knife with a carved bone handle, sticking right out of her chest. Looks like she's been stabbed in the heart."

Chapter Two

Mr. Ulises Bellows, pastor of the Christian Church of Boynton, Oklahoma, stepped up to the graveside, and the mourners fell silent. "Brothers and Sisters," Mr. Bellows began, "we're here today, the ninth day of July, in the year of the Lord, 1912, to mourn the passing of our sister in Christ, Louise, wife of Walter Kelley. Sister Louise's short life came to a sad end, but we cannot judge her heart. Only God can do that. We may question why our sister was taken from us in such a way, but we rest assured that even this is part of God's plan, and on the day of Glory, all things shall be revealed."

Alafair Tucker stood in the back of the small group with two of her daughters and surveyed the congregation while Mr. Bellows spoke of death and the hope of resurrection for Louise Kelley. Alafair hadn't known Mrs. Kelley all that well, but since the poor woman's body was found on their property, she felt honor bound to attend the funeral. Shaw and the boys, who had actually done the finding, were standing closer to the front, nearer Louise's family.

On the near side of the grave, Alafair could see the back of the widower's head. When he turned to look at a well-wisher and Alafair could see his face, she thought he looked stunned. It must have been quite a shock for him to be called home from a trip to Kansas City because of the brutal murder of his wife. The Kelleys had been in Boynton for about five years. All Alafair knew of them was that they had moved to the area from Kansas City because Louise's sister lived on a farm west of town, and Louise had wanted to be near her.

On the far side of the grave, this very sister, Nellie Tolland, stood almost collapsed with grief, weeping profusely on her husband's shoulder. The husband had been weeping, too, judging from his eyes. He gazed morosely into the grave where Louise's coffin lay.

Alafair recognized a number of the people who had attended the funeral; there was Mrs. Bellows, and two or three people that Alafair knew to be neighbors of the Kelleys, besides many of Mr. Kelley's barbershop regulars. Standing far in the back was Sheriff Scott Tucker, eyeing the crowd, looking for a murderer, Alafair expected. After the short graveside service was over, and the mourners were filing slowly forward to have a word with the bereaved, Alafair turned to walk back to the Masonic Hall where their wagon was parked.

"I'll be along directly, Mama," her daughter Alice said to her. "I want to offer my condolences to Mr. Kelley."

Mildly surprised, Alafair paused and looked up at the tall eighteen-year-old from under the brim of her best hat with the cherries on the band. She understood why Martha had come to the funeral with her, but Alice hadn't known the Kelleys at all. None of Alafair's other daughters had shown any interest in coming. "Go ahead, then," she said to Alice. "Try to round up your daddy and the boys directly. I'm getting tired of standing. Martha and me will be back at the Hall."

"Yes, Mama," Alice said, and hurried off as Alafair and Martha turned to leave the cemetery. As they passed out of the gate, they walked by a young woman standing close by the fence. She was engrossed in the proceedings going on inside the cemetery, and paid Alafair and Martha little mind as they walked by her. Alafair, however, eyed the girl closely, from her mess of nondescript colored hair to her bare brown feet. She was sure she had never seen this young woman before and considered speaking to her, but before she could approach, the girl slid her a shy glance and moved around behind a slim elm, obviously in no mood for conversation. Alafair suddenly changed her mind about leaving the funeral. Something about the sight of that girl who didn't want to be spoken to set Alafair's senses to quivering. "Let's go back in," she said to Martha.

Martha paused when her mother did and gave her a quizzical look. "I thought you were tired."

Alafair walked back inside the cemetery grounds with Martha at her heels. "I'll just sit here a spell," she said, parking herself on a little bench which was situated beside the path just inside the gate. "You can go on back to the church hall if you've a mind."

Martha sat down beside her, intrigued but not surprised by her mother's reversal. "No, I'll stay here with you."

Alafair patted Martha's knee and turned her attention back to the service, which was finally breaking up. Walter Kelley was now standing off to one side, surrounded by well-wishers. He was a popular man in town, the busiest barber, the owner of two or three town buildings, as well as the proud owner of one of the town's growing number of automobiles—a shiny black Ford touring car. He also had electric lights and indoor plumbing in his white house on Elm Street, and a telephone in his barber shop that he would let anyone use, free for local calls, though the town was small enough that it was probably easier to holler out the window. For long distance calls, most people paid the barber a nickel. He was a young man to be so well-off, Alafair thought. Late twenties or early thirties, tall and good-looking. But he worked hard, Alafair admitted to herself, even if he was too glib and a bit "hail-fellow-well-met" for her taste. He looked ill-at-ease and at odds with himself now, though, with all the people crowding around him, like he'd rather be anywhere in the world but here.

Alafair had lost sight of the other bereaved party, Louise's sister Nellie, and she cast a glance around the crowd. She finally saw the woman, still supported by her husband, walking down the path toward her. Like other local farm people, the Tollands were known around town, but that was all. They bought their supplies at the Boynton Mercantile. They had taken out a loan at the First National Bank. They went to the Baptist Church, which Alafair did not, so she knew them only slightly. As far as she knew, they paid their debts and got by. When they passed her on their way out of the cemetery, Alafair nodded at them. Mrs. Tolland didn't seem to notice her, but Ned Tolland nodded back.

Nellie suddenly stopped in her tracks, and her husband, unprepared, stumbled. Alafair followed the woman's gaze and was not surprised to see it riveted on the half-hidden girl outside the fence. There was a long moment of silence as Nellie stared at the girl and the girl stared back, and Alafair stared at them both. Finally, Nellie Tolland's face screwed up with distaste and she spat on the ground. Without a word, she and her husband turned around and left the cemetery another way. The girl didn't move.

Martha made a little sound of surprise, but Alafair's attention was already back on the barber, who had extricated himself from his knot of well-wishers and was trudging their way with his eyes on the ground and his hands in his pockets. He touched his hat brim as he passed the two women on the bench.

"Miz Tucker," he said softly. "Miz Martha."

"Our prayers are with you, Mr. Kelley," Alafair said to him.

"Thank you," he responded. He took one more step, then froze as he caught sight of the girl. His right hand came out of his pocket and unconsciously covered his heart, as though the surprise was just too much. He turned toward the east exit, but paused when he saw Ned and Nellie Tolland's retreating backs. He looked desperate for a moment, trapped, but he recovered quickly and smiled at Alafair and Martha. "I'm glad y'all come," he said, then turned around and walked back toward the grave site. Alafair looked back over the fence, but the girl was gone.

"Well, that's strange," Martha observed. "Who do you suspect she was, to cause the family such distress?"

"That's a good question, honey," Alafair replied.

~~~

Shaw listened to the tale of the mysterious woman with interest as he steered the team of mules down the road toward their farm. He cast a glance at his dark-haired wife sitting in the buckboard seat next to him, and smiled when she finished her story. He knew that no one was more sensitive to disturbances of the heart than Alafair. "And just what do you make of all these goings-on, darlin'?"

"I don't know, Shaw," she admitted. "But there's a story here that we don't know nothing about, that's for sure. Could that gal have anything to do with Miz Kelley's murder?"

"Scott told me that as far as he's been able to find out to now, Miz Kelley was last seen alive in the company of a young fellow, the day before she turned up in Cane Creek. He didn't mention anything about a girl."

"Do you suppose Scott saw her standing there by the fence?"

"Scott don't miss much," Shaw assured her.

"Maybe we should mention it to him just in case."

Shaw laughed in spite of himself. "Don't get yourself all fretted, honey," he admonished. "I'll say something to Scott next time I see him, but I'll bet you he will have already asked Kelley and the Tollands about her."

"I just don't want that poor woman's murderer to get away."

"He won't," Shaw reassured.

As Shaw spoke, one of the mules sidestepped and the left front wagon wheel ran over something with a noisy bump. Charlie jumped up from where he was seated in the back of the wagon next to Martha, Alice, and Gee Dub. He leaned over the side behind his father's back to scan the road. "It's a shoe, Daddy!" he exclaimed.

"A shoe?" Alafair repeated.

"Stop the wagon, Daddy," Charlie begged. "I'll fetch it."

Shaw obliged, and Charlie leaped out of the wagon onto the road as the rest of the kids stood up for a better look. The Tuckers' dogs had been following the wagon, and as soon as Charlie hit the ground, all three dashed to his side for a sniff and a better look. Charlie ran around behind the wagon and scooped up the object, then darted over to the side of the road a few feet back. "Here's the other one," he called. "Hey, maybe the dogs can track them back to whoever lost them! Come here, dogs." Crook and Buttercup, the hunting hounds, and Charlie-dog, the kids' pet, pressed around the boy and snuffled eagerly at the shoe. Charlie-dog had never been much of a tracker, so was more interested in trying to get Charlie-boy to play. But the two hunting dogs knew their business and set about immediately to pick up a scent.

The people in the wagon watched with interest for a few moments as the dogs methodically swept back and forth across the road, noses to the ground, running a few yards afield, then back to the road.

"Them dogs can't find a scent," Gee Dub said, as they circled back and forth.

Charlie shook his head impatiently. "Wait a minute."

"No, Charlie," Alafair admonished. "Come on back up here. There's no trail for the dogs to find, and we have to get home."

Resigned, Charlie whistled sharply, then trotted back to the wagon with the dogs wagging and panting around him. He handed the shoes up to his father. Shaw passed them over to Alafair before he hauled the boy back up into the wagon by one arm, then picked up the reins.

Charlie thrust himself between his parents on the wagon seat. "Whose shoes are they, Mama?" he asked.

"Don't know, son," Alafair told him. "Well, look here, Shaw. It's a perfectly good pair of men's dress shoes. And right out in the middle of the road! Look almost new, except that this run-over one has been chewed on by some critter."

"One was in the road, Mama," Charlie corrected her. "The other was way up under a bush to the side of the road."

"Somebody must have lost them out of a wagon," Shaw speculated. "They look expensive. Somebody is mighty sorry he lost those."

"Can I have them, Daddy?" Charlie asked.

"You'd have to grow a bunch to be able to wear those," Shaw told him with a laugh.

"How about me, Daddy?" Gee Dub asked from the back.

"They look to be too big for you, too, son. Even too big for me, I think."

"We're just going to hold them for whoever lost them," Alafair assured them firmly. "I'll ask Hattie at the Mercantile to post a notice."

"What if nobody claims them?" Charlie wondered.

"Well, they're too good to waste," Alafair admitted. "One of you boys will have to get down to growing big feet." She placed the shoes on the floor of the buckboard and Charlie fell back into his place beside his brother. Alafair shook her head. "Mysteries by the bushel," she observed to herself. She looked over at Shaw. "You know, this has been a strange couple of days. I got a funny feeling about it all."

Shaw looked at her askance. "Uh-oh," he teased. "Sounds like you think God is trying to tell you something again."

Alafair took the jibe good naturedly. "Oh, don't worry. There's not a thing that's happened in this last week that has anything to do with me or mine."

"I hope it stays that way," Shaw said.

"So do I," Alafair seconded, in all sincerity.

Chapter Three

Kelley's Barber Shop was doing a booming business on this Saturday before Easter in the year 1913. Besides the need to get the top trimmed and the sides shaved for the holiday, the men from town and the surrounding farms had plenty to discuss. Cotton futures looked to be unchanged. The price of crude oil was up. You could count on that. March had been cooler than normal, thus far. The new president had just been in office less than a month, not long enough to judge him rightly. He was, after all, a Democrat, and that couldn't be good. However, he did preach against big business, so he wasn't all bad. Then there was this business in Mexico. Should we really have sent troops? And Governor Cruce! What a disgrace. The man should be impeached.

Walter Kelley was holding forth with the best of them. It had been eight months since his wife had been found in Cane Creek, murdered, and folks were finally beginning to treat him like they had before the tragedy. Walter was a gregarious man, and having people tiptoe around him, afraid to laugh and gossip for fear of upsetting him, had been torture. His business had suffered, too, at first, until the sheriff had satisfied himself that Walter could not possibly have killed his wife himself. He had been in Kansas City at the time, and numerous witnesses had testified to that fact. Which was a good thing, too, because he had originally planned to be home the very day Louise was found in the creek. If his uncle hadn't dropped in unexpectedly and caused him to extend his trip, he'd have probably been home in time to be the prime suspect.

Walter had been in a fog for several weeks, after the sheriff had wired him to come home because Louise had been stabbed. He was just beginning to feel normal again. He didn't miss Louise, but he was sorry that she had died that way. Everyone knew that they hadn't been particularly happy together. Walter had an eye for the ladies, and he liked to have fun. He hadn't meant to hurt Louise. He just was who he was.

And Louise was not blameless, to Walter's way of thinking. First, she had threatened to leave him, or at least to start stepping out on him. He had suspected for quite awhile before she had met her unfortunate end that she had a lover, since she would disappear at the oddest times. But then she had gotten religion so bad that it was annoying. She had kept praying at him to change his ways.

For weeks after the funeral, all the ladies of the Christian Church had kept him fed like a king. Every single night one lady or another would stop by the barber shop at closing time, toting a casserole, or a roast, or some fried chicken. When business was slow and he went outside to sit on the bench in front of the shop, every woman who passed by would pause and offer her sympathy. During the last couple of weeks, he began to notice that some of the ladies were stopping by with their marriageable daughters in tow. He was, after all, quite well to do, and a good catch, if he did say so himself.

Today, Shaw Tucker was in the shop with his two sons, which made Walter happy. He liked the voluble Shaw and both the boys, and he liked the fact that when Shaw was in town with the family, it was likely that Walter would get to pass a few words with some of Shaw's vivacious daughters. All the Tucker girls were sharp and friendly, but the elder two, Martha and Mary, didn't seem to appreciate his banter as much as the next two, fraternal twins Alice and Phoebe. Phoebe had married their neighbor boy, John Lee Day, last winter, which was all right with Walter. Phoebe was sweet and pretty, but he had eyes for Alice.

It had taken him a long time after Louise's death to realize that he was free to court a nice girl, and Alice Tucker suited him right down to the ground. She was tall, blond, blue-eyed, and flirtatious. She had a tongue like a razor and an iron will, which daunted most men, but Walter felt he was easily her match. Walter hadn't broached the subject with Alice, or tested the waters with Shaw. He had just become aware himself of his interest in the girl. He thought, too, that she might be interested in him, since she had taken the time to talk to him at Louise's funeral. One problem he did foresee, however, was Alice's mother, Alafair. He really didn't think she liked him.

"So, Mr. Tucker," Walter found himself saying to the man in his chair, "how's Miz Tucker lately? I ain't seen her around town in a bit."

"She's doing fine, Walter," Shaw assured him. "The new baby keeps her close to home nowadays. The little gal is getting up big enough, though, that I expect Alafair will begin ranging farther from home before long."

"How many girls is that for you, Mr. Tucker?"

Shaw laughed before he answered. "That's eight girls, and a prettier bunch of butterflies you'll not find. And I'll tell you, little Grace is one lucky imp. She's got seven mothers besides her own. You never saw such a doted-on baby."

"What do you boys think about another sister?" Walter asked the two youngsters, who were sitting in bentwood chairs, waiting their turn.

"We're used to being outnumbered," Gee Dub told him. "And she is mighty cute."

"She's funny," Charlie admitted, "but you got to watch her every minute. I swear she'll eat anything. Mama caught her about to chomp down on a big green caterpillar the other day. I'd have liked to see that. Grandpapa said it would have made her bonny. Grandma and Grandpapa come over a lot since she got born."

"He thinks his Grandpapa hung the moon," Shaw informed the barber.

Charlie looked over at his father. "Are Grandma and Grandpapa coming over for Easter, Daddy?"

"No, we're going over to their place, son," Shaw told him, "along with all your aunts and uncles and cousins." Shaw dropped his head forward onto his chest to afford Walter access to the back of his neck. "What are you doing for Easter, Walter?"

Walter shrugged in the midst of his clipping. "Go to church and then home, I reckon. I have lots of family back in Missouri, but none of them live out here."

"What about your late wife's family?"

"Oh, I think they'd just as soon shoot me as look at me," Walter told him mildly.

Shaw paused, then let the comment pass. "Why don't you come out to my folks' farm for dinner after church on Sunday," he invited. "Don't seem right to be alone on Easter."

Walter paused, pretending to consider the offer. He didn't tell Shaw that he'd already had three invitations to dinner. "Why, I'd be right pleased, Mr. Tucker, if you think it would be all right with your mother," he finally answered. His heart perked up a little at the thought of having dinner with Alice.

⌐◦⌐◦

"Walter Kelley!" Alafair exclaimed. "You invited Walter Kelley to Easter dinner?"

Shaw was taken aback at her tone. Alafair was usually the first one to claim the lonely, and comfort the bereaved. "Well, yes, seeing as he didn't have nowhere else to go, and there will like to be so many people at Ma's tomorrow that no one will even notice one more. Don't you like Walter?"

They were sitting in their bedroom after dinner while the kids cleaned up the kitchen and Alafair nursed six-month-old Grace. Shaw was sitting on the bed, and Alafair was in her rocking chair with a baby blanket thrown casually over her shoulder and the baby's head for modesty. Her dark eyes gazed at Shaw accusingly. Alafair huffed at his question, but her expression softened. "Truth is, I don't know him but to speak to him," she admitted. "I don't like what I hear about the way he treated his poor murdered wife. Her sister Nellie Tolland hates him like the devil for making her so unhappy. According to Miz Fluke, over at the post office, Nellie isn't convinced at all that some passing tramp done Louise in, like Scott thinks. She thinks Walter was involved in some way."

"I'm surprised at you, Alafair," Shaw scolded gently, "listening to gossip and all. Nobody but the ones involved knows what goes on in a marriage. I wasn't acquainted with the late Miz Kelley, but I've known Walter for years, and a better natured person I never did meet, always smiling and laughing. I'm thinking that the wife was the discontented one. What was she doing while her husband was out of town that got her knifed and dumped in a creek, anyway?"

Alafair shifted in her chair to ease the leaden weight of the baby on her arm. "Well, maybe you're right," she conceded. "Louise Kelley did seem like kind of a sour woman to me. Of course, maybe she had reason to be. I do know that Walter is just a big flirt."

"So's my papa," Shaw pointed out. His mustache twitched ironically.

Alafair laughed. "Yes, but as far as I know, your papa never did anything but flirt."

"And you know that Walter Kelley did?"

"Well, no, not for sure," she admitted.

Shaw stood up and grabbed the baby's toe, and was rewarded by a coo from under the blanket. "You always take the woman's side," he teased Alafair, "even when there's no earthly reason to."

She reached up and smoothed back his newly trimmed and oiled hair. "We poor put-upon creatures have to stick together," she informed him. "But you're right, I guess. I don't really know the man, and I trust your judgment. So bring him along and any other poor bereft soul you come across."

Shaw brushed her forehead with his lips. "Good. You'll see he's a nice fellow, and it's always good to be neighborly."

"I expect," she said to his back as he left the room. She pulled the blanket off her shoulder and looked down at Grace, who had finished lunch and was lying with the nipple in her mouth and a look of utter contentment on her face. Her enormous black button eyes popped open and gazed at her mother with interest. May I help you, her expression said? Alafair stifled a laugh and her heart melted in her chest and ran right down into her shoes. Grace was the twelfth little baby to gaze up at her like that, with eyes full of mischief, or fear, contentment, rage, or adoration. Two had died and ten had lived, and Alafair loved every one of them with a love so big that it was a miracle her body could contain it. She tapped the baby's nose with her finger and sang to her softly.

> *"Oh, you beautiful bumble bee.*
> *Don't you bumble yourself at me.*
> *There's no honey inside my head.*
> *Won't you bumble the flowers instead?*
> *Oh, you beautiful bumble bee,*
> *Beautiful bumble bee."*

Grace gave her a toothless grin and struggled to sit up. Alafair buttoned herself up and arranged Grace on her lap. "Yes, indeed, Grace," she said as she wiped the baby's milky mouth with the corner of the blanket, "it's always good to be neighborly, and it's always good for your mama to trust the little voice in her head."

When the sun began to rise a little after 6:30 on Easter morning, Alafair left the hullaballoo of her family preparing for church and went out on the porch. For the past many years, she had made a ritual of going outside by herself early in the morning to walk into the copse of woods behind the house and feed the wild turkeys. It was a chilly, clear morning, and the sky was pinking up nicely in the east. The canny birds, normally impossible to see in the woods, seemed to sense that Alafair meant them no harm when she appeared in the mornings with her pan of bread crumbs, and clustered around her feet like chickens. On this Easter morning, Alafair sank into a meditative state as she scattered the crumbs, seeing herself back in the Holy Land on that first Easter so long ago, trying to imagine the despair of the disciples turning to wonder when it began to dawn on them what had happened at the tomb. The thought filled her with the deep religious awe of the true believer.

Her moment of reverence was short-lived, however, as were all solitary moments for any mother of ten. As she walked back up the porch steps with the empty pan in her hand, two of her youngest, seven-year-old Blanche and impish Sophronia, aged six, banged out the front door with brushes and ribbons and hairpins in their hands.

"Mama," Blanche complained, "Martha and Mary are busy with packing up the food and Alice says we have to wait until she gets done doing Ruth's hair before she can do us."

Sophronia threw her arms around her mother's waist in an excess of affection. "Daddy said he'd braid our hair for us, Mama, but when he gets done there's always one way up here and one all skewed around here." She demonstrated with her hands flying about her head.

"Besides, Daddy always pulls our hair," Blanche added, holding the brush out toward Alafair.

Alafair took the brush from Blanche and sat down on the porch swing. "Well, come here, then," she said, arranging Blanche between her knees while Sophronia climbed up into the swing beside her.

She began brushing the dark brown hair briskly. Blanche had the most beautiful wavy hair, Alafair thought, and enough of it for two little girls. "You girls look mighty pretty in your new dresses," she observed, prompting Sophronia to leap off the swing and pirouette around the porch a few times before flinging herself back up beside her mother.

"Do me some French braids, Ma," Blanche begged. "I want fancy hair to go with my fancy dress."

"I aim to," Alafair assured her with a laugh. She dropped the brush into her lap and divided the hair into two bunches on either side of the girl's head. She twisted one side up and pinned it to keep it out of the way, then began to braid the other side high up on Blanche's crown.

"Can I help?" Sophronia asked.

"Don't let her, Ma," Blanche protested. "She's messy."

Alafair gently pushed away Sophronia's little hand while managing not to drop any of the three hanks of Blanche's hair that were precariously threaded through her fingers. "Sit down, Fronie," she ordered. "Wait until I get down to the bottom here and I'll let you twist a couple of times."

"Can I tie the ribbon?"

"Mama!" Blanche wailed.

"Don't be bothering me, now, Fronie," Alafair said to the bouncing child. "Blanche wants to look especially pretty today. Don't you? Now sit down."

Sophronia sat down with as much grace as she could muster while her mother expertly finished off one of Blanche's braids and most of the other. When Alafair paused and looked over at her, Sophronia gleefully climbed into her mother's lap.

"Stick out your hands, here," Alafair instructed. "Now take these two hanks here in this hand and this one here, and go slow. This one over, and over, and over, and that's good. Now hold it tight while I tie the ribbon. There, that's good. And it looks real neat, Blanche. Thank you, Fronie. You were a big help. Blanche, go in the house and admire yourself in the mirror, then go see if you can help in the kitchen."

Blanche bounded into the house and Alafair swung Sophronia off the seat and set her between her knees. Before she could begin braiding Sophronia's auburn curls, her oldest daughter, Martha, appreared at the front door, holding the baby.

"Grace is ready for her breakfast, Mama," Martha said.

Alafair made a noise of confirmation and stood. "Is she changed?"

"Yes, Ma." Martha handed Alafair the fussy baby. "Mary's washing out last night's diapers right now. I've yet to pack the baby's things to take with us to Grandma's."

"Thank you, sweetie, but I've already done it. The bag is in my bedroom. Would you do Fronie's hair for her?"

Alafair and Grace disappeared into the house and Martha took her mother's place on the porch swing with Sophronia standing before her. "You want French braids like Blanche?" she asked as she began to brush.

Sophronia had reached the limit of her ability to remain still. "Naw, just braid them regular, Martha. The other takes too long."

Martha had just finished the second braid and was tying it with a ribbon, when Sophronia leaped forward out of her grasp and ran down the steps into the yard. "Martha, Mama!" she yelled. "Here comes Phoebe and John Lee." She skipped through the gate to greet her sister and new brother-in-law with a dimpled smile as they came up the path from their adjoining farm. They were carrying a big picnic basket between them. Martha, Sophronia, and the newlyweds converged at the gate just as Mary and Alice came out the front door lugging their own huge baskets of food, and their father pulled up to the house with the buckboard, all neatly swept out and covered with clean quilts to protect all the pretty dresses and pressed suits. Shaw's two hunting dogs, Crook and Buttercup, were bounding around the wagon, excited at the prospect of a trip. Shaw spoke to them sharply and, chastened, the dogs retreated under the porch.

"Let's go, let's go, boys and girls," Shaw called. "We've got to drop all these vittles off at Grandma's before we go to church, and the sun's already up, now."

More children poured out the door, and they all arranged themselves on the quilts in the bed of the wagon with much chatter and laughter. Alafair was the last out of the house, with the baby on her hip. She climbed onto the seat next to Shaw, who turned to inspect the load of offspring he was carrying: Martha and Mary, Alice and Phoebe, his boys Gee Dub and

Charlie and his young girls Ruth, Blanche and Sophronia, his son-in-law John Lee, and perched next to him, his wife Alafair and baby Grace.

"Looks like I'm toting a wagonload of flowers," Shaw observed, and was answered with a chorus of giggles.

"Do I look like a flower, Daddy?" Charlie demanded, affronted.

"Charlie-boy," Shaw answered him with a big white grin, "you look like a bright red apple, all polished and ready to eat. Now settle, you kids, and let's get to Grandma's." He picked up the reins and clucked at the mules.

⌐⌐⌐

An hour later, in the red brick Masonic Hall, where met the congregation of the First Christian Church of Boynton, the family was sitting with Shaw's mother and stepfather, his three sisters and their families, his two brothers and their families, and his two younger half brothers. The Tucker-McBride amalgamation took up nearly a third of the hall. Because of the baby, Shaw and Alafair sat in the back, at the end of the row, and Alafair was afforded a fine view of the rest of the congregation. Since it was Easter, the hall was packed, all the aisles filled with overflow worshipers in cane-bottomed chairs. Alafair waved at Shaw's cousin's wife Hattie Tucker, sitting near the front with Scott and their four nearly grown boys. Two rows up and directly across the aisle from Alice, Alafair caught sight of Walter Kelley, scanning the crowd with bright brown eyes and waving and calling to everyone he knew. His gaze crossed Alafair's and he gave her a cheerful nod. She responded with a tight smile. His gaze slid onward and lit on Alice. He leaned across the aisle to speak to her, and Alice leaned in to hear him. Her blonde hair fell off her shoulder and she casually tucked it behind her ear. She gave the barber a languorous smile.

Alafair straightened. The young people were close enough that she could hear their conversation clearly over the chatter of the congregation, and she eavesdropped unabashedly.

"I reckon I'll be taking Easter dinner with you and your family after church," Walter opened.

"I heard. The family will be mighty glad to have you."

"Will you be glad to have me there, as well?" Walter teased, grinning.

Alice grinned back. "Why, yes, I will. In fact, my grandfolks have the best apple orchard in the Creek Nation, so they tell me. I'd be pleased to give you a tour after dinner. It's just blooming like glory this year."

"I would love to see it, young Miss Alice," Walter assured her.

There was no time for more conversation, since the new minister, Mr. Bellows, stepped up to the pulpit and a hush fell over the crowd.

Alice! Alafair thought, as the minister greeted the congregation. He called her Alice, just like that, so fresh, and Alice flirted back at him as brash as you please. Don't fret yourself, her inner voice admonished. I'm pretty sure they don't even know one another. You just don't like the fellow, and there's no good reason not to like him. It's just his personality, too flip for you, and that big old grin that's way too friendly, and that sly look that sets your teeth on edge. It doesn't mean he's a bad person.

A bad person. Alafair anxiously called to mind his murdered wife. If anybody would be drawn to a flip personality, it was her darling Alice. If only Shaw hadn't invited him to dinner, she thought. She had a sudden fear that she was looking at the first meeting of fire and tinder.

Chapter Four

Grandma and Grandpapa's very large farm was located a scant mile outside of Boynton, on a prime section of land bordered by Cloud Creek on the east and dissected across the southeast corner by Cane Creek. The pearl gray, two-story Victorian house sat at the end of a long, curving drive that wound down from the gate, and was surrounded by native oaks and elms. A massive roofed and railed porch wrapped around the front and both sides of the house. Grandpapa had surrounded the house with a low picket fence to create a pleasant yard, much of which Grandma had turned into mixed flower and vegetable gardens. Behind the house, Grandma had planted a tiny orchard of fruit trees, two of each of pear, cherry, and peach. Just outside the fence stood a couple of rangy persimmon trees, a black walnut, two or three massive hackberrys, and a forked path, one branch of which led to Grandma's stand of native pecan trees, and the other to Grandpapa's justly famous apple orchard.

As soon as Shaw pulled the wagon into the yard, Charlie spotted several age-mate cousins. He made a break for it, but his mother caught him by the collar before he got away and pressed him into service carrying food baskets.

They entered the house through the tall front door with the oval, etched glass window. The foyer led to a short hallway. To the right of the entrance, a carved wooden stairwell ascended to the bedrooms. To the left, glass-paned French doors opened onto a huge, airy, multi-windowed parlor. Alafair and her troop of helpers went straight down the hall with their baskets of food, through the dining room that used to be a breezeway before it was enclosed, heading for the big kitchen at the back of the house.

The younger children had divested themselves of their burdens and skipped out the back, except for Charlie, who tugged Alafair's skirt.

"Ma, can I have some of them boiled eggs? Uncle Bill said me and the boys can hide them for the little kids to find later."

Distracted, Alafair pointed him toward the large milk pail full of hard-boiled eggs that she had just set on the cabinet. "You can have about a dozen, honey. That means twelve and not one more, now. Take them and scoot."

Normally, when Alafair's family went to her mother-in-law's for dinner, no one was allowed into the kitchen to help with the cooking. Grandma Sally informed all who asked that she could cook up a meal infinitely more efficiently if she was left alone. When guests came to her house, she insisted on doing the entertaining. When Sally did the visiting, she expected to be entertained herself. However, on a big holiday like today, when the entire tribe was in residence, the rules were eased. Most of the food was already prepared and hauled in by the wagon loads by the various daughters and daughters-in-law and granddaughters. All that was left to do after church was to make the potatoes, both mashed and fried, heat up the quarts of home-canned vegetables, and make the biscuits and gravy.

While the women were toiling in the kitchen, the men set up the long plank-and-sawhorse tables and benches under the elms by the side of the house. By the time all the tables were set up, the women were beginning to haul out platters and bowls of food to set on the makeshift banquet table. Many of the plates and bowls were covered with dishcloths to keep away the flying critters, but several medium-sized, disgruntled children were pressed into service with leafy twigs and paper fans to stand over the food and wave threateningly at the flies.

The kitchen was literally a hotbed of action. The spring day was cool, but the heat of the wood-fired, cast iron stove, combined with the harried activity of nearly a score of women, served to make Grandma's big kitchen uncomfortably hot. Grandma Sally herself stood in the center of the floor at the head of the kitchen table, directing the action like a trail boss. Sally stood five feet tall in her bare feet, a plump, birdlike woman, all brown and bright-eyed, always flitting from this to that, never still. She wore her still-dark hair pulled straight back into a bun, and her Cherokee ancestry showed plain on her face. She was imperious, ordering everyone about without shame, but she was so good-natured and even humorous about it that no one could manage to be insulted.

Alafair was standing at the cabinet next to Shaw's sister Hannah, mashing potatoes in a big pot. Mashing potatoes for sixty-five people is a daunting task. Alafair was using a two-handed, twisting method that took a certain amount of upper body strength. She paused occasionally to add cream from a pint jar at her elbow. She had just reached a point where the potatoes were smooth and creamy enough to serve when her daughter Ruth, just turned fourteen, sidled up to her through the crowd and plucked her sleeve.

"Who's watching Grace?" Alafair said to her in lieu of a greeting.

"Alice has her," Ruth said, and Alafair grunted her approval.

"Hand me that serving dish over there," Alafair instructed. "What do you want, honey?"

After handing her mother the bowl, Ruth leaned in confidentially. "Mama, can I eat at the grown-up table today?" She was striving to keep a pleading tone out of her voice.

Alafair tried not to smile as she began to ladle the silky potatoes into the bowl. "You can eat anywhere you want to, puddin'."

"Such a pretty, grown-up dress you've got on there, Ruth," Aunt Hannah noted. "You shouldn't let any sticky little hands anywhere near it. Go find your cousin Liz and tell her to sit at the grown-up table with you."

Ruth straightened with a grin and made a little hop as she turned to go back outside. "Thank you, Aunt Hannah. Thank you, Mama." She moved toward the door, but Grandma Sally grabbed her arm before she made good her escape.

"Not so fast, there, my girl," Sally admonished. "Take these couple of bowls out and put them on the table." She loaded Ruth down and draped some dishtowels over the girl's shoulder. "Throw these over the bowls," she instructed. "Now, scoot."

"That'll teach her to come in here while Grandma's in charge," Alafair noted to Hannah with a smile. She plopped a scoop of butter into the well she had pressed into the top of the potatoes.

As she turned to place the bowl on the table, she found Sally close at her side.

"Tell me about this handsome young barber y'all invited along to dinner," Sally opened.

"The barber is here already?" Alafair asked.

"He drove in a few minutes ago in his shiny black automobile, with his fancy blue racing cap on his head, and his blue braces to match. All the kids were crowding around wanting a ride, but he jumped out right smart and went to sit in the shade with some of your girls."

Alafair's eyebrows shot up. She wiped her hands and dabbed her cheeks with the tail of her apron as she regarded the shrewd look in her mother-in-law's eyes. "Funny you should ask me about him, Ma. I was hoping you and me might have a little time to talk about that sometime today."

Sally's gaze darted around the kitchen, taking in the chaos of preparation. "Josie," she said to her eldest daughter, at the stove, "you do the directing. Me and Alafair are going outside for a spell."

Not ones to waste effort, Sally and Alafair grabbed dishes to convey to the table before strolling off together through the crowd, on their way to the pecan orchard. As they passed, Alafair eyed Walter Kelley, sitting in a chair under the budding elms with Alice, Mary, and John Lee Day. Phoebe and Martha were busying themselves at the table. Grace and two of her infant cousins were rocking back and forth happily on a blanket spread on the grass at the young people's feet. Walter was being his ever-so-charming self, judging by how much the girls were laughing.

Alafair hadn't noticed before that Buttercup the hound had followed them from home. The dog had insinuated herself among the young people and was intently snuffling around Walter's feet. Alafair shook her head. Even the dog was beguiled. When Walter reached over and patted Alice on the knee, Alafair bridled. Alice didn't seem to mind.

"You don't like him much, do you?" Sally observed, as they walked out the back gate.

Alafair looked over at her, startled out of her reverie. "I guess I'm not too good at keeping my feelings hid, am I?"

Sally took her eyes off of Alafair's face and began to scan the multitudinous buds on the pecan trees. "He seems like a pleasant enough fellow to me. Just what is it about him that riles you?"

"Shaw asked me the same thing," Alafair said with a shrug. "Something about him seems false to me. He just likes the sound of his own voice too much, and preens like a cocky old rooster." She hesitated, gathering her thoughts, then went on. "I'm bothered about what happened to his wife. I know Scott says that it looks like she got herself in with some bad types—and I know that she was seen at the road house the night before she ended up in Cane Creek—but still…"

Sally nodded. "Yes, that was a bad thing. Louise wasn't a real good friend or nothing, but I knew her as well as any number of women around here, from church and all. It surprised me that she was sporting around in a road house before she got killed. She hardly ever missed a church service." Sally paused to examine a pecan bud on a low branch. "We visited some when the barber first brought her here from Kansas City, back a few years ago. She seemed happy enough back then, I reckon. Said her family and Walter's knew each other from way back. He had flirtatious ways, but I think she expected he would change after they married. It didn't set well with her when he didn't. She often prayed with the ladies in her Bible group that Walter would become a better Christian. That's the story I heard, anyway."

"Always a mistake," Alafair noted, "to expect them to change for you. I didn't know the woman as well as you, but I could tell well enough that she was unhappy. Maybe it would have helped if they had had some babies."

"Maybe not."

Alafair twitched out a smile and her shoulder lifted in a gesture of resignation. "Maybe not," she agreed. "Who knows what goes on in a marriage? Was she too hard to please? One thing, though. He seems to have got over it pretty quick. I don't care for how he likes the ladies."

"You don't care for how he likes Alice," Sally stated, and Alafair looked over at her.

"No," Alafair admitted. "I don't. If he was turning his attention to Martha or Mary I wouldn't worry as much. But Alice likes his brand of guff, and she's got a will like granite if she decides she wants something."

"What does Shaw think about this?" Sally wondered.

"Well, I haven't mentioned to him that I think Walter has his eye on Alice, because truth be told, I haven't seen any real evidence of it. He flirts just the same with all the pretty girls." She paused and gazed into space for a minute before she added, "It's just a hunch."

"I always follow my hunches when it comes to my kids," Sally assured her. "I'm right most of the time, too. I notice that you're pretty good at it yourself."

Alafair shook her head. "But I don't know what to do, Ma. Nothing has happened that I can sink my teeth into. Did I ever tell you about that strange gal that showed up at Louise's funeral? If I only knew what really happened to Louise Kelley, and why..."

Sally stopped walking and turned to face her daughter-in-law. "Maybe you'd better find out, sugarplum. Ask Scott about it. Alice would cool off considerable if she found out that the apple of her eye had drove his wife to despair. And if it turns out that Walter is just the wronged party, you'd feel a bunch better."

The circular path they were following through the pecan grove turned back toward the house, and as the women rounded the furthermost tree, they caught sight of Sally's twenty-three-year-old son, Bill McBride, along with Charlie and two or three other Tucker boys, chucking boiled eggs at a fence post. The youngsters' aim left something to be desired, since most of the eggs lay intact on the far side of the fence. There had been a couple of bull's-eyes, though, and yolky remains smeared the top of the post.

"Charles Tucker!" Alafair hollered. The gang froze. Charlie's arm hung in the air, mid-windup, and the boys and their uncle stared at the women like a bunch of startled rabbits, ears pricked and noses aquiver.

"What in the name of good John are y'all boys doing?" Sally demanded. "Bill, what kind of example are you setting these lads? You're making a mess and wasting perfectly good food. Y'all clean that up right now and get back to the house."

It was Bill who made the first move. He straightened slowly and slipped the egg he was holding into his pocket. His mouth quivered in a heroic effort not to guffaw. One twinkling brown eye closed in a sly wink at his mother. "Hitch 'em up, boys," he said to the nephews. "Let's take our punishment like men. Looks like we're caught red handed."

Alafair and Sally resumed their walk amidst a murmer of apologies and a scurry of cleanup. As soon as they were out of earshot, they both burst into laughter.

"What a pitiful bunch of throwers," Alafair managed. "I could have beat the lot of them with my eyes closed."

~~~

Alafair was seated near the head of the table with Ruth and Cousin Liz on one side of her and Hannah on the other, and baby Grace in her lap. Shaw, Gee Dub, and Shaw's half brother, that erstwhile troublemaker, red-haired, brown-eyed, freckle-faced Bill McBride, were across from her. Alafair could see Alice and Walter Kelley seated next to one another halfway down the table, chatting warmly. She was gratified to notice that her mother-in-law had placed herself opposite the two young people. Alafair could expect a full report later. She busied herself with peeling a hard-boiled egg, attempting to keep Grace from eating eggshells, and trying not to pay attention to Alice and Walter.

Grandpapa Peter McBride sat at the head of the table. He wasn't the biggest of men, but he had a booming voice that served well for delivering an interminable and slightly irreverent Easter grace. His prayers edified, entertained, and whetted the appetite, and he always knew that when mischief began to break out at the children's table, it was time to stop. Grandpapa Peter had come to the United States from Ireland in 1864, when he was sixteen years old, and he spoke with an accent that was an amazing mix of Northern Irish and Arkansan. He had brought two things with him from the old country—a set of Irish bagpipes and a love of gab, both of which had stood him in good stead with the natives of the Ozarks.

"Grandpapa," Ruth said, "tell us again how you and Grandma met."

Peter's blue eyes lit up and he sat up straight in his chair, delighted at the opportunity to hold forth. Shaw and Bill laughed and groaned at once.

"Haven't you heard that story enough, Ruthie?" Bill asked.

"Aw, it's a good story, Uncle Bill," Cousin Liz protested.

"Come on now, boys," Grandpapa Peter interjected, "I reckon you can stand it just one more time."

Shaw smiled. His stepfather loved nothing better than to entertain anyone who would listen to a story, the longer the better. And all the children in the family particularly loved the story of how their grandparents had met, even if they had heard it so many times that they could all repeat it verbatim. That was part of its charm, Shaw supposed. "Go ahead on, Papa," he said.

"And so I will," Grandpapa assured them. "Now listen up, lassies. When first I came to Lone Elm, I got a job at the sorghum mill on the Old Wire Road. It was there that I became best of friends with your great-uncles, Paul and Albert and George Tucker, the selfsame men who went together with me to buy that sawmill in Mulberry a few years later. 'Twas they who told me that they had had a brother, Jim, who died of the fever just the year before, leaving a young wife and six sprightly children. She lived in a dog-trot cabin a few miles outside of town, they said, said they, and on regular occasions some member of their family would make the trip out there to see if anything needed doing. This widowed sister-in-law, they told me, was a fine and feisty woman who was slow to take a handout and was determined to make a living and raise up her half dozen young'uns on her own. It was so fascinating that they made her seem to me, with all their stories of how Sally did this and Sally did that, that I became resolved to have a look at this fine example of womanhood. So I attached myself as big as you please to Paul Tucker the next time he told me that him and his wife were going out there.

"Oh, it was such a raggedy little cabin she lived in, boys and girls, down in the holler between two hills, but it had a fine garden and a tin roof. And when we rode up the trail, I got my first sight ever of your grandma. And what do you think she was doing?"

"Fixing the roof!" chorused his listeners.

"She was fixing the roof!" Peter exclaimed. "She was on the roof on her hands and knees, with tin shears in one hand and a hammer in the other and a mouth full of roofing nails. She had on a pair of man's overalls and a shirt. Her little brown feet were bare as the day she was born. She had a long black braid as thick as my wrist hanging down her back. Boys and girls, Cupid's arrow nearly knocked me clean off that horse. She was a vision.

"Now, boys and girls, my hair may be white as the driven snow today, but back then it was orange as a carrot. I was struck dumb when your grandma peered down off that roof at us, but she had all her wits about her, I'll say. After she greeted her kinfolks, she looked at me, and do you know what she said?"

"Who set your head on fire!" chorused the listeners.

"Who set your head on fire!" Grandpapa affirmed.

～～～

"Looks like your grandpa is telling a story," Walter observed to Alice. "Looks like everybody's enjoying it, too."

"Grandpapa does love to tell his stories," Alice acknowledged. "Over and over and over again."

"Mr. McBride is a fine old gentleman. And this is a fine place they have here. I knew that y'all were kin, but for a good long time, I didn't know Miz McBride was Mr. Tucker's mother. I always sort of figured the McBrides were your Ma's folks."

"Mama's parents still live in Arkansas," Alice told him. "Grandpapa is Daddy's stepfather. Daddy's born father died when Daddy was little, and Grandma married Grandpapa two years later. Uncle Bill and Uncle Howard are Grandpapa's natural sons, but he raised up Daddy and his brothers and sisters like his own children."

"It must be hard to step into a family like that."

"Daddy loves Grandpapa a lot, but he told me once that he always remembers his own father in his heart."

Alice glanced at her grandmother across the table. Sally appeared to be engrossed in conversation with one of the cousins. Alice leaned in toward Walter. "My Aunt Josie told us once that Grandma nearly expired of grief when Grandpa Jim died. Said she just worked herself to a frazzle so as to stay busy and not have to think, and never smiled or laughed once from the day Jim died until Peter came along. Josie said they all love Grandpapa for making Grandma laugh again."

"I expect it's wonderful to have a fine person come into your sad life and teach you to be happy again," Walter mused.

Alice picked up a radish and crunched it thoughtfully. "I reckon you've had a sad life since your wife died."

"It's been lonesome."

Alice languidly rearranged her napkin in her lap. "From what I hear, you're not lacking female companionship, Mr. Kelley," she said.

Walter's fork paused between plate and open mouth as he glanced at her. His fork completed its trip and he chewed for a moment before he replied. "I'd be pleased if you'd call me Walter, Miss Alice," he said, at length.

"All right, Walter. And you're not obliged to use the 'Miss.'"

"Thank you, Alice. As for your observation, it's true. Since my wife passed on, several ladies have been kind enough to accompany me to the picture show or have me over to supper."

"But you're not looking to remarry just yet?" Alice was aware that Phoebe, seated on her left, had been listening in on her conversation for the past few minutes. As soon as Alice had asked her question, her twin-sense had picked up a thrill of alarm from her sister. Alice nearly laughed. Proper Phoebe.

Walter shrugged. "I always figured I would remarry some day. I like having a female in the house. But I haven't yet come upon a young lady who I'd like to spend my life with."

"But the idea doesn't exactly repel you," she observed.

"Well, no," he admitted, and smiled, amused at her brass.

"And what are your requirements in the way of a female to spend your life with?"

Phoebe hastily leaned across Alice. "My husband John Lee is mighty intrigued by your automobile, Mr. Kelley," she said. "Where did you acquire it?"

Alice did laugh, now, as Walter described to Phoebe how he had found the Ford in Muskogee. Delayed, but undaunted, she asked an uncle to pass the potatoes.

The meal drew to an end and people began to straggle away from the table in ones and twos, with armloads of dishes or leftovers, or a child by the hand. Alice made a show of stacking the dishes in her vicinity, but it wasn't difficult to foist them off on a passing sister and make her escape with Walter through the crowd. They walked down a long hill behind the house and into a large hollow that was filled with nearly an acre of mature apple trees, all of which were covered with a froth of white blossoms as delicate as sea foam.

"Bless me!" Walter exclaimed. "You can see this orchard from the road, but it's quite a sight up close like this. All this sun-struck white is like to blind me!"

"I used to like to cut across the orchard on my way home from school when it was in bloom like this," Alice said. "I'd gather up armloads of flowering branches to take home. Mama would scold me and say that each blossom was an apple that would never get made. But she always put them in a jug on a table in the parlor."

"Looks to me like there's blossoms enough to spare," Walter said.

"In the summer they make wagon loads of the tastiest little red apples. They're tart and sweet all at once. Every restaurant and bakery and greengrocer in the county wants Grandpapa's apples. Then in the fall, it's the same with the pecans."

"Your grandfather raises saddle horses, too, don't he? Sometimes I see him gliding through town on some real fine animal, sitting back and looking like he's managed to throw a saddle over the back of a cloud."

"Kentucky walkers," Alice informed him. "He used to raise work horses and mules like Daddy does, but he's given that up. Said he just wants to enjoy breeding and training the smooth steppers now that he's old."

"Do any of your folks have oil wells? I saw a shale outcrop yonder as we came over the hill."

"Daddy had some surveyor out to our place not long ago, but I never heard what came of it. Grandpapa has never mentioned oil wells that I know of. You seem to know something about oil, Walter."

"Well, I've got me a couple of wells up north of town. Pretty good producers, too."

"Why, Mr. Kelley," Alice teased. "Are you trying to impress me with your wealth?"

Walter laughed. "I hadn't thought to. But if I had, would that do it?"

Alice smiled and clasped her hands behind her back as they strolled among the trees. "Might," she said. She shrugged. "Truth is, wealth is nice, but other things are more important, to my way of thinking."

"Well, now, Miss Alice, a while ago you asked me what my requirements were in the way of someone to spend my life with. So let me ask you the same question. A charming young lady like yourself must have many admirers to choose from."

"As far as I've been concerned, Walter, they can all admire me from afar. I'm mighty particular where I bestow my affections."

"I hope you are. What are the high standards you hold your potential suitors to, if it ain't too bold to ask?"

"I'll tell you this. I ain't marrying a boy. I'm not starting out dirt poor on a tenant farm, like Phoebe. I'll be looking for somebody who has got himself established, at least. A grown man who knows how to treat me like a lady."

"You sound mighty adamant on the subject," Walter noted with a chuckle.

"I am. And now that I've told you what I'm looking for in the way of a future, I'll repeat my question to you. What are your requirements?"

Walter shook his head. "I'm not as certain of my requirements as you are. Seems like things don't always turn out the way you hope. When I married Louise, I thought we'd make each other happy forever, but everything went wrong and I don't exactly know why. I never did know how to satisfy her. She's the one who wanted to leave Missouri, to get a fresh start, but once we came here, nothing changed. We had no more than got here than Louise started in on her old ways. She couldn't stand me to be away from her for a minute. She wanted all my attention, all the time. If I as much as looked sideways at another female, young or old, she'd fly right off the handle. Why, she just couldn't get it into her head that I never meant nothing by it. They never meant anything to me. I'm just too friendly for my own good, I guess…" He paused, and gave Alice an abashed glance. "I'm sorry," he said. "I don't mean to be going on. I'm sure you don't want to hear this."

"Oh, but I do," Alice said. She leaned toward him, sincere. "I'm flattered that you'd feel comfortable enough to talk about such a hard thing with me. And I do understand. With her dying that terrible way, I expect you feel that now you'll never know what troubled her."

"You do understand. Even though Louise went looking for comfort in the arms of another, I could have forgiven her. I didn't want a divorce, but if she was so unhappy with me, I'd have given her one, if she had only asked."

"No husband of mine will ever have to guess what's on my mind," Alice assured him. "If something bothers me, I want it out in the open so it can be fixed."

"You're a rare girl, Alice," Walter said. "The fellow who wins your hand is going to be mighty lucky."

The breeze picked up and stirred the branches over their heads. White petals showered down on them, and they stopped walking. "Hush-h-h," the trees told them. And they did.

They stood and looked at one another for a long moment as the swirling snow of petals settled around them. Walter removed his linen cap and held it to his breast. Alice felt the hair rise at the back of her neck.

"Alice!" Sophronia's childish voice calling her name caused Alice to start violently and she whirled around.

"Here, Fronie," she called in reply.

The little girl burst through the trees at a skip. "I found you!" she exclaimed, and threw her arms around Alice's waist in triumph. Her deep dimples gave her grin a particularly impish quality. "Phoebe said y'all might be in the orchard, and she was right! Mama wants you, Alice. She said we got to get ready to go and Grace needs changing."

"All right, Fronie," Alice said. "You go on back and we'll be along directly."

"I'm supposed to bring you back my own self," Sophronia protested.

Alice and Walter exchanged a glance. Alice could feel the heat in her cheeks. She sighed. Walter seemed to take the intrusion in stride.

"Well, then, Miss Sophronia," he invited. "Lead on."

Chapter Five

Four days after Easter, on a cool, cloudless spring morning bursting with forsythia and flowering fruit trees, Alice Tucker came waltzing into her mother's kitchen with a bucket full of spring greens. She really was waltzing, too. She glided through the back door, extended her arms, and made a couple of lazy turns around the kitchen before setting the bucket on the cabinet and giving Alafair a kiss on the forehead. Alafair smiled but didn't pause from kneading the enormous mound of bread dough in front of her.

"You're in a mighty good mood," she observed to her daughter.

"And why not?" Alice wondered. "It's a fine day and I have nary one thing to complain about."

Alafair laughed at that. "I've never known that to stop you if you're of a mind to complain."

"Well, I ain't," Alice assured her. "Phoebe sent over these greens. I'm going to wash them and put them in some cool water so they'll still be crisp for dinner."

"How's her garden?"

"It's not as far along as yours, Ma. I noticed coming in that there's a passel of radishes that could use to be pulled."

"We'll make a nice wilted salad for dinner. Did you see Daddy on your way back to the house?"

"Yes, he's back in the mule paddock with the two new hired men."

"Fetch me the loaf pans, would you, honey? I like both those boys that Daddy hired last month. Both polite and hard workers. I hope they stay awhile. Both easy to look at, too. Micah's a charmer, but that Dutch boy, Kurt, I can't understand a word he says."

Alice, busily rinsing the greens in spring water, sniffed her disdain. "I hadn't noticed."

Alafair crooked an eyebrow and looked over at her. "This is a red letter day. I thought there never was a fine looking boy that you didn't notice."

"I've decided to set my sights high, Ma," Alice informed her with a grin. "No farmers for me. I'm going to marry a businessman, or a man with a profession, and live in a fine house in town. Drive around in an automobile. Going to wear fancy dresses and get fat."

Normally, Alice's sass would make Alafair laugh, but today, something in the girl's tone made her heart leap with dread. "My, my," she responded, with calculated calm, "do you have somebody in mind?"

"Maybe I do," Alice admitted. She walked out the open back door and through the enclosed back porch to toss the gritty water she had used for the first rinse of the greens out into the bushes. Alafair punched the dough nervously until Alice returned to the kitchen and dumped the greens into a second pan of water.

"Do I know this paragon?" Alafair continued.

Alice blinked at her across the table, mentally shifting back to the interrupted conversation. The corner of her mouth quirked up ironically and she shrugged. "Well, there isn't anybody, really," Alice admitted. She wiped a stray lock of blond hair out of her eyes with the back of one wet hand. "Or, he doesn't know it yet, I should say. But maybe I've got my eye on somebody."

Alafair kneaded intensely while she pondered her next move. Should I say it, she wondered to herself? Alice was a beautiful, funny, life-loving girl, but she was contrary. If she got it into her head that her mother, or anybody, for that matter, didn't approve of the man she had set her sights on, she would be twice as determined to have him. Alafair schooled her voice to be as bland and noncommittal as possible.

"Is it Walter Kelley?" she asked.

Alice laughed. "Why, yes it is, Ma. How'd you know?"

Alafair gave her bread dough a violent punch. "Well, I ain't blind, darlin'," she answered sweetly. "You two were practically in each other's pockets over at Grandma's on Easter Sunday."

"I didn't know I was that obvious," Alice said, not abashed in the least.

"I'm surprised you'd be interested in somebody who is so much older than you. He's thirty if he's a day."

"I want somebody older," Alice informed her. "No boys for me. Walter has had time to get himself established. He's a successful man, with his own business and a nice house. Knows how to treat a lady, too, having been married and all."

"Yes, about that…" Alafair began carefully, picking her way through her objections as though they were spring traps.

Alice gave her mother a piercing glance over the greens. "I knew you'd be worried about that, Ma, but you shouldn't be," she said firmly. "The poor man has had his share of troubles, but they weren't his fault."

"I just don't want you to get yourself into a situation where you might get hurt," Alafair ventured.

"I know, Ma," Alice conceded. "But I think you should trust me. I'm not a child."

She rose to throw out the second pan of rinse water, and as soon as she was out of the room, Alafair slumped over her well-kneaded dough with a sigh. Oh, child, she thought. Lord, watch over my daughter, and gird my loins for a fight if one is coming, because I've got a bad, bad feeling about Walter Kelley.

⌇⌇⌇

There was no one at the house except Alafair and the baby when Grandma Sally came riding up on her big chestnut thoroughbred late the next morning. Martha had ridden her bicycle to her job as secretary to Mr. Bushyhead at the First National Bank of

Boynton, Alice and Mary were visiting Phoebe, and the younger children were at school. Thursday was Alafair's sewing day, so she had a basket of mending beside her rocking chair on the porch, but it was such a pretty morning that she was having trouble making herself get down to business. Instead, she and Grace were playing a rousing game of peep-eye with one of Shaw's workshirts when Sally rode up to the gate and dismounted.

The long-legged thoroughbred was entirely too big for Sally, and Alafair thought that she looked rather like a baby astride a barrel. She was dressed in a blue poke bonnet and a long-sleeved calico shirt, and was wearing a pair of men's trousers and boots under her skirt. Sally had never been one to be swayed by fashion.

Alafair smiled as Grandma Sally swung out of the saddle and jumped to the ground. Sally stretched up and removed the saddlebags before she walked up to the porch.

"What did you bring me, Ma?"

"A peck of sweet peas." Sally sat herself down in the cane chair next to Alafair and traded the bags for the baby.

"Delightful!" Alafair exclaimed. She dug into one of the flour sacks in the saddlebag and pulled out a couple of fat pods. She slit one open with her thumbnail and popped the sweet English peas into her mouth. Alafair loved English peas, but she and Ruth were the only ones in the family who did, so Alafair never wasted good garden space raising them herself.

"Where's the kids?" Sally wondered as she bounced Grace on her knee.

"Young ones in school and most of the older ones over at Phoebe's pulling up green onions and planting squash."

"Good. I've been meaning to get over here for a while and tell you about my talk with Walter Kelley on Easter."

Alafair smiled as she picked up a ripped shirt and began rummaging through her sewing basket for matching thread. "I've been curious," she admitted. "Just yesterday, Alice told me she's got her eye on Walter, but I didn't want to question her too close. If Alice thinks I'm snooping into her business, she'll shut up so tight I'll never find out another thing."

"I know what you mean," Sally commiserated. "When Hannah was young, she was just like Alice. Drove me to distraction. But Hannah turned out all right, and I'm sure Alice will, too. She's a smart girl. You know, on Easter, I made a point of sitting across from Walter and Alice, and I must say he's a personable one."

Alafair rolled her eyes. "That's the problem." She measured off a length of thread and bit it off the spool with a snap.

"I know. Anybody would think, just to look at them together, that they make a good match for one another. They both love to talk and laugh, and neither of them ever met a stranger. They're both mighty good looking, too, and used to being admired. He's pretty worldly, though, next to her. He's had some trouble in life, and she never has, yet."

Alafair looked up from threading the needle. "You think he's out to take advantage of her innocence?" she asked, concerned.

"No, not necessarily," Sally said. "I do think he's interested in her, though. A man who's been married can find it hard to live without a woman, and she's a good catch, so pretty and lively. Alice sure looked to be interested in him. I guess she is, too, after what you told me. He's well off, after all, besides being good looking. He could buy her lots of things and provide for her very smartly."

"But is he a good man?" Alafair asked fretfully. "Would he make her happy? Would he be a good husband and father?"

Sally managed to shrug while making a goofy face at the baby. "That's the question. And young girls aren't the best judges of these things, either."

"No, they ain't," Alafair agreed. "I can't help but keep thinking about that poor wife of his. What drove her to take up with such low types that she got herself murdered while her husband was out of town?"

"Well, now…" Sally began. The baby began to fuss and Sally sat her down on a blanket on the porch. Grace rolled over on her back and began to chew happily on a cloth dolly.

"Well, now?" Alafair prompted.

Grandma Sally eyed her for a second before deliberately removing her bonnet and sitting back in the chair. "Hattie told me something that don't reflect well. But it's just gossip, now, so you've got to take it for what it's worth."

Alafair's expression didn't change, but her sewing immediately became more like stabbing. "I've been warned," she acknowledged. Since her husband Scott was the law in Boynton, gossip from Hattie carried a little extra cachet.

"As you know, it seems that Louise Kelley's sister Nellie Tolland hates Walter like poison. Nellie thinks that Walter is a tomcat, and it was that very catting around that drove Louise to her downfall. You know the Crockers over by Council Hill?"

"Don't believe I do."

"I used to know a Crocker boy back in Arkansas," Sally filled her in. "A bunch of them come out here right after statehood and got them a place. Well, old Adam Crocker has him a daughter named Peggy, a girl of about twenty now, I reckon. Used to be betrothed to Billy Bond."

"I know of the Bonds. Somebody in that family buys a mule from Shaw every year or so."

"It seems that Peggy got herself enamored of Walter Kelley a couple of years back and ended up in a delicate condition. Whether the daddy was Walter or Billy was a matter of some discussion thereabouts. The tale is that Peggy broke up with Billy and tried to talk Walter into leaving his wife, but Walter was having none of it. Miz Kelley wasn't the least happy about the business, don't you know. Seems that Walter had strayed before, when they lived in Kansas City, and had promised his wife he'd mend his ways. Well, after that, seems their life together was a misery. In fact, Hattie thinks the reason he went to Kansas City that week was that Louise caught him making eyes at some pretty gal and went at him hammer and tongs. He expected he'd better leave town for a spell and let her cool off, I reckon."

Alafair rolled her eyes at the folly of it all, and Sally chuckled before she continued. "Anyway, Peggy lost the baby, I hear, but she and Billy ended up with broken hearts, and Peggy's daddy

Adam swore to tear Walter limb from limb. Louise probably wouldn't have objected much."

Alafair had stopped sewing and sat looking at her mother-in-law in frozen horror. "Peggy was the girl at the funeral!" she exclaimed.

"I think so," Sally agreed. "She must still pine for Walter."

"Why have I never heard a breath of this before now?"

"It ain't exactly the kind of thing the family would bruit about."

"I guess not," Alafair admitted. She dropped the sewing into her lap. "Ma," she said, troubled, "do you think it's possible that Walter Kelley killed his wife?"

"Walter was in Kansas City at the time," Sally pointed out.

"Well, could he have paid somebody to kill her or something like that?"

Sally blinked at her before she answered. "Anything is possible, Alafair. Walter don't really seem to me like the type to hire murderers, though. And even after Louise died, he didn't end up with Peggy, did he? I have in mind that he's just too fond of the female sex. I've seen many a man like that, you know. They don't mean to hurt anybody at all, but they just can't help themselves. They just don't think. Then they feel bad when their wives suffer, until another pretty young gal comes along and they do it all over again. I expect it was just like Scott thought. Louise was unhappy in her marriage, but got to looking for comfort in the wrong places."

"And met up with a villain," Alafair finished for her.

"Just so."

"But…" Alafair appended, and Sally smiled.

"Anything is possible," Sally repeated. "If he did, he wouldn't be the first man to find a way to rid himself of an inconvenient wife."

Alafair's gaze wandered off into space as she pondered this possibility. "Do you remember," she said at length, "after we had first moved into the soddy just after Gee Dub was born, that time that Alice got away from me? It was in the spring, just before her and Phoebe turned two. Martha was four and Mary was three, Gee Dub was just a baby, and I was expecting again. To say I was tired would be a faint word for it. That was a pretty day, mild and breezy, if I remember right. Me and the kids had had a boisterous morning. It was impossible to keep things clean in that soddy, and the kids were all in a fractious mood. By the time I got them all down for a nap, I was ready to fall over, myself. Usually I'd try to get some work done in the rare times I got them all to nap at the same time, but that day I was so tired that I fell asleep with them on the bed. When Gee Dub woke me an hour later by crawling all over me, three of the girls were playing together on the bed, but Alice was gone.

"She was nowhere to be found. I hunted all over that soddy and the yard, and was about to load the bunch of them up in a wagon and head to the pasture to find Shaw, when Miz Eichelburger from the farm over next to ours came riding up with Alice on the pommel of her saddle. Told me she had found the imp running down the side of the road in nothing but her drawers, heading for who knows where, happy as a basket full of puppies."

"I'll declare!" Sally laughed. "That's a pretty far piece, from your old soddy to the road."

"She must have took herself off as soon as I fell asleep. That's the way Alice has always been. She rushes off into adventures without a worry in the world, certain sure that nothing bad could ever happen to her. I could rein her in when she was a kid, but she's no kid any more, and where she's rushing off to now, I can't follow."

She stuffed the mending back in the basket. "Would you watch the baby for a spell until the girls get back, Ma? About an hour, I expect."

"I'd love to," Sally assured her. "Where are you going?"

"Into town to talk to Scott."

Sally nodded. "What do you want me to tell the girls, or Shaw, if he comes back to the house before you do?"

"You can tell Shaw the truth, though he'll just think I'm a busybody. Tell the girls I'm looking for pokeweed or some such.

I'll cast my eyes about for some on the way home to make you honest."

Grandma Sally smiled. "All right then, go and set your heart at ease. Take my horse. He's a fast one." She picked Grace up off the blanket and sat her in her lap, waving the baby's fat little fist at Alafair's back as she retreated down the porch steps. "Say 'bye-bye, Mama,'" Sally instructed. "And good luck."

Alafair swung herself up into the saddle, arranged her skirt to cover her black-stockinged knees, and turned the horse's head toward town.

<center>~~~~</center>

At a canter, Alafair covered the two miles into Boynton in fifteen minutes. She swung out of the saddle and threw the horse's reins over the hitching post in front of the sheriff's office, then bounded up the wooden steps, still moving quickly from the brisk ride. Sheriff Scott Tucker was pouring himself a cup of coffee when Alafair entered the office. He lowered the pot gently back down onto the Franklin stove and smiled when he recognized Alafair. Shaw's cousin Scott Tucker was a medium-sized man, running to plump, with thinning hair, a pleasant face, and twinkly blue eyes. He owned the mercantile and a small hotel in Boynton, both of which his wife ran. He had gotten himself elected Sheriff several years before, and he took the job very seriously.

"Good day to you, Alafair," he greeted. "What can I do for you this fine day?"

Alafair sat herself down in the bentwood chair beside the sheriff's desk and came right to the point. "Scott, what can you tell me about the murder of Louise Kelley?" she asked.

Scott sat down on the edge of the desk. "Louise has been singing in the choir celestial for most of a year now," he noted. "Being as her earthly remains were discovered on your land, I'm surprised you haven't asked me about this long before now."

"I didn't know that Alice was interested in Walter Kelley before now."

"Ah," Scott breathed, enlightened. He stood up. "Can I get you some coffee? No?" He moved around behind the desk and took his seat, then leaned forward on his elbows. "Here's what I propose," he said. "I'm going to tell you what I found out about that affair, little as it is, just to set your mind at ease about Walter Kelley, because as I see it, it's most unlikely that he could have been involved in the murder of his wife. But before I do, I want you to promise that you won't go off half cocked, like you did last year when Harley Day got hisself shot in the head. You remember how that turned out. You almost got your own head stove in."

"I learned my lesson, Scott," she assured him grimly. "But if you can set my mind at ease about Walter, I would be much obliged."

Scott leaned back comfortably and gathered his thoughts for a moment. "Here's the bare facts," he began. "On July second last year, at about one-thirty in the afternoon, Walter left Muskogee on the train with a ticket for Kansas City, where his mother lives. He had told some of his customers that he was planning to get home late on the morning of the sixth, but according to his mother, Walter's uncle made a special trip up from Joplin on the day before, just to see his nephew. So Walter decided to stay, and changed his return ticket to July 10. Instead, I wired him that his wife was dead, and he ended up coming home late on the seventh.

"After Miz Kelley got murdered and her husband came home, I sent my deputy, Trent, on the same trip Walter took. I told him to talk to everybody he could find from here to Kansas City who may have seen or spoken to Walter. Walter was the only person to board the Wichita train in Muskogee that day. He makes that trip regular, and him being such a friendly fellow, they know him well at the Muskogee depot. The conductor remembers him, and so do two or three people at the station who saw him get on. Likewise, witnesses saw him change trains in Wichita for Kansas City, and we have plenty of witnesses who can testify that he got to Kansas City on time, went to his mother's home, and was seen there and around the neighborhood every day after that for a week. There ain't two hours together that he was in Kansas City that he can't account for—certainly not enough time for him to get back to Boynton and kill his wife without anybody in Kansas City noticing he was gone."

"How do you know that he didn't hire somebody to do the deed while he was well away?" Alafair asked. "It was common knowledge that him and Louise weren't happy together."

"It's possible, Alafair," Scott admitted. "But if he did, I can't find one single bit of evidence of it. No money went missing from his bank account, nor was he seen consorting with known thugs and wastrels. The Kelleys weren't happy, that's true. Plenty of people were quick to point that out when I went to asking questions. But nobody could say for sure that there was ever any violence or even loud words in that marriage. Discontentment ain't enough reason to indict a man for murder.

"On the other hand, there was lots of evidence that Louise had been leading a shadow life of her own for some time. And it seems that when Walter went to Kansas City, Louise cut loose. The last time I can prove that anybody saw her alive was the fifth of July, the night before the boys found her in the creek. She had been dancing that evening at the Rusty Horseshoe roadhouse outside of town, sneaking out and drinking home brew behind the building with a young man. Got herself falling down drunk, the proprietor says, and made quite the fool of herself. Then several people tell me that she left the place a little after dark on the night of the fifth with the same fellow, who was as plastered as she was. And that was it. No one has seen hide nor hair of this man since. I did get a good description of him and the horse he rode in on. The law in three states is on the lookout for him. I expect he holed up a spell, but he'll be feeling safe eventually, and may be out and about by now. Somebody will spot him sooner or later, and we can at least give the poor woman some justice, even if she didn't have no happiness."

Alafair, who had been listening with a troubled expression on her face, pondered for a moment, then shook her head. "But what about Walter's straying? I'm guessing you did talk to the Crockers."

Scott laughed. "Scandalous news does spread, don't it?" he observed. "Yes, I looked into all that. Neither husband nor wife was faithful in the Kelley marriage, I'm afraid. Who knows who drove the other to it? Walter says they hadn't been as man and wife for a couple of months or so before Louise's unfortunate end. Now, Alafair, I think I can tell you fairly certain that Walter didn't kill his wife, but I'm sad to say that I can't tell you that Walter Kelley was much of a husband."

"I'm distressed to hear it."

"It may not have been his fault, you know, that unhappy marriage," Scott ventured.

"You're a charitable man," Alafair observed, with a sour smile.

"I've always known you to give a person the benefit of the doubt."

"Not where my children's welfare is concerned," she assured him.

Scott hid his amused expression by passing his hand casually over his face. "In any case," he said, "whoever killed Louise was a pretty low character. She had a bruise on one side of her face, like she had been struck by a fist. Doc Addison said that she was stabbed with one furious blow that broke her breast-bone and plunged right into her heart. It was an unusual knife, too—a big carving knife with a white bone handle that had a design of a ship whittled into it. Scrimshaw, they call it. She was dead before she hit the ground. And then the murderer—or murderers, I think, judging by the tracks—somehow toted her body, knife and all, from wherever it was they killed her down to Cane Creek, where they stuffed her under the cottonwood roots up nigh the bank. Probably not eight or ten hours before your boys found her."

Goose bumps rose on Alafair's arms at the thought. "Mercy. I don't like the thought of bad sorts like that being on the loose, and for so long."

"Sometimes it takes a while to catch them if they go into hiding. I doubt if they're still close around here," Scott soothed her. "But whether they are or they ain't, we'll get them soon enough."

"Do you have the names of these men?"

"We know the name of the man who was seen at the road-house with Louise."

"Would I know him?"

"I doubt it," Scott assured her.

Alafair nodded. Cousin Scott was the most easygoing of men in his daily life, but she had never known anyone more doggedly persistent in the pursuit of justice. "So you don't think Louise was killed there on the banks of Cane Creek?"

"I didn't find no evidence of it. The ground around the creek bank was pretty churned up by the time I got there, but I did find prints going off away from the creek out toward y'all's back forty. Looked to me like two people on horseback and one pony —or maybe a jenny or a jackass—with a triangle-shaped nick in the left rear shoe. I tracked them through the woods onto the Eichelburger property, cut right across the corner of their pasture, then I lost the trail on the road. They were heading away from town, I think. South."

"Well, Scott, they could be in Mexico by now, couldn't they?"

"They could be all the way to the South Pole by now, but I don't think so."

"Why not?" Alafair persisted.

"Now, Alafair," Scott said, "you don't expect me to give away all my secrets, do you?"

She blinked at him, disappointed. Of course, that was exactly what she was hoping for. But Scott had just informed her gently but firmly that if he had suspicions who these miscreants were and where they were hiding, he certainly wasn't going to tell her.

"If you know who they are, though, why haven't you put up their pictures? Don't you want folks to be on the lookout?"

"Maybe we do have certain folks on the lookout. Maybe we don't want the villains to know we're hunting 'em, so they'll feel comfortable enough to come out of hiding."

"Ah," Alafair said, enlightened. "Local fellows, then."

"Local enough. Leave it to us lawmen, Alafair. I expect we know what we're doing."

Scott smiled, and Alafair flushed. "I never thought otherwise," she assured him. She stood up, and Scott did likewise. "Thank you for so kindly telling me all this, Scott," she said. "I can't say you exactly put my mind at ease, but at least I don't feel so ignorant about the man Alice has her eye on."

"I'm glad I could be of help, such as it is," Scott said. "You know, if Alice was my girl, I'd be concerned, too. Are you going to talk to Shaw about this?"

"I surely am. I can't imagine what he'll say about it. He likes Walter Kelly a lot."

Scott sighed. "So do I," he admitted.

⌐⌐⌐⌐

Alafair unhitched the horse from the rail in front of the sheriff's office, but didn't mount. Instead she took the reins and led the horse down the street. She felt like she needed time to think. As she walked down Main Street, absently greeting several acquaintances who were going about their business, she passed Elm, and on a whim, took a left turn and walked up the street, past Kelley's white frame house.

It was a nice neighborhood. The long, brick-paved street was lined with American elms, not yet massive trees, since the town of Boynton itself wasn't very old, but big enough to cast a pleasant lace of shade over the sidewalk. A haze of pale green leaves gave the light that filtered through the branches a soothing pastel hue. Most of the houses were large, often two stories, and painted white, with red brick foundations that flowed all of a piece into long brick walks leading from the porches to the street. The Kelley house, sitting on the corner of Third and Elm, was smaller, only one story, with a gabled attic. But it was well appointed, with fancy gingerbreading along the porch and a leaded glass window panel in the front door.

Grandma Sally's big red gelding clopped placidly along with Alafair, his enormous head next to her shoulder, nodding along with each step as though he approved of her detour. An occasional snort of sweet, hot horse breath warmed the flesh of her arm.

She began to talk to the horse under her breath as they ambled along, up and down Elm Street. "I don't know what I think I'm going to see, here, Horse," she murmured. "I reckon I ought to be getting on home, before your mistress takes exception to being left alone with a squally little mess of a baby."

Her gaze swept Kelley's neat yard as she passed it for the second time. "Do I think Louise's unquiet ghost is going to march right out here and tell me who killed her? You know what I'd say to her if I could, Horse? I'd say: 'Louise, I'm sorry you got killed, and if I could find out who murdered you, I sure would. But, you know, what I really wonder is, what kind of a man is your former husband?' That's mighty bad of me, ain't it, Horse?"

She passed Kelley's house a third time, sighed with annoyance at her own folly, and headed back toward Main Street. She was just walking by the neighbor's gate, when the front door opened and two women came out of the house and walked down the steps toward the street. Alafair and the horse stopped abruptly.

"Good afternoon," she called, before she had thought what she would say to these people.

The older woman paused, her hand on her front gate, and looked up at Alafair with a smile, not thinking it all odd that a stranger leading a horse down her street would greet her. "Afternoon," she called back.

The two women were obviously mother and daughter. Their round, red-cheeked faces and sturdy builds were exactly the same. If you subtracted twenty-five years and twenty-five pounds, the daughter was a perfect picture of what the mother must have looked like in her youth.

"Fine day, ain't it?" Alafair said, as she led the horse over to the sidewalk.

"It surely is," the woman agreed.

"My name's Alafair Tucker. My husband is Shaw Tucker, and our farm is just out west of town. His mama is Miz Peter McBride, you may know of them. Sheriff Scott Tucker is my husband's cousin."

"Yes, indeed," the woman responded. "I know of y'all's place out there. My daughter here is friends with Maxine Cecil. I believe Maxine's mother is your husband's sister. My husband voted for Sheriff Tucker last time. He's a good man." Alafair wasn't surprised that the woman was familiar with her family. It would be hard to swing a cat without hitting a Tucker here in Muskogee County.

The woman extended her hand. "I'm Wanda Grant, and this here is my daughter Susan. My husband is the local representative for the Muskogee Tool Company."

"Hello," Susan managed to wedge in.

"Hello, Susan. Yes, Miz Grant, my husband has dealt with yours, I believe. Proud to meet you."

Now that they had properly placed themselves in the great scheme of local society, Alafair prepared to get down to business. She noted that the Grant women were both nicely dressed in fashionable high waisted cream-colored frocks and wing-brimmed hats. On their way out, either for shopping or calling, she figured. Alafair was going to have to get right to the point.

"I was just visiting with Scott," she said. "We was talking about the murder of your neighbor, Miz Kelley, last summer, and how nobody has been caught, yet. Got my curiosity up, I confess, and I just decided to wander past and have a look at the house. Pretty nosy, I guess. I reckon you must have known Miz Kelley, though! That was a sad story, wasn't it, about some devil doing her in and dumping her in the creek?"

Mrs. Grant pursed her lips and shook her head. "Well, I don't like to malign the dead..." she began, in a way that told Alafair she was about to do just that. "...Nobody ought to get murdered like that, no matter what they're up to, but I must say that I wasn't surprised that Louise got herself in a bad situation and came to no good. Yes, we knew Miz Kelley pretty well, and a more unpleasant woman you'd never meet..."

"Now, Mama," Susan interjected, "Miz Kelley wasn't so bad, just demanding. Her and Walter just wasn't suited, I think, her being serious and him so sociable. She wished he was different than he was. Why, they probably never knew how to make each other happy."

Alafair looked at Susan with renewed interest. Because of her earlier silence, she had made a quick assumption that the daughter was retiring, but the girl was more spirited than she had first appeared.

"Thank you, Susan," Mrs. Grant was saying. "Yes, I shouldn't be so hard on Louise, since things turned out the way they did."

"I heard there was some talk that her husband may have had something to do with it," Alafair ventured.

Both Mrs. Grant and Susan made indignant noises at that. "Why, I'd just fall right down dead from shock if Walter ever had a mean thought, much less killed his wife," Mrs. Grant assured her. "He was a saint for putting up with her for as long as he did, is what I think."

"Now, Mama," Susan chastised.

Mrs. Grant gave her daughter an indulgent smile. "Susan has been listening to her father, I think. He don't like us talking bad about Louise now she's dead. My husband is a good Christian man, and tries not to pass judgment." She turned to Susan. "But tell the truth, now, honey. You didn't care much for Miz Kelley, either."

Susan shrugged. "Well, she wasn't very nice to me, I admit. She'd give me a look that would wither a post every time I walked by."

Mrs. Grant leaned toward Alafair. "Jealous," she said under her breath. "And her husband is the nicest man, always with a good word to say to anybody."

"Wasn't there some rumor a while back that Mr. Kelley had a dalliance?" Alafair asked.

"Rumor, is all! I heard that, too. But I've been neighbor to the Kelleys for five years, Miz Tucker, and I just can't credit it. In fact..." Mrs. Grant hesitated and bit her lip, wondering whether to spill a tidbit that was too scandalous even for her. She didn't wonder for long. "In fact," she continued, "it was the other way around. I know Louise was seen in the company of someone other than her husband the night she was killed, but I had the feeling for a long time before that that she had her a fellow somewhere."

"Mama," Susan admonished.

Mrs. Grant had the good manners to blush. "I know I'm being mean. But I like Walter Kelley a lot, and I'm sorry to hear there's stories about him going around."

You must like Walter indeed, Alafair thought, to go on so readily about his late wife to someone whom you just met in the street. But she said, "I understand, Miz Grant."

"The Sheriff asked us a lot of questions in the weeks after the murder," Mrs. Grant continued. "Why, he must have been over here half a dozen times. I could tell he suspected Walter might have had something to do with it, but you know, there wasn't a bad thing we could say about Walter." She sighed. "Poor man. He was all at odds after Louise died. We took food over to him every night after he got back from Kansas City, or he would have starved to death. After a week or so, I volunteered Susan to keep his house for him. She goes in to clean a couple times a week. I figured it might cheer him to be around a fine young woman for a while. You should have seen what a mess he let that house get into. Men are just helpless, I declare."

Now Susan was blushing. So that was it, Alafair decided. Wanda Grant had her eye on the barber for her daughter. And Susan may have looked embarrassed at her mother's indiscretion, but her little smile said she wasn't displeased by the implication that Walter would benefit from her company.

"I expect I'm keeping you," Alafair said. "I'll be on my way so you can get to wherever you're going. I apologize for my curiosity. Sure was nice to meet y'all."

The Grants continued down the street and Alafair swung herself up into the saddle and headed out of town. "Well, Horse," she mused. "I don't know if I just found out anything helpful or not. Maybe Louise had her a boyfriend. Maybe a jealous boyfriend who saw her with the fellow at the roadhouse? Surely

Scott has looked into all of Louise's social contacts, respectable and otherwise. Miz Grant, who doesn't have a lick of sense, wants Walter for her girl. Well, I hope she gets him, and they have joy of each other, and Alice never speaks to the man again."

Chapter Six

Alafair leaned back against the headboard of the tall four-poster bed she shared with Shaw, and propped herself up with a pillow as she watched him getting ready for bed. She found herself staring at his sinewy, brown back as he hung his work shirt on a peg on the wall. It's no wonder we have so many children, she thought, then smiled at her own brazenness. Her mother would faint dead away if she knew.

"I rode into town today and had a little talk with Scott about the murder of Louise Kelley," she opened.

In the dim light of the coal oil lamp on the bedside table, she could see his honey-hazel eyes skew an ironic look over his arm as he reached for his nightshirt in the wardrobe. "Still worried about that, are you?"

She sat up straighter and folded her hands primly in her lap. "I told you that Alice has got her eye on that barber, and I'll be switched if I'm going to let her get involved with a murderer."

Shaw sat down in the rocker and pulled off his boots. "Walter ain't no murderer."

Alafair sighed. "Maybe not," she admitted. "But I fear he was no prize as a husband, either. Your ma told you the story about him and the Crocker girl, didn't she? I'm pretty sure she's the one I saw at Louise's funeral, standing outside the fence, still hoping to catch his eye."

Shaw leaned forward with one sock dangling in his hand and placed his elbows on his knees. He regarded her for a moment before he replied. "Yes, I know about that, and it troubles me. But if he was still interested in her he's had plenty of time to do something about it. Now, I know that Alice may have told you that she's set her cap for this fellow, but I haven't seen no sign that he returns the sentiment. I know they were chatting it up at Ma's Easter dinner, but it could be that he was just being friendly and enjoying the attentions of the pretty girls. He's a good ten or twelve years older than she is, I'm thinking."

Alafair gave him a brief wag of her index finger. "There's another problem."

"I've known plenty of happy marriages with more than fifteen years between husband and wife," Shaw noted.

"Still…if that were just the only problem."

Shaw leaned back in the rocker and smiled. "Yes, if only…" he conceded.

A moment of silence fell as they regarded each other across the dim room.

"So what are we going to do?" Alafair said, at length.

Shaw shrugged. "What do you suggest, hon? Alice is eighteen years old. She's of age. If she's of a mind to marry the barber then she's got a right to do it. He's good-natured and well to do. He'd be a good provider. Maybe that's what's most important to her. I can lock her up, I reckon, but I expect that would just make her more determined to do it. I'm thinking that if we don't push her one way or the other, she may decide herself that she could do better."

"Alice may be of age," Alafair said, "but that don't mean we can't try to talk some sense into her."

"Now, Alafair," Shaw warned, "you know how contrary Alice is. You start arguing with her and she'll have him just to spite you."

Alafair leaned forward in the bed, anxious and suddenly on the verge of tears. "Shaw, I'm not worried about the idea that they might get married. I'm worried that…well, what if they don't get married? She's young and thinks she's smart, but she's just innocent. I mean, I don't want her to marry somebody who would make her unhappy, and I think Kelley might. But I'd much rather that than…oh, Shaw, what if he ruins her?"

She couldn't see his expression very well in the darkness but he fell very still for a moment.

"Well, then I'll just kill him," he assured her quietly.

Alafair said nothing to this. She knew Shaw well enough to know that when he was serious, he never exaggerated, and he never lied. She snuggled down under the covers, satisfied.

The cock crowed at five o'clock the next morning, and Alafair and Shaw rolled out of bed in half-conscious silence. Pre-dawn in late March was a chilly time of day, and Shaw hustled into the parlor in his stocking feet and nightshirt to fire up the stove while Alafair lit a coal oil lamp and spread up the bed before changing and nursing her sleepy baby. She had buttoned her petticoat and was just pulling on her stockings when Shaw returned.

"Did you wake up the boys?" she whispered through chattering teeth.

He laughed. "Naw. They're sleeping like a pair of logs. I don't think they'd have been bothered if I had pounded on the stove with the tongs. I heard some girls stirring, though."

"Martha, probably," Alafair speculated. She drew on a long-sleeved shirt and pulled a dark skirt on over her head, sat on the side of the bed to put on her shoes, then ran her brush briskly through her long dark hair before twisting it up into a knot at the back of her head.

She left Shaw in his britches with his galluses hanging looped down his sides, standing in front of the mirror over the dresser, mixing up his shaving soap in a ceramic mug with a boar bristle brush. With Grace on her hip and the diaper pail in her hand, she passed through the parlor where her sons lay sleeping on their cots and into the kitchen to make up the fire in the enormous old iron cookstove. She put the diaper pail on the back porch, then sat the baby in her highchair and gave her a cracker before she checked her supply of wood and kindling—enough for today, but she made a mental note to tell Gee Dub to split some more and fill her fire box before the day was out.

She raked out the ashes from the fire box into a bucket, laid her kindling and starter, and lit it with a long match. After the kindling was well alight, she began feeding the fire with larger pieces of wood, until her practised eye told her it was big enough and the stove hot enough to cook breakfast. Before she had the burner covers adjusted, Martha padded into the kitchen, still tucking her calico shirt into her skirt.

"Aren't you going in to work this morning?" Alafair asked, eyeing her daughter's casual outfit.

"I have the day off," Martha told her, chucking the giggling baby under the chin. "Mr. Bushyhead said he'll be making some calls out of town today and won't be needing me."

"Are the other girls awake?"

"I am," Mary said, appearing in the kitchen door out of the dawn gloom, still braiding her honey-colored hair. "Ruth is getting around, but Alice and the little girls are still asleep."

Alafair nodded. "Mary, honey, start some biscuits, and that pot of oats I've been soaking. Martha, wake up them boys. They need to get to milking before the day gets too much further along. I'll get the girls."

Fifteen minutes later Alafair and Shaw were directing their army of frowzy-headed, mostly dressed children in the tasks of starting the day. Mary and Alice were cooking, Sophronia setting the table and entertaining Grace, Ruth and Blanche were drawing water. Charlie and Gee Dub were making a chilly dash across the dew-covered yard with buckets in hand, just ahead of their father, heading for the barn and the animals to be fed and milked.

"Martha, come with me to the hen house," Alafair asked. Martha looked at her askance, since her mother rarely asked for help gathering eggs in the morning, but she complied quietly, grabbing an egg basket and shrugging into her jacket.

"Bring me another slab of bacon from the smokehouse on your way back," Mary called to them, as they walked out the back door.

Alafair liked the hen house. It was always warm, even on nippy mornings like this one, and she enjoyed the soothing clucking music of the chickens. She was fastidious about keeping the hen house and the chicken yard clean, and the smell of corn and chicken feathers was rather homey. She and Martha worked in silence for a few minutes.

"I always liked gathering eggs," Martha said out of the quiet. "Don't get to do it much anymore since I went to Tulsa for my typewriting course and then started working at the bank."

Alafair was not surprised that Martha was verbalizing the same thoughts that Alafair herself was having. She and her eldest were, to all intents, not that far apart in age, and she had always felt a special bond with her dark-eyed, dark-haired Martha. Even though their lives and desires were quite different, Martha resembled her mother more than any of the other children, both in looks and in nature.

"You haven't been talking much about work for the last few weeks," Alafair observed. "Are you still enjoying yourself at the bank?"

"Oh, yes. It's just been very busy lately. Lots of new people moving in around here, you know. Lots of new accounts and loans. Lots of papers to type and file. Mr. Bushyhead is teaching me about how the bank makes loans, about interest, and what they do with the money they get, about investing."

"Mercy," Alafair said. "It sounds too complicated for me."

Martha chuckled. "I like it."

"Must be nice to feel so independent, make your own money and all." Alafair wasn't being insincere. Options for women had always been few, especially on the frontier, but times were changing, and Martha was one of a new breed of woman. Alafair genuinely admired her daughter for taking her own fate in her hands. Not every one of their neighbors and relatives were quite so tolerant of Martha's unconventionality, but if disapproving looks bothered Martha, she never gave any indication of it. "Tell me, honey," Alafair continued. "Do you ever see much of Walter Kelley there in the bank?"

In the gloom, Alafair couldn't see Martha slide a glance at her. "Yes, quite often," Martha answered. "He does a lot of business with Mr. Bushyhead. Besides that barbering business he has, he owns a bunch of property around the county, including the building on Main Street that his shop is in, I think. Some oil wells, too."

"Is that so?" Alafair exclaimed. "So he would be pretty well-to-do."

"I expect everybody knows that already," Martha said. She straightened up from bending over the nest boxes. "Now, Ma, don't go telling anybody I was blabbing to you about bank customers," she admonished. "Mr. Bushyhead would not be pleased."

"I won't," Alafair said. "I was just interested in Kelley because Alice told me she likes him."

Martha bent back over the nest. "I figured."

"So has Alice said anything to you about this?"

"Oh, she's set her cap for him, all right," Martha confirmed. "Trouble is, she hasn't bothered to tell Mr. Kelley about it yet."

"Well, I'm glad of that, at least. But why this Kelley man, Martha? With all the trouble around him, what does she possibly see in him?"

"It's like you said, Ma. He's got money, and Alice is determined not to marry a farmer."

"What's wrong with a farmer?" Alafair wondered, stung.

"Too much work," Martha said. "Alice wants nice clothes and a house in town and trips to St. Louis and Kansas City and who knows where. Besides, Mr. Kelley is right good looking, and charming as all get-out."

"But a womanizer!"

"Alice is sure she can tame him, Ma," Martha informed her with amusement. "Alice has always had a good opinion of herself."

Indeed, Alafair thought. Alice was the beauty of the family, tall and imposing, with wheaten blond hair and sky blue eyes and a complexion like milk, and such personality that she could charm the birds out of the trees if she was of a mind to. Alafair paused with her hand over her egg basket, remembering her dancing little Alice, always laughing and singing. She had been the wittiest child Alafair had ever seen. She was too smart, Alafair thought, too easily bored and into mischief if she wasn't constantly busy and amused. As sassy and troublesome as she had always been, none of her children could make Alafair laugh like Alice could. Yes, if she were hard pressed, she might say that Alice was her favorite. Alafair felt tears start to her eyes, and she blinked them back fiercely. Alice was a grown woman, now, and a willful one at that. If she was determined to marry, she would do it whether her mother approved or not. But this man! If there was anything that Alafair could do to forestall grief for her daughter, she would, come the Devil. Even if Alice was a grown woman.

"Well, I'm thinking we've got enough eggs," she said to Martha. "We'd better get back to the house and get this day to going."

⁓⁓⁓

Unlike dinner, the family didn't sit down as one to eat breakfast. Instead, the first meal of the day was done more or less in shifts as groups of family members finished chores and made it to the table. Six-month-old Grace had already had her breakfast, but she sat at the end of the table, where she could see all the action, in the venerable highchair that Shaw had made by hand for Martha over twenty years before. She gnawed cheerfully on whatever her mother deemed appropriate for her that morning. The soda cracker she had started out with had long since been gummed into oblivion, and when Alafair came back into the house, she found that one of the older siblings had made the baby a "sugar tit" out of a spoonful of sugar knotted inside a clean dish towel. Since the baby had begun teething, she appreciated chewing on the hard knot. Martha picked up the baby and took her into the bedroom for a change while Alafair delivered the eggs and bacon to the girls and inspected the food preparation.

Mary and Alice had already taken the biscuits out of the oven and placed pitchers of sweet milk, Karo syrup, sorghum, and cream on the table, along with a couple of loaves of pale spring butter and two sugar bowls. An enormous pot of oatmeal was biding its time on a back burner. The girls had already fried up one slab of bacon, the still sizzling slices of which were on a towel-covered platter on the cabinet, and Alice was just making gravy from the pan drippings. Mary took the eggs from her mother, poured more bacon grease from the drippings jar into a second iron skillet, and began expertly cracking eggs into the hot grease to fry. As soon as one egg was done she scooped it out onto a plate and cracked another into its place in the skillet. She cooked the eggs to order. Ruth liked her fried eggs over hard, Sophronia and Blanche over easy. Shaw and both the boys liked to sop egg yolk with their biscuits, so Mary made their eggs sunny side up. Alafair liked to sop a little, too, but she was adamant that the whites of her eggs be well set, so Mary "blindfolded" her mother's eggs by flipping hot grease over the tops with the turner. Martha's taste agreed with her mother's. Alice decided to forgo eggs altogether in favor of extra biscuits and gravy along with her oatmeal and bacon. Mary cracked a couple of eggs in a bowl and scrambled them up with fresh whole milk and a little butter for herself.

The younger girls had finished and gone off to get ready for school, and Shaw and the boys and the two chefs of the day, Mary and Alice, were sitting around the table, ravenous after their early morning tasks. Alafair prepared a bowl of oats for Charlie-boy with lots of cream and sugar and a pat of butter slowly melting in the middle. Charlie-dog was sitting on the floor next to his boy's chair, watching with blazing attention as the people at the table ate their bacon.

"You know," Alafair said to anyone who might be listening, as she sat the bowl down in front of the boy and gave the dog a surreptitious pat, "my daddy always said that when he was growing up, his grandpa would never eat his oats but what he was standing up."

"Now, why would that be, hon?" Shaw asked, always keen to encourage a tale.

Alafair sat down in her chair and reached for the platter of bacon. "I don't rightly know. I reckon my daddy never knew, either. But he swears that his Grandpa Gunn took his oatmeal with cream and a pinch of salt, and always stood up when he was eating it."

"Salt!" Gee Dub exclaimed. "Now, that don't sound good at all."

"Did he ever stand up to eat anything besides oats?" Alice asked, skeptical.

"Not that I heard of," Alafair admitted. "But your grandpa swears it's true, and you know your grandpa ain't much of a one to make things up. His old grandpa was from the old country, and I expect they have different ways of doing things over there."

"Was he from the same old country as Grandpapa McBride?" Charlie asked.

"I don't know, punkin'. Next time we're over there you should ask Grandpapa if he ever heard such of a thing."

"I'm sure he'll tell you all about it, whether he ever heard of it or not," Shaw said, with a mischievous glint in his hazel eyes.

～～～

After breakfast, while Mary washed dishes, Martha made up five bacon sandwiches and wrapped them in clean sacking, then packed them along with a big square of dried-apple cake into a tin bucket for the kids to take to school. Gee Dub and Ruth, armed with books and lunch pail, then herded Charlie, Blanche and Sophronia out the door for the two-mile walk into town.

Alice was conscripted to baby-sit while Alafair went out on the back porch to wash diapers. The diaper pail was a tall, modified milk can with a tight-fitting lid. Alafair kept it partially filled with a mild lye-water solution, and every time she changed one of Grace's cloth diapers, she threw it into the pail. Now that Grace was a little older, Alafair didn't have to wash quite so many diapers, but she still had that task to look forward to at least a couple of times a day.

On a bench, Alafair kept a wash tub and a rinse tub at the ready. She drew water from the pump near the back door to fill her tubs, then swished the diapers around in the lye water a few times before she transferred them to the wash tub to soak in soapy water. She smiled to herself, remembering that when Martha was a baby, she had used a stick for the task. Twelve infants later, she used her bare hand. She scrubbed the diapers on the washboard, rinsed them in clear water, ran them through the hand wringer, and hung them to dry on the line she had strung across the porch.

She filled a bucket with a strong lye solution, then took it and the used diaper-soaking water to the outhouse, one pail in each hand and an old broom tucked under her arm. She dumped the diaper water down one of the holes, then splashed the lye water around the interior of the outhouse, furiously scrubbing it down with the broom. She returned to the porch to clean the diaper pail, refill it with disinfectant, and dash the wash water onto the bushes next to the back door.

When she went back inside, Martha and Mary were putting the dishes away, and Alice and Grace were on the floor, engaging in a riotous ticklefest and laughing hysterically, much to the older girls' amusement.

"Alice, if she wets her drawers, you'll be cleaning up after her," Alafair warned, more amused than annoyed.

Alice caught her breath, wiped her eyes, and stood up with the giggling child under her arm. "I reckon to go into town today and buy me some material for a skirt, Ma," she said. "Neither Martha nor Mary want to go. Is there anything I can pick up for you while I'm there?"

"Not so fast, sugar," Alafair cautioned. She ladled some water into the wash basin and lathered up with her soft, pale yellow, homemade hand soap. "This morning I noticed that the hen house needs to be cleaned and raked out. I don't want no sick birds on my hands. A couple of you girls can do that, while the other one turns the manure into that end of the garden that I dug up yesterday. Then in a couple of weeks I can plant some tomatoes in that section." Alafair raised her voice to be heard over the groans that greeted this pronouncement. "...*And* the green beans need to be picked over for bugs and weeded."

"I wish I'd gone to work, now," Martha said.

"Who'll be taking care of Grace?" Alice asked.

"I'll take care of Grace," Alafair told her, as she toweled her hands. "I want to start cleaning out the kitchen cabinets before dinner. Put in some fresh bay leaves to keep the critters out of there."

"Let me do that, Mama," Alice requested. "I'll get dinner, too. That way I can still go into town this afternoon without having to wash all over and burn my clothes."

Alafair looked at her other daughters. "Do y'all girls object?" she asked.

"Not if Alice promises to return the favor," Martha said.

The corner of Alice's mouth quirked. "I'm sure you'll get back at me one way or the other."

Alafair shrugged. "It's all right with me, then. I don't mind digging. Just see to it that you keep a good eye on Grace while you're working, and call us in plenty of time to wash up before dinner."

Chapter Seven

Later that afternoon, Alice Tucker was strolling down Main Street in Boynton, window shopping. She had had a busy day. Following a morning of chores, she had borrowed Martha's bicycle after dinner and ridden into town to visit a girlfriend. From there she had called on her aunt Josie and cousin Maxine Cecil, then dropped in for some gossip with Mrs. Fluke, the postmistress. She followed that with a visit to Cousin Scott's wife Hattie, at the Mercantile. She had bought several yards of material while she was in the store—a light green poplin that would make a pretty spring frock. Hattie had thrown in a piece of pale blue grosgrain ribbon that matched Alice's eyes. Alice tied it around the crown of her white straw boater, and was feeling quite jaunty as she biked down the street with her package in the basket that hung from the handlebars. The tails of her ribbon bounced off the brim of her hat as she rode along the brick pavement.

The street was busy with traffic on this weekday afternoon, mostly wagons and buggies and a few horseback riders. The odd automobile, however, was no cause for excitement in these modern times, so Alice paid no particular attention to the vehicle coming toward her until the driver came to a stop in the middle of the street and honked his horn at her. She stopped pedaling and put on her best smile when she saw who it was.

Walter Kelley doffed his hat grandly. "Afternoon, Alice," he called. "Where are you off to with all them bundles in your basket?"

"I'm on my way to Williams' Drug Store for a flip," she told him. "Shopping makes me dry."

"Care for some company?"

"I might."

He jumped out of the driver's seat. "Throw your packages in here, then. I'll strap your bicycle to the back and give you a lift."

The fact that the drugstore was less than half a block away was of no moment whatsoever. Alice tossed her bundle onto the seat, gathered her skirt in one hand, and hoisted herself into the auto as Walter strapped Martha's precious bicycle over his spare tire on the back of the automobile.

"You look mighty pretty," Walter observed, after he was settled in his seat again.

"Thank you."

"What would you say to a short spin?" he suggested. "It's such a nice day."

"I don't have all the time in the world," Alice told him, "but I expect I could spare half an hour or so."

Someone behind them in a horse drawn dray hollered at them to move, and Walter put the car in gear.

"What say we drive out north of town a bit," he said. "One of my customers tells me that the cranes are coming in."

"I'd like that."

Once they left the brick-paved streets of town, Walter drove very slowly in order to raise as little dust as possible and spare Alice's hair, clothes, and respiratory system. The road north to Tulsa was well-maintained, but the dry weather that made it easy to navigate also made it a dusty ordeal for an automobile driver. Fortunately, they didn't have to drive far before they reached an elongated stand of trees that spanned the road on either side. From a distance, the trees appeared to be covered with enormous showy flowers, but as the Ford approached, the flowers transformed into birds that took to the air on snow white wings. The quarter-mile-wide copse was watered by Cloud Creek on one side of the road and several farm ponds on the other, and served as a comfortable rookery for a flock of small, white egrets. The egrets appeared every spring to spend the warm season raising their families. They were a beautiful sight.

Walter pulled off onto the side of the road and shut off the engine, and after a moment, the swirling flock settled back onto their perches.

"I know it's really spring, now that the cranes have come back to roost," Alice said.

"We have big old cranes and herons on the river, up around Kansas City," Walter said, "but these here ones are pretty small. Do you know what kind they are?"

"I don't," she admitted. "My sister Martha thinks they're some kind of egret. My sisters and I used to come up here and gather white feathers all season long. Sometimes boys from town come out and shoot at them. I don't know why. They don't do anybody any harm and they aren't good to eat. They're just pretty."

Walter dropped his arm across the back of the seat. "Some folks don't appreciate beauty. But I surely know a beautiful thing when I see it." The arm dropped casually over Alice's shoulders.

She turned her head and looked at him from under her lashes. One corner of her mouth turned up. "Are you going to buy me that flip or aren't you?" she said.

He removed his arm from her shoulders. "I will if you'll answer me a question."

"More questions? And what would this one be?"

"I expect you know that I hold you in high regard, Alice," he began.

She said nothing, but the sly half-smile broadened a little. She looked back toward the birds.

"What I was wondering," Walter continued, "was if you thought you might be able to return the sentiment some day."

"I might," she said, after a pause. She looked at him out of the corner of her eye. "I already do, truth be told," she added.

Walter grinned. "Well, now, that's fine," he exclaimed. "So we might step out together some time?"

Alice studied his face critically for a moment. "I'd like that, Walter, but my folks think it's too soon after your wife's death for us to do any sparking."

"Too soon? It's been nearly a year since Louise died. There's plenty of ladies around town who would be only too happy to see me go around with their daughters." He knew he had made a mistake the minute the sentence left his mouth. From where he sat, he could feel the air chill between himself and Alice.

"Go out with one of them, then," she said.

"No, I didn't mean to say...I didn't mean it the way it sounded. I just mean, well, I don't want anybody else, Alice. Until you came along, I didn't have no interest in forming an attachment to any young lady at all."

Her expression thawed slightly. "Are you talking about a serious attachment?" she asked. "Because I ain't interested in wasting my time, otherwise."

She was making him work harder for her good opinion, Walter thought, than anyone he had known before. He smiled and shook his head. He was enjoying it very much. "I never thought I'd be saying this again, at least not for a long time, but yes, I am talking about a serious attachment." He turned in the seat to face Alice directly. "You're different than any girl I ever met. Ever since that walk in the orchard at your grandfolks' place, I can't hardly get you out of my mind. You're mighty special, is all I've got to say."

Alice was pleased by his declaration, and even excited, but she wasn't surprised. She was entirely aware of her worth. "What I have to say, Walter, is that I feel the same way. I wouldn't object a bit if we got to know one another better."

"When can I call on your folks?"

"I don't expect my folks need to know about this just yet," Alice said. "I'd just as soon wait until they catch the fellow who killed your wife and that's all cleared up. If I don't have to, I'd rather not have to put up with the hard time my mother would give me."

"Why, Alice, sugar, it could be months before that happens, if it happens at all. I'd feel mighty bad not to be able to see you for all that long time."

"I didn't say we couldn't see one another. I'd just prefer that my parents don't know about it."

Walter's face registered confusion, surprise, and admiration, one after the other, within the space of a second. "How do you propose we go about in secret in a town the size of Boynton?" he wondered.

Alice didn't answer right away. Deep in thought, her gaze swept the egret-festooned trees in a slow arc. "I have an idea how we can meet. My sister Phoebe had the same problem when she and John Lee were courting, and she didn't want Mama and Daddy to know. They found themselves a secret place to rendezvous." She looked back at Walter. "But before I agree to go behind my parents' back to see you, I'll ask you to tell me what happened between you and Peggy Crocker."

Walter leaned back in the seat. "Oh," he said, looking none too comfortable. "All right. I expect you have a right to know. I'm not proud of that, Alice, I promise you. I tried to put the girl off for a long time. But Peggy wouldn't let it go. Things went farther than they should have. Louise and I hadn't…well, we had slept in separate bedrooms for months by that time, and Peggy was more than willing. I felt so bad about it after awhile that I broke it off. That story about her being with child, I don't believe it. I believe it's a tale she concocted so I'd leave Louise, or else drive Louise to divorce me. In fact, she came to the house when I was at work and told Louise about it. I was riled about that. But then when I told Peggy that there was no possibility of us getting married, she had a mighty convenient miscarriage. That's why I think it was a story."

He paused, grasping for the right words. "Louise…Louise lost her mind after that, I think. I hate to say it, but I don't know what else. She'd sneak off at night to meet paramours, yet she got religion so bad that she was at church or praying every spare minute of the day. She wouldn't let me touch her, yet she accused me of running around on her so many times that I figured I might as well be hanged for a sheep as a lamb." He turned in the seat and took Alice's hand. "It would never

have happened if I hadn't been drove to it by her suspicions."
His dark eyes brimmed.

Alice believed.

"My ma thinks you're a natural-born cheater, Walter, but I
expect there's only so much a man can stand," she said.

"If I had an honorable wife, Alice, I'd be the picture of an
honorable husband."

Alice regarded him thoughtfully, then gave a decisive nod.
She extricated her hand from his grip and sat up straight. "This
is a real nice spot, close by the nesting birds. It's a shorter walk
for me to get from home to here than into town. If we were to
meet here on Monday afternoons, when your shop is closed.
Say two or three o'clock. We might have an hour or so to stroll
together, or even take a spin in your Ford."

"That's a fine plan," Walter acknowledged.

"Then, after Cousin Scott catches the men who killed
Louise, you can talk to my father, if we both are still of a mind
by then."

Chapter Eight

Less than a month after Alice and Walter conceived their plan, Alafair was making a trip to the mercantile, accompanied by Crook, the hound, who loved to ride in the buggy. She was just outside of town, going over in her head the list of necessities she intended to buy, when she spotted a rangy, stooped figure coming out of the entrance to the cemetery.

Ned Tolland. Alafair tugged on the reins to slow the horse.

The man apparently was unaware of her presence, for he didn't turn around or look toward her as she pulled her buggy to a halt in front of the cemetery gate. Alafair hadn't had in mind to visit the cemetery. She had no reason to go there. All the members of her family who were wearing the starry crown were buried in the Tucker Cemetery located on her parents-in-law's farm. In fact, she didn't really have time to make a side trip, since Alice had taken baby Grace to visit Phoebe, and Alafair expected the baby would be fussing for a meal when they got back to the house in a couple of hours.

None of those logical reasons stopped her from parking the buggy right next to the gate and calling, "Ned!"

Ned Tolland was a tall, morose man who always looked like he was bearing the weight of the world on his narrow shoulders. He was dressed in overalls and a straw hat that was drawn down over his forehead as a concession to the gusty wind. Crook jumped out of the buggy, trotted up to Ned, and began sniffing the strange man up and down. Ned reached down and rubbed the hound's ears, before tilting his head back a little to gaze at Alafair from under the shadow of his hat brim.

"Morning, Miz Tucker." Ned seemed not at all surprised to see her.

"I haven't seen you since the funeral, Ned," Alafair began. "I never did get a chance to tell you and your wife how sorry I am that Louise got killed."

"Thank you, Miz Tucker. My wife used to be real close with her sister. When Louise died, it left a real big hole." He ran the back of his hand under his eye.

"Y'all must miss her terrible."

"We do," he acknowledged. "Louise was a ray of sunshine. I still can't hardly get over it."

Alafair blinked. She had never heard Louise described as a ray of sunshine. "You know," she ventured, "I was surprised to see Peggy Crocker lurking around during the funeral. I remember that Nellie looked mighty unhappy to see Peggy there that day."

If Alafair was expecting a revealing reaction, she was disappointed. Ned shook his head sadly. "Yes, Nellie don't have no use for her," he admitted. "Peggy was after Louise's husband. She wanted to run away with him a while back." He sniffed again. "I wish they had."

Intrigued by something on Ned's boot, Crook stuck his nose into the man's arch and snuffed loudly. Alafair slapped her thigh to get the dog's attention. "Crook!" she scolded. "Get back up here." For an instant, the dog looked as though he was considering whether he wanted to obey, but he finally did as he was told and jumped back up into the buggy beside his mistress.

Alafair turned her attention back to Ned. "Do you think Peggy had something to do with Louise's murder?"

"Naw, I don't think so," he said. "Such a pitiful little gal."

"So you think it was that man that was last seen with her at the roadhouse, after all?"

Ned shrugged. "I just stopped by here to talk to Louise, like I do, sometimes, to say I was sorry."

"What are you sorry for, Ned?"

Ned hesitated before he answered, but rather than looking like a man who was considering his answer, he resembled an ox bothered by flies. "Why, I'm sorry Louise died, Miz Tucker," he said.

⌐∾⌐∾⌐∾

After Ned mounted and rode off, Alafair drove the buggy right through the gate and parked half way up the narrow road that divided the burial ground in two. She looped the reins around the whip mount before she stepped out of the buggy and began meandering up and down among the scattered stones, reading the names.

She didn't want to believe that Ned Tolland could have had anything to do with the murder. The big old sad thing hardly looked like a killer, and besides, it was obvious to her that he must have had feelings of some sort for Louise. Were they the kind of feelings a brother-in-law shouldn't have? Louise had been gadding about with a man the night she was killed. Could a rejected lover of Louise's have seen them, and taken out his rage and frustration on her afterwards? Ned Tolland? It was not the first time that Alafair had wondered if jealousy had been the spark that set off this impulsive murder. She decided that she should probably mention her odd encounter with Ned to the sheriff.

The Boynton Cemetery wasn't very large. The first occupant had been buried there less than twenty years before, shortly after the town began to grow up on the trail between Okmulgee and Muskogee, before it was surveyed and named. Fewer than a hundred graves were dotted around the enclosed grounds, and Alafair found herself purposefully picking through the longish grass to find the newer ones.

It didn't take her long to find the stone marked with the name of Louise Kelley. She stood and looked down at it for a few minutes, thoughtful and more than a little curious about her own motivation for being there at all. The small, gray, granite stone didn't look to have been laid long, since the earth around it was still disturbed and the carved letters were sharp and unworn. *Louise Boyd Kelley,* the stone read, *February 10, 1882 - July, 1912.* No day of death. Had to have been late July 5, after Louise was seen at the Rusty Horseshoe, or early on July 6, the day the boys found her in the creek. Alafair squatted down on her haunches before the grave and gathered her coat collar closer in her hand. Someone had placed a ragged branch of redbud blossoms on the grave. Ned, she thought. It was a chilly day, for the third week of April. The wind was up pretty good, and the sky was overcast with low scudding clouds. Alafair wiped a flying strand of hair out of her eyes and thought of Louise.

What was on your mind, Louise, she wondered? What made you think that dragging yourself through the gutter could possibly cure whatever ailed you? Did consorting with low men make you feel better about yourself? Did it make your husband love you?

To her own surprise, Alafair's eyes filled with tears of pity. No matter how low Louise Kelley may have sunk, she didn't deserve to be stabbed in the heart and dropped into a creek. "Who did you in, Louise?" she wondered aloud. She lifted her eyes from the grave stone and stared into the middle distance for a long moment. The cutting wind was shaking the pale-leafed elms and oaks that shaded the cemetery, making a disturbing sound that reminded Alafair of the rustling crinoline petticoats her aunts and grandmothers had worn when she was a girl. Lost in her own reflections, it took a moment for Alafair to realize that there was a strange, faint odor on the wind, and she blinked herself back to consciousness and took a cautious sniff of the air.

Ammonia. The odor was so unexpected that she glanced around curiously, half expecting to see a dog urinating on some poor soul's monument. But Crook was still sitting obediently in the buggy, and aside from her horse, who was standing at the side of the road quite content, she saw no other living creature. The acrid smell grew stronger, and it became apparent to her that she was smelling nothing more than common household ammonia. It was a smell that was familiar enough to her, though she would never spend the money to buy ammonia for cleaning when she could make her own very serviceable soaps and disinfectants from lye or vinegar.

Now, where is that coming from, she wondered, and rose to turn a circle where she stood, trying to pinpoint a direction. The wind was blowing out of the northwest, but the odor was no stronger from the northwest than it was from the southeast. It was almost like she was standing right on top of it.

Before Alafair could further ponder the mysterious smell that had come to her out of nowhere, she became aware of two people walking toward her from the cemetery gate. She immediately recognized the new pastor, Brother Ulises Bellows, and his wife, Sister Norma.

Alafair forgot her dilemma and sighed when she saw them. She liked the pastor, a short, cheerful, rather pompous man of middle age with a hearty laugh, but his religion was too scrupulous and legalistic for Alafair. Mrs. Bellows was a bit prim, but outgoing, and made no secret of the fact that she held a very high opinion of her husband's quality as a preacher. Alafair suspected that being the wife of a Christian Church pastor was the end all and be all for Sister Norma, and she was inclined to be forgiving of the woman's minor shortcomings.

"Sister Alafair!" Mr. Bellows called as they neared and recognized her. The three people greeted each other, the women clasping hands cordially, before the preacher continued. "What brings you out to the cemetery on such a blustery day?" he wondered. "I didn't think you had any family here to visit."

"I don't," Alafair confirmed, "but, the strangest thing, I was just passing by on my way to town and I felt a need to stop and pay my respects to Miz Kelley here. If you'll remember, my sons found the poor woman's body in a creek that runs through our property."

Mr. and Mrs. Bellows both crinkled their foreheads and shook their heads sadly. "I do remember," Mr. Bellows said. "That unfortunate incident happened only a few months after my wife and I took up our ministry here. I knew that unhappy woman well for those few months, since she came to us several times for spiritual guidance before she was so cruelly murdered by those passing wastrels."

"Did she now!" Alafair exclaimed. "I have heard that she spent a lot of time in church."

"She did," Bellows affirmed. "We prayed together many times. She was real concerned about the state of her soul, and that of her husband, as well. Why, I told her that any time she felt the Tempter at her heels, she could come and find me or my wife, day or night, at church or at our home, and we'd cast him out together. But sadly, the devil had too strong a hold on her, and here you can see the sad outcome."

"Ulises sweated drops of blood over Sister Louise," Mrs. Bellows interjected, "just like Jesus did over his disciples at Gethsemane. Ulises fought like a soldier of the Lord against the devil that possessed that woman's soul."

Alafair was taken aback at hearing Mr. Bellows compared to Jesus, but she added it up to his wife's devotion to her husband and her faith in his calling, and she smiled, amused.

"She was a soul in need," Mr. Bellows was saying. "Norma and I tried to help her as best we could."

"If she could have been saved, my husband would have saved her," Mrs. Bellows assured Alafair.

"She was too weak," the preacher said, accepting his wife's accolades as his due.

"Why, I came home late the very night she died," Norma said, "from helping Doctor Ann Addison deliver Miz Click of a fine boy. Doctor Ann brought me home in her buggy near on to nine o'clock. I was probably on the road at the same time as the devil that ruined and killed Miz Kelley." She slipped her hand into the pastor's, looking overcome at the thought. "You know it had to be Satan who was behind that death."

"Satan," Mr. Bellows seconded.

"Yes, I'm sure," Alafair said noncommittally, not wanting to embark on a lengthy theological discussion. "Well, I'm afraid I must be on my way. I didn't really have time to stop in the first place, but the unfortunate woman was on my mind, don't you know."

Mr. Bellows nodded solemnly. "My wife and I often come to the cemetery to pray in the presence of the saints who have gone before and will be waiting for us in our heavenly mansions. It's too late for Louise, I fear, but I always pray that the Lord will allow me to save souls by using her life as a sad example of the Deceiver's wiles."

"Amen," said his wife.

Oh, dear, Alafair thought, but she too said, "Amen."

"Sister Alafair," Mrs. Bellows said, warming to Alafair's apparent religious enthusiasm, "my husband and I would be proud if you and your fine family would take Sunday dinner with us at our home."

"Indeed!" Brother Ulises seconded.

"Why, we'd love to," Alafair said, "if you're sure you're up to feeding such an army all at once." She was teasing, but Mrs. Bellows missed the humor.

"Why, I've had bigger broods than yours over, Sister. Mr. Bellows and I weren't blessed with a family of our own, since the Lord wants us to minister to his Christian family, so I make a point of surrounding us with as many of the sheep in our flock as I can."

"We live in fellowship," the preacher added.

Alafair thought that the minister and his wife might not find her family very sheeplike, but she kept that thought to herself. "We'd be pleased," she said. "What can I bring?"

"Not a thing, Sister," Norma assured her. "And I'll have all the help I'll be needing. You may know that colored girl, Sugar Welsh, who lives over yonder toward Taft. She does most of the cooking for me when I have folks over. Why, she'll have the meal done and waiting for us by the time we get out of church."

"Yes, I know Sugar. Her brother and his family are tenants of ours. But I reckon we could bring the dessert, save the gal some baking."

Norma shook her head, firm. "It's a blessing to provide for my guests."

Alafair hesitated, surprised that the preacher's wife would feel able to feed such a large family without some contribution. "All right, then," she said finally, unsure of how to protest graciously. "When do you want us?"

"Two weeks from next Sunday, I'm thinking," Mrs. Bellows said. "Is that the tenth day of May? I think that it is." She clapped her gloved hands together delicately. "What a joy!"

"Yes, indeed," Alafair agreed brightly. "And now I'd best get going. I have a baby at home who'll be fussing up a storm before long." She walked a few steps toward the buggy, then hesitated and turned to look back over her shoulder at the pastor and his wife. "Brother Ulises," she said, "do you think that Walter Kelley contributed to his wife's downfall?"

Mrs. Bellows said nothing, but her mouth thinned to a lipless line, which gave Alafair a pretty good idea of her opinion. Mr. Bellows looked thoughtful for a minute before he replied.

"Well, Sister Alafair," he said, "Brother Walter cannot be held blameless, but I believe the wife's demons were the main reason that marriage soured."

⌐⌐⌐

When Alafair arrived home at about eleven o'clock, she found Alice and Phoebe playing with the baby in her kitchen. The table was already set for dinner and several pots were simmering on the stove. Phoebe rose to help her mother unload the boxes of staples.

"Nice to see you, hon," Alafair greeted her newlywed daughter. Little auburn-haired Phoebe, Alice's fraternal twin, had married their neighbor John Lee Day only a few months earlier. They lived in a tiny newly built cottage on the adjoining eighty acres, which Shaw owned but leased to John Lee for a share of his crops. John Lee also assisted his father-in-law with the horses and mules that Shaw raised and sold, and was consequently learning the business. Like most newlyweds, John Lee and Phoebe were poor as church mice, but John Lee, with his liquid eyes and serious demeanor, was a hard worker with good prospects. Alafair particularly loved him for his devotion to gentle Phoebe.

"Are you and John Lee joining us for dinner?" Alafair asked.

"I will, Ma," Phoebe told her. "But Daddy asked for us to send some dinner for him and John Lee and the hands out to the stables. I think they're checking shoes or shaving hooves or some such."

Alafair nodded as she hung her coat on the peg by the back door. "He's got an order for a dozen mules from Fort Sill for next week. I expect he's getting them ready. Well, let's get something up for them. Where's Mary?"

"Oh, we've already done it, Ma," Alice informed her from her seat at the table. "Mary's on her way out there right now with Charlie's little pull-wagon piled up with food."

"She volunteered," Phoebe interjected with a laugh. "I think she can't decide which of those new hands she's sweet on, that gray-eyed Micah or the big tall blond one."

"That's Kurt, the Dutch fellow," Alafair reminded her, tying on her apron. "Nice polite boy. Your daddy likes him. I wish he'd learn to speak English in a way that I could understand him."

"He told John Lee that he's from a place called Bavaria, over in Germany. Only been here in America for a few years."

"That Kaiser over there is crazy," Alice said. "I read that he might be spoiling for a war."

"All that has nothing to do with us," Alafair informed them, as she relieved Alice of the baby and lifted the lid off of a pot. "So it's just us females for dinner. Let's see what you girls have come up with—why, chicken and dumplings, my favorite! What with y'all fixing dinner for everybody while I go off gallivanting to town, I'm the one getting spoiled."

"Don't worry, Ma," Alice teased. "You'll get us all married off one of these days, then you can do all your own cooking again."

Alafair gave Alice a sharp glance. "That's what I'm afraid of."

The women sat down at the table, and after saying grace, continued the conversation.

"I've got more carrots coming up than I know what to do with, Ma," Phoebe said. "I thought I'd pull a mess of fingerlings and can a bunch of them. If I can borrow some canning jars from you, I'll give you a couple of quarts."

"I had the same plan," Alafair told her, "so I don't need any of yours, darlin', but you're welcome to as many jars as you need."

"Mercy me," Alice said, "be sure and tell me when y'all intend to be canning, because I'll make plans to be somewhere else."

Phoebe and Alafair snorted with laughter and Grace waved a cracker at her. "Alice, I'll swear you're as lazy as Uncle Ed," Alafair told her.

"I didn't know that was possible, Mama, at least by your way of thinking. Nobody is as lazy as Uncle Ed."

"Why, sugar," Alafair assured her, "Uncle Ed hated to work in the field so much that he cut off his own toe with an ax so he wouldn't have to chop cotton any more."

"I'd have liked to have seen that," Alice said. "Well, I don't think I'd go to cutting off any body parts to keep from canning, but maybe near to it. I like to make pies, because I like to eat them, but sewing is my calling, I expect."

"You're quite the tailor," Phoebe acknowledged.

"I am," Alice stated matter-of-factly. "Not as good as Mama yet, but I aim to be."

"I think you will be," Alafair told her. "You like it better than I do. But I've had so much practice what with eight daughters I reckon I could sew dresses in my sleep."

"I'd like to have a couple of new dresses," Alice said.

"Summer's coming," Alafair noted. "Everybody needs some new things. Maybe tomorrow we can pick through the rag bag and find some nice pieces to make some new shirts and blouses."

Alice shook her head. "I'll help you with making things for the kids, Ma, but I saved a couple of dollars and bought myself some material. I intend to make myself some pretty new frocks."

"I think Alice is going sparking," Phoebe interjected, raising her voice to be heard over the baby's babbling. Grace began to squirm in her highchair and Phoebe lifted her out and set her on her lap.

Alafair looked over at Alice, gimlet-eyed. "You still have your eye on that barber?"

"I do," Alice admitted gaily.

"Even with all the talk about what happened to his wife?"

Alice's blue eyes snapped her opinion of the woman in question. "Don't waste your pity, Ma," Alice said tartly. "Louise Kelley didn't deserve it."

"Alice!" Phoebe admonished. "Speaking ill of the dead and all!"

Alafair was taken aback. "Well, Alice, what makes you have such a hard opinion?"

Alice lowered her spoon. She was an outspoken girl, but she looked somewhat abashed at her outburst. But only for a moment. She shrugged, unrepentant. "She was loose," Alice assured her mother. "She didn't honor her marriage vows and shamed her husband and drove him away."

"Now, how are you so sure of that? Maybe it was the other way around."

"Walter told me, and I believe him."

"Walter?" Alafair's heart fell. "When did you talk about such a thing with Mr. Kelley?"

Alice hesitated before she replied. Eighteen years of her mother's gentle tyranny had left their imprint on even such a lively and independent soul as Alice. She glanced at Phoebe, who was gazing back at her, curious but unhelpful. Too passionate to be deterred for long, she looked back at Alafair. "I've been seeing Walter for a couple of weeks now, Mama," she said. "I've met him outside of town on Monday afternoons, when his shop is closed, and we talk for a spell. I've even taken a ride with him in his automobile once or twice."

The look of disapproval and even fear in Alafair's eyes gave Alice a moment's pause, but encouraged by her mother's silence, she continued. "I believe what Walter told me, Ma. Louise was a bad, bitter person. He couldn't please her no matter how he tried. And he tried, Ma. He's a good man."

"You went for a ride in his automobile?" Alafair asked. She seemed to have forgotten about Louise for the moment.

Alice blinked. "Just for a little ways out of town. Nothing bad happened." She paused, then added, "I think I love him, Ma."

The look in Alafair's eyes turned to horror. Phoebe said nothing, but turned to cleaning the mashed cracker off of Grace's face with desperate concentration.

"Alice," Alafair managed, "you've got to be careful. You don't know this man…"

"Yes, I do," Alice interrupted.

"You don't know this man after only a few weeks," Alafair insisted. "I know he's rich and all, but…"

"Rich," Alice echoed. "You think that I only care that he's rich? That isn't so. You're the one doesn't know him, Mama. He don't have a mean bone in his body. He's just a happy, laughing man who wants nothing more than a good life and a loving family, which I would like to give him. I love him, Ma. He makes my heart sing."

Alafair didn't respond. She couldn't. She realized to her dismay that there was nothing she could say that would make any difference.

Encouraged that the explosion she expected hadn't materialized, Alice continued. "Walter loved his wife when he married her. He told me so. He tried his best to make her happy but she wasn't having it. She broke his heart. She got what she deserved."

"Nobody deserves what she got," Alafair said.

"Well, not murder, maybe," Alice amended. "But she had everything, and she sold herself cheap."

Alafair shook her head. "Honey, she may have done bad, but howsoever stupid she was about it, she set about to make herself feel better about something. It's human nature. She's at the mercy of the Lord. There's no help for her now on this side of Heaven, but we can give her our pity, and, if we can, justice."

Alice said nothing, but her expression conveyed a less forgiving assessment of Louise's situation than Alafair had given.

"You know about the Crocker girl?" Alafair asked. Phoebe began bouncing Grace on her knee with reckless abandon.

"Yes," Alice said without hesitation. "He told me about that right up front. She made eyes at him and he was weak. He knows it. She knew he was married. He didn't lead her on. If his wife hadn't driven him away, it never would have happened."

Alafair puffed out a noncommittal noise. "Alice, I believe you when you tell me that you have feelings for this man. You're grown up now and can cast your affections where you will. But you've only heard Mr. Kelley's side of this story—which may be the true one, I'm not saying it ain't. However, there's something about this whole thing that don't smell right. Now, you know that I would do just about anything to keep you from getting hurt, don't you? Don't you?"

"Yes," Alice answered cautiously.

"Good. Because I'm going to ask you not to see Mr. Kelley for a little while—a month or so—at least until we really know what happened with his wife."

"Ma, if you really don't want me to be hurt, then don't keep me from Walter."

"If Walter Kelley is the man you say he is, then you'll have the rest of your life to be with him, if that's what you want."

"It is," Alice assured her.

"Then let it be proved. Besides, if he really cares for you, a short separation won't make any difference in his feelings. And if it does, then you'll be glad you found out now."

Alice looked over at Phoebe, who had given up all pretense of entertaining the squirming Grace and was watching the proceedings avidly. "What do you have to say about this?" Alice asked her twin.

"Nothing," Phoebe assured her.

"Oh, I don't believe that," Alice challenged.

Phoebe put Grace on the floor and watched the baby pull up on her hands and knees while she considered her answer. "I'll tell you, Alice," she answered at length, "I think you ought to do as Mama says, at least for a while."

Alice made a sound of protest, and Phoebe looked up at her, her hazel eyes resolute. "If it weren't for Ma, I wouldn't have John Lee now," she said. "It was her helped clear his name after his daddy got shot. He'd have been hanged by now, otherwise. And nobody's saying that Walter killed his wife himself. I think you ought to give Ma a chance to lift that cloud off of Walter, and then y'all can be together without anybody even looking sidelong at you."

Alice pondered this while gazing at her mother critically. "All right, Ma," she said. "I really don't care if people do look sidelong at us, but if it'll make you and Daddy feel better, I'll give you a month and not see Walter all that time."

Alafair hadn't even realized she had been holding her breath, but a great sigh escaped her when Alice agreed. She made a resolution to bake Phoebe one of her favorite chess pies tonight. "Thank you, sugar," she said to Alice. "One month, then. Will you promise me?"

"I promise. The only thing is that Walter will get hurt feelings if I just disappear without saying anything to him."

"Daddy and I will talk to him," Alafair assured her.

"Good. And when you do, be sure and tell him that this isn't my idea."

⌐⌐⌐

When Phoebe went home, Alice went with her. Grace sat in her highchair with a rattle and watched Alafair mop the kitchen floor, highly entertained. But Alafair had things on her mind. It was hard to describe how relieved she was that Alice had agreed to stop seeing the barber for a month. She had to get cracking, now, if she wanted to convince her daughter that she could do better than Walter Kelley.

Had he killed his wife? It didn't seem possible. Had he paid someone to do it for him? There was no proof that he had. Had he made his wife so unhappy by his continuous dalliances that she lost all respect for herself and got herself into a dangerous situation? Of course, Alafair wanted to be fair if she could. Perhaps Louise Kelley was just an unforgiving and spiteful woman, and her demise was not her husband's fault in any way.

Even that scenario didn't give Alafair much pleasure.

As she mopped, her mind kept returning to her odd meeting with Ned Tolland that morning. He was sorry that Louise had died. He had put redbud flowers on her grave—the grave that he visited regularly, he said. She had only seen Ned and his wife together the one time that she could remember, at Louise's funeral, and as far as she could determine at the time, they seemed close enough. Ned had been comforting Nellie, and she had been clinging to him.

If Louise had nearly broken up her sister's marriage, apparently all had been forgiven.

Alafair pondered and mopped, remembering the strange smell of ammonia that had seemed to come out of nowhere. At first, she had unfairly blamed the dog…

The dog. She straightened, visualizing the dog snuffling around Ned's feet. She put her mop back into the bucket and leaned it against the wall, then picked Grace up out of her highchair and carried her into the bedroom. She placed the baby in the crib, then reached into the bottom of her chiffarobe and withdrew a package wrapped in butcher paper. She sat down in her rocker, unwrapped the bundle in her lap, and sat for a moment staring at the pair of weather-beaten and animal-chewed shoes that the family had found by the road last summer.

Charlie had let the hounds sniff the shoes. Shaw's raccoon hounds were renowned trackers, but would Crook have remembered the scent after nearly a year? Surely one event couldn't have anything to do with the other. Those hounds smelled everything they came in contact with. A memory floated up into her head of Easter dinner, and Buttercup snuffing around Walter Kelley's feet while he was sitting under the elms with the girls. She began rocking, and tried to think over the din of Grace banging her rattle against the side of the crib.

She was thinking, so what? Perhaps the shoes did belong to Ned Tolland, or even to Walter Kelley. That didn't mean they had anything to do with the murder of Louise Kelley. Did it? She wondered if she should discuss her musings with Shaw, or even with Scott. She imagined herself telling Scott that Crook had been interested in Ned's feet, and maybe that had some connection with a pair of lost shoes the dog had smelled almost a year before. She could just visualize Scott's face.

Alafair's cheeks reddened, and she stopped rocking. She re-wrapped the shoes and put them back in the bottom drawer of her chest. No, not yet. If there was any connection, it was too tenuous to mention. She wouldn't forget, though. You never knew.

She picked Grace up. "Come on, cookie, we've still got work to do."

Chapter Nine

Walter Kelley made his way home from the restaurant on Main Street with his hands in his pockets, whistling a happy tune. The last light of day lingered on the horizon. The blustery weather had abated when the sun went down, and it was a beautiful, cool evening. Walter figured he would sit on the front porch for a little while before he went to bed and maybe visit with any of his neighbors who might decide to do the same.

He turned off the sidewalk and put his hand on his front gate, but paused when he saw two people standing on his porch, waiting for him. He recognized the couple immediately, and an unaccustomed feeling of wariness overcame him. He put a smile on his face and pushed open the gate. "Well, hello there, Mr. and Miz Tucker," he said, as he mounted the steps. "This is a nice surprise. What brings y'all into town this evening?"

Shaw shook the man's hand. "We're sorry to spring ourselves on you all unannounced," he said, "but Miz Tucker and me would like to talk to you for a bit, if you don't mind."

"Well, sure," Walter responded. "Come on in." He pushed open the front door and stood aside to allow his guests to precede him. It was dark inside, so he switched on a table lamp and seated himself in an armchair across from where the Tuckers had made themselves comfortable on the settee.

Alafair took in the room thoroughly while trying not to be too conspicuous about it. The white clapboard house was neat and well appointed. The front door led into a small, nicely furnished parlor with a settee, two chairs, a tea table and three or four side tables. Two electric lamps with cut glass shades cast a cheerful light over the room. A long, maple wood sideboard with eight drawers and fancy scroll work along the bottom sat against the back wall. The wooden floor was highly polished, with a colorful handmade rag rug that stretched along the floor in front of the settee, under the tea table.

"I have some tea in the ice box," Walter told them. "I was planning on fixing myself a glass of ice tea. Can I offer you some?"

"That would be right nice, yes," Alafair answered for both of them.

Walter leaped up and disappeared through the French doors that led to the sitting room and the kitchen in the back. For a moment, they listened to the crack of an ice pick chunking pieces of ice off of the big block in the ice box.

"Nice house," Shaw observed to Alafair. "Do you know who keeps it for him?"

"The neighbor girl, Susan Grant," she said, nodding toward the north, where the Grants' house abutted the Kelley property. "I talked to her and her mama some while ago. I got the feeling that Miz Grant would be pleased to have Walter for a son-in-law. She's not the only one, either. There's any number of single women in town would be happy to keep his house for him."

"He is well-off," Shaw admitted. "And at least he keeps things nice around him." He shook his head ruefully. "I swear, Alafair. If it wasn't for all the talk about the wife's death, I'd be pleased that Alice fancies Kelley. He could sure take care of her, and I always liked him. I'd be happy, though, if one of our girls went for a man who wasn't wrapped up in a murder investigation."

"You and me, both," Alafair agreed.

Walter came back into the room with three glasses of iced tea and a plate of sugar cookies on a tray, which he placed gingerly on the table before them. "I hope y'all will help yourselves to some cookies. My neighbor lady's daughter brought me a whole box full of 'em that she made herself just yesterday."

They all partook of tea and cookies, with appropriate words of appreciation, for several minutes, until enough time had passed to satisfy propriety.

"I expect you know why Miz Tucker and myself have come to see you," Shaw opened.

Walter lowered his tea glass to the table. "Yes, sir," he admitted. "I'm guessing it has to do with Alice."

"You guess right," Shaw said. "I must say, Walter, my wife and I are surprised that you think it's all right to be seeing Alice socially without approaching us first."

Walter shifted uncomfortably, but Alafair noted that he looked Shaw in the eye before he answered. "I don't blame you folks for being concerned. I'd more than likely feel the same way. But I promise you that my intentions are entirely honorable. It's just that, well, I have to say that I didn't realize myself what was happening between me and Alice until just recently. What with all this business about Louise getting killed while I was in Kansas City, and Alice being so young and all, I didn't expect to be feeling the way I do about her. It just sort of snuck up on me."

"What do you think is going to come of this friendship?" Alafair asked.

"I have to admit," Walter said, after a pause, "that after things settle down a mite, and with your permission, that I'd like to marry Alice, by and by."

There was a long moment of silence while all present considered the implications of this statement. Alafair glanced at Shaw, who was studying Walter speculatively. He didn't seem to be blindsided by the prospect of Alice marrying, not like he had been about Phoebe. He had a calculating look on his face, as though he was totaling up Kelley's strengths and weaknesses as a prospective son-in-law. Alafair looked back toward Walter, who was sitting up in his chair, patiently awaiting their verdict. He didn't appear nervous, not like a young swain would. He was a grown man, and well aware of what he had to offer a bride.

Shaw turned his head and gazed at Alafair for a moment, his hazel eyes quite green in the electric lamplight. He gauged the look on his wife's face, then smoothed down his black mustache with the back of his index finger. He turned back to Walter.

"Walter, my wife and I think that things are moving along too quickly for our liking. Alice is young, and for all her sass, she's very innocent about these things. Now, you know how the world works, even if she don't. It looks bad, what happened to your wife, like maybe you drove her to her bad behavior…"

Walter started to protest, but Shaw held up his hand to cut him off.

"I'm being plain," Shaw said, "because this is our daughter we're talking about, here, and I want you to understand the situation aright. Alice likes you, and I think you could provide a good life for her. But her mother and I would feel much better if a few things were cleared up before we give our blessing to this match. That's why we asked Alice to promise not to see you or talk to you for the next month. We're thinking that in a month's time we can learn more about your situation, and also, it'll give you and Alice time to breathe and think about if this is what you really want. A young girl's affections are sometimes lightly given. If she still feels the same way after a month, well, then, we'll see."

Walter chewed his bottom lip, then nodded. "I understand. And I'll do as you wish. I admire your care for Alice. I think, though, that my feelings won't change in a month, because I've never known a girl as full of life as Alice. Every time I'm around her I feel like the world is a mighty fine place because she's in it. And I promise you I'd never do anything to hurt her, and if she were to marry me, I'd make sure she never would regret it."

Alafair wondered why she didn't feel better at Walter's attestation, but all she could think was that fine words were easy to say. She noticed that Shaw's mobile eyebrows had disappeared under the shock of black hair that had fallen onto his forehead.

"Well, that's fine," Shaw said, echoing the very word Alafair had been thinking. "I appreciate that you're going along with this. We'll see how things stand in a month."

Walter smiled a beguiling smile. He is a handsome man, Alafair admitted to herself. Tall and well put together, with a square, chiseled, clean-shaven face and black eyes. His wavy dark hair was combed back and pomaded into a glossy shine, a perfect advertisement for his barbering skills.

"I hope you and the boys will still come in to have your hair cut in the next month," he said.

"I imagine our hair will still grow," Shaw acknowledged. "I think we'd better get on home, now. It's getting late."

The men rose to shake hands and Alafair leaned forward to place her dish on the tea table in front of her. As she did, a half-eaten cookie slid off of the china plate and landed on the rag rug close by her feet. She stooped down to scoop up the cookie in the handkerchief that she had pulled from her sleeve, and as she did she was immediately aware of the acrid smell of ammonia coming from the rug. It was exactly the same odor she had smelled at the cemetery, at Louise's grave. She absently picked up the cookie, and bent down a little closer to the rug, sniffing delicately to make sure she wasn't mistaken.

No, that was one smell that was unmistakable. Surreptitiously, as the men moved their conversation out onto the porch, she picked up the corner of the rug to check the underside. The nether side of the rag rug was covered with a large brown stain.

Alafair stood up quickly, unconsciously stuffing cookie, handkerchief and all into her coat pocket, and followed Shaw out of the house.

⌒⌒⌒

"Where on earth are you, Alafair?" Shaw asked her.

She looked over at him, surprised at the question, until she realized that they were half way out of town and she barely remembered climbing into the buggy. "Shaw, I think Louise Kelley was killed right in that room where we were sitting."

Shaw blinked at her, processing this unexpected information before he replied. "What did you see?" he asked, intrigued. He knew Alafair well enough to know that she had to have some pretty strong evidence to make such a shocking allegation.

"Just as we were getting up to leave I dropped a piece of cookie on the floor, and when I reached over to pick it up, I smelled ammonia on the rug."

"Ammonia," Shaw repeated, not following yet.

"Ammonia. When you've got a bad stain on something, sometimes a solution of ammonia and water will lift it. Not always though. I picked up the corner of the rug and looked underneath. Almost the whole underside of that thing is covered with a brown stain that looks like blood."

"Oh!" was all that Shaw said, before he pondered a minute or two. "It could have been something else besides blood, don't you expect?" he wondered at length.

"Could have been," Alafair agreed. "But I don't think so."

They were just outside of town now, but Shaw pulled on the reins and the horse came to a stop. "We'd better tell Scott about this."

"I need to get home to the baby. Can't you carry me on home first?"

Shaw turned the buggy in a wide circle in the road and headed back for town. "You're the one saw this stain," he said. "The girls know how to take care of Grace if she gets fussy."

⌒⌒⌒

"I don't smell no ammonia," Sheriff Scott Tucker said. He was on one knee in front of Walter Kelley's settee, leaning down toward the rug.

Alafair, Shaw, and a concerned and puzzled-looking Walter were ranged in an arc on the other side of the tea table. "Look under the rug," Alafair instructed.

Scott stood and placed his hands on his hips, eyeing the long yellow, brown, and cream rug for a minute. Then he squatted down, pushing the table aside and turning the rug completely over. The underside looked almost as if it had been dyed a rusty brown color, with only one corner largely free of stain. Scott's forehead wrinkled as he examined the rug. He scraped at the stain with his thumbnail, sniffed it a bit, then pulled up one edge so he could examine the front and back sides together.

"I was wondering why, if this is blood, and a lot of it, too," he observed in a conversational tone, "that it didn't soak through to the other side, or stain the floor. But I see now that it did seep through the seams, at least. See here how these rusty streaks on the other side look like they're part of the pattern? Still don't see none on the floor, though."

"Rug might have been moved," Shaw offered.

"Might have," Scott ceded. He stood up. "Walter, did you know these stains were on this here rug?"

"No!" Kelley assured him, still looking stunned.

"Have you moved this rug since you got home from Kansas City last summer?"

Walter sat down heavily in the armchair. "I never moved it, Sheriff," he said. "I never even noticed that rug was under the table there until just recently. Louise was always buying things for the house and moving things around. It must have been somewhere else in the house before. Since Louise died, I pay Miss Grant next door to come in once a week and clean. She must have put it there. She could move anything in the house and I'd hardly pay any attention to it."

"You mean to tell me that this rug could have been laying around this house all covered in bloodstains since last summer and you wouldn't have known nothing about it?"

Walter shrugged. "I guess so."

"Somebody tried to clean it, if Miz Tucker smelled ammonia."

"Wasn't me," Kelley assured him.

Scott stood for a moment mildly observing Walter's demeanor. "Miss Grant, you say," he said at last. "Anybody else come to the house regular?"

Walter looked up at him, resigned. "Nellie Tolland, Louise's sister, used to come a lot, and so did Nellie's husband Ned, but not since Louise died, of course. Several ladies from town have been to see me since Louise died. Sugar Welsh, the colored woman from over east of town, does the laundry for me. Folks from the church been here so many times I can't count, both before and after Louise died. They was always on to Louise, trying to save her soul, I guess," Walter rattled on nervously. "It was all right for Louise, I figure. Now they're trying to do the same with me, but I like my religion a little quieter. Can't think of anybody else right now, but I'll tell you if I do think of anybody else."

Scott grunted an acknowledgment. "Make a list for me. I'll go around and talk to all of them, whether I already did or not. It seems strange to me that somebody didn't come across this bloody rug last summer when we were investigating your wife's murder."

"Maybe it ain't blood," Walter said hopefully.

"Maybe," Scott begrudged. "Now, step on over to the Grants' for me, Walter, and ask Susan to come talk to me for a minute."

Walter obliged. Scott crossed his arms over his chest while they waited and looked at Alafair with an expression she might describe as amused. "Alafair, how is it you manage to get yourself tangled up in my murder investigations?"

Alafair felt her cheeks flush, but it was Shaw who answered. "She does have a rare talent, don't she?"

"It's not like I aim to get myself into these things," she protested, affronted. "Have you heard any more about the fellow that was seen with Louise at the roadhouse?" she asked, to change the subject.

"I think there's been some progress on that front," Scott began, but before he could continue, Walter returned with all three Grants in tow, Susan and her parents.

After introductions all around, Mr. Grant turned to Scott, slightly put out. "We were just sitting down to supper, Sheriff. What has happened that you're so all fired eager to see us?"

"It's Susan I have a question for, Mr. Grant. Susan, I understand that you've been keeping Mr. Kelley's house for the past few months."

The Grants looked at each other in confusion. "Sheriff, what…" Mrs. Grant began, but Scott cut her off.

"I reckon Susan can answer the question without any help, Miz Grant. Can't you, honey?"

Susan blinked, but answered straightforwardly. "Yes, sir. I've been doing Mr. Kelley's housekeeping since August or so, if I remember right."

Scott unfurled the rug that he had been holding under his arm and held it out for her inspection. "Have you ever seen this?"

"Yes, sir. A couple of weeks ago, when I was cleaning the floor, I moved the sideboard and found that rug stuck up under it. I expect it got kicked up under there somehow and lost. I took it home and tried to wash it, but that big old stain it has on one side there is set, and I couldn't get it out. It still looks pretty on the other side, though, and I thought it kind of matches the settee, so I put it under the table."

"Did you use ammonia to try and get that stain out?"

"No, sir. Just soap and water."

Susan's answer surprised Alafair. Why did she smell ammonia if it hadn't been used to clean the rug?

Scott was watching Susan's reactions closely, but if his questions distressed her, she didn't show it. "Do you know what this stain is?" he asked.

"I figured it was chocolate, or gravy, or something like that."

Mrs. Grant understood Scott's implication at once. "Sheriff, does this have something to do with Louise Kelley's murder?"

"That's what I'm trying to find out."

"You think that stain is blood?" Susan asked, horrified.

"Maybe, young lady," Scott said. "Have you ever seen anything else unusual around this house that you'd like to tell me about?"

Mrs. Grant made an indignant sound. "Sheriff, this house was in disarray when Susan started keeping it, like any house without a woman in it. I'm sorry, Walter, but it's true. I'm sure you did the best you could."

Scott ignored her. "Susan, have you ever seen other stains like this anywhere in the house, on the floor or walls, rugs or sheets, maybe?"

"No, sir, Sheriff. I'd have noticed."

"Sheriff, you've already questioned us about this more than once," Mrs. Grant insisted.

"If you think of anything, you come tell me right quick," Scott said to Susan.

Alafair was watching Mr. Grant during this exchange, thinking it odd that he wasn't coming to his daughter's defense. He was standing back, by the door, looking uncomfortable. He was a traveling tool salesman, Alafair remembered. She also remembered that his wife had told her he had been at home the night Louise died.

When Scott told them they could go, Mr. Grant murmured something and herded his family out the door, leaving Scott to gaze thoughtfully at the space they had vacated.

"Walter, what is your opinion of the Grants?"

Walter was wearing an expression that said he wanted to sink through the floor. He started when Scott spoke to him, and rallied. "Susan is a nice girl. Modest and friendly. I've never had no complaints about her cleaning. Her mother is overmuch, though. Miz Grant always treated me fine, but her and Louise didn't get on at all."

"Do you know why?"

"Wasn't nothing much. They just rubbed one another the wrong way, is all. Louise complained about how she put on airs, things like that."

"What about Mr. Grant?" Alafair interjected, unable to keep quiet a moment longer. "Did him and your wife get along?"

Walter blinked at her. "I don't know as they were much acquainted, Miz Tucker."

Scott had other things on his mind. "Now, Walter, is there anything else you've noticed since your wife died, or anything strange that you've remembered, or maybe something you just didn't mention that you should mention now?"

"Well…" Walter said.

"Well, what?" Scott urged.

"I never mentioned it at the time, because it didn't seem like it had to do with anything, but there was a couple odd things went missing after Louise died. One of my best razors, and…" He hesitated, then continued. "…and a good pair of my shoes."

"Shoes!" all three listeners said at once, Scott in disbelief, and Alafair and Shaw in enlightenment.

"I knew it!" Alafair exclaimed. "I knew the shoes had something to do with the murder."

"We found them shoes on the day of the funeral, Scott," Shaw told him. "Don't you remember? We had Hattie post a notice in the store."

"We found them on the way home," Alafair added, "right outside of town. We ran over one in the middle of the road. Looked like an animal had chewed it and dragged it into the road. Charlie-boy tried to get the hounds to track it, but they couldn't pick up a trail. I just thought about that yesterday, because I saw Ned Tolland at the cemetery visiting Louise's grave, and Crook seemed mighty interested in his feet."

"Ned was visiting Louise's grave?" Walter asked.

"Wasn't the first time, either, seemed to me. Looked like he had left some flowers."

"Why does that surprise you, Walter?" Scott interjected. "Is there some reason Ned wouldn't be interested in paying his respects to his late sister-in-law?"

"Well, no, I reckon not. Ned and Louise got to be friends in a way, a while back, when him and Nellie had a falling out. Louise took his side in that dust-up, for some reason or another."

"I doubt if Crook being interested in Ned's feet meant anything, either, Alafair," Shaw added. "Crook is interested in just about everybody's feet."

Alafair shrugged, not totally convinced that all these coincidences meant nothing. Her eyes narrowed and she peered at Walter, who was staring at the wall, looking as though he wished he were invisible.

Scott pondered the new information. "My, my," he mused. "So maybe the murderer stabs Louise right in this house, so quiet that the neighbors don't hear a thing. Then he cleans up the mess, steals Walter's shoes and razor, and dumps Louise's body in Cane Creek. Ain't this a poser?" He rolled up the rug and stuck it under his arm. "We'll see what Doc Addison says about this stain."

⌐╾╾⌐

After Scott left, the three people stood gazing at one another in an uncertain silence for a few moments.

"Do you suppose Louise was killed in this room?" Walter wondered. His habitual cocksure expression had been wiped right off his face. He looked horrified. Neither Alafair nor Shaw answered his rhetorical question, and Walter continued. "I don't believe I want to sleep here tonight, not until I hear what the sheriff has to say."

"Where are you going to stay?" Shaw asked him.

Walter's discomfiture was so genuine that Alafair felt sorry for him, but not so sorry that she wouldn't have objected had Shaw asked him to stay out at the farm with them.

"I got a cot in the back room of the barber shop," Walter said, to Alafair's relief. "I reckon I'll sleep there a night or two." He shook his head. "Mercy, this is bad business!"

"Then you understand why we don't want you seeing Alice right now," Alafair interjected. She didn't want anyone to lose sight of the main objective of this visit.

Walter looked at her with an expression of sorrow and maybe even remorse in his black eyes. "Miz Tucker," he said, "I wish you didn't feel so bad about me. Louise and I both made some mistakes in that marriage, but I promise you that I never meant to hurt her. I always wanted to be a good husband, but Louise and I just weren't cut from the same cloth. I got nothing but the highest regard for Alice. I'll do whatever you want to set your mind at ease."

"We know you will, Walter," Shaw replied, but Alafair said nothing. She knew very well that Walter Kelley never set out to be a bad husband. He just was. He was the kind of man who gleefully went off and lived his life without a single thought for his wife, and then was truly surprised that she was unhappy about it. Alafair knew that he might even love Alice, but it would take a miracle to change his nature. And all she could do about it was pray with all her might that this break that she and Shaw had imposed on them would be long enough to cool their ardor.

As she walked down the porch steps with Shaw and Walter coming up behind her, she caught another whiff of ammonia, almost as though it were on the night breeze. "Y'all smell that?" she asked.

"What?" Walter asked.

"I don't smell nothing, sugar," Shaw told her.

Alafair nodded, but didn't pursue it. For the first time, she wondered if what she was smelling was an earthly odor at all. "All right, Louise, you've got my attention," she murmured under her breath.

※※※

On Monday morning, Alafair's mind was still trying to untangle Walter and Louise Kelley's complicated relationships with their neighbors and relatives. She couldn't make sense of the rat's nest of bitterness, jealousy, cheating and lies that she had uncovered, nor decide if any of it had anything to do with Louise's murder. She had to admit that the more she found out about Louise, the less she liked the unfortunate woman. Sadly, none of it made her like Walter any more, either.

Martha and Mary were working and Alice was baby-sitting and making dinner, so Alafair's only assistant with the family wash on this bright, windy morning was her occasional helper, Georgie Welsh, wife of their colored tenant farmer. Georgie's sister-in-law was Sugar Welsh, and Sugar, Alafair remembered, did laundry for Walter.

The two women finished the huge wash in good time, and between them lugged the baskets of wet clothes over to the lines. Georgie started at one end and Alafair at the other as they ran damp rags over the lines to remove the dust, then they gauged the wind direction before deciding on which corner of clothesline to begin hanging. If they started hanging clothes to windward in the stiff spring breeze that was blowing, they would be flogged to death by snapping shirttails before they could finish.

The work of washing was too labor intensive for much conversation, but clothes hanging was a more companionable task, suited to catching up on each other's lives. However, Alafair's mind was running in only one direction these days, and she plunged right in.

"Georgie, do you see much of Sugar, these days?"

"All the time, Miz Tucker. She stays with us quite a bit, especially when she's got a job of work in Boynton."

"She must be a good worker. I hear she cooks and cleans and washes for a bunch of folks in town."

"Yes, ma'am," Georgie agreed proudly. "Sugar works hard. She's been helping Miz Ross quite a bit lately, since the poor lady took sick. She cooks up Sunday dinner for Miz Bellows regular, whenever she has folks over after church."

"We're going over to have dinner with the Bellows' in a couple of weeks," Alafair noted.

"Yes'm. Sugar will have dinner all ready when Miz Bellows gets in from service, and be gone by the time you folks get there."

"Yes, so Miz Bellows told me. I reckon Miz Bellows couldn't possibly manage such a feed all by herself."

Georgie laughed. "Well, Sugar admires Miz Bellows a heap. Say's she's a good Christian woman, but cooking and housekeeping ain't her greatest strength."

"She does the washing for Mr. Kelley, the barber, I hear."

"She does."

"Does she like working for him?"

"She likes working for Mr. Kelley. He's right kind, she says."

"How long has she worked for the barber?"

Suddenly aware that she was being pumped for information, Georgie looked at her askance. She liked Alafair well enough, but voicing opinions on white folks to other white folks could be a risky business. "Since right after his poor wife was killed," she said warily.

Alafair sensed the subtle change in the atmosphere between them, but it didn't deter her. "Does she ever cross paths with Miss Grant? I hear she's doing his cleaning."

"Yes, ma'am, once in a while. Sugar helps out over at the Grant place, too, sometimes."

"Does she?" Alafair sounded casual. "I reckon the Grants were mighty shocked when their neighbor woman was killed so cruelly like that."

Georgie shrugged and kept her eyes on the wet skirt in her hands. "I reckon. Sugar don't talk much about the folks she works for."

Alafair nodded, feeling guilty for putting Georgie on the spot. She knew that Georgie wouldn't like for word to get around that Sugar was indiscreet. She tossed out one last crumb. "Shocking, though…"

A fleeting smile passed over Georgie's face as she pinned a work shirt to the line. All right, just this final morsel. "Yes, ma'am. Sugar allowed as how Mr. Grant was right broken up about Miz Kelley's death. Said he was mighty low about it for a long spell."

Alafair perked up. She flipped out a pillowcase with an authoritative crack. "Really? I wouldn't think him and Miz Kelley was that well acquainted."

"I wouldn't know, Miz Tucker. Maybe he's just got a tender heart. It was a sad thing, after all."

Alafair took mercy on Georgie at last. "How's that big boy of yours, Georgie? You haven't brought him over in ages."

Chapter Ten

Martha Tucker kept lifting her head from her typing to gaze out the window of the First National Bank of Boynton. The two-story, red brick bank building was situated catty-whompus on the corner of Main and First Street, and from her desk in the reception area in front of Mr. Bushyhead's office, Martha had a fine view of both streets. There seemed to be a lot of activity on Main Street today. Boynton was a busy little town by virtue of its location in the midst of a fertile farming area, exactly half way between the county seats of Okmulgee and Muskogee. The five-and-a-half-year-old state of Oklahoma was one of the fastest growing in the nation in 1913, and the First National Bank of Boynton was flush with business from a continual influx of new settlers, as well as from a number of established families, mostly Indian and part-Indian, like the Tuckers, who had been in the area since before statehood.

Martha was typing financial reports for Mr. Bushyhead, a task which she could practically do in her sleep. And therein lay the problem. Martha's fingers were so adept at expressing at the typewriter keys what her eyes were seeing on the page that her brain hardly needed to be engaged. So she had developed a number of techniques to keep her mind from wandering. One technique consisted of pausing at the end of each page of figures, fingers on keys, and looking out the window, trying to see how many passers-by she could identify in half a minute.

At the end of page five, she looked up to find her view blocked by the body of one of the tellers, Mr. Keane, who was standing in front of her desk with a flushed, squat little woman in tow. Martha's eyes widened in surprise, since she hadn't heard them approach, but she recovered quickly and gave the pair a businesslike smile.

"Excuse me, Miss Tucker," Keane said, "but Miz Tolland is here to make the loan payment for her husband this month."

Martha nodded at the woman by way of greeting before addressing the teller. "Thank you, Mr. Keane. Mr. Bushyhead isn't here right now, Miz Tolland, but I can take care of you."

Keane briskly returned to his cage, leaving Mrs. Tolland standing uncertainly before Martha's desk.

Martha gathered up her papers into a neat pile and put them aside. "Have a chair, ma'am," she invited, gesturing at the slat-back chair beside her desk. "It's nice to see you, Miz Tolland," she said, once the woman was settled. "It's always been your husband made the loan payments before now. I hope he isn't sick or some such." Martha was intrigued by this turn of events, since Nellie Tolland was Louise Kelley's sister. She had no idea how she could gain information that might be useful in resolving Alice's plight, but she was determined to become Mrs. Tolland's dearest friend in the next five minutes, in case the opportunity should present itself.

Nellie shifted in the chair, obviously out of her element and not happy with the task she had been given. "No, he's fine, Miss. He just can't leave the cotton field right now. He done told me what to do, said I was to bring him a receipt."

Martha nodded. "Like I said before, Mr. Bushyhead and the assistant director Mr. Cecil are out of the office right now. You're welcome to wait, but I can take the payment and give you a receipt. I often do that when the bank managers are away."

"Well, how long do you think it's like to be before Mr. Bushyhead comes back?" Nellie wondered.

Martha tugged at her ear thoughtfully. "He and Mr. Cecil have been making calls since ten o'clock this morning. They've gone over by Checotah to inspect a plot of land that a client wants to put some wells on. After that, Mr. Cecil told me they'll be calling on Mr. Greyeyes in Council Hill. I don't expect them back 'til three or four o'clock."

Mrs. Tolland winced. "I got to get home before that. I reckon my husband won't be bothered if I get a proper receipt from you."

Martha smiled and rose to take the receipt ledger from the shelf behind her. "I do it all the time," she assured the woman. "I've taken the payments from your husband once or twice before when the bank officers were out."

That information seemed to relieve Nellie. She relaxed back into the chair and began rummaging in her handbag for the money. Martha sat back down.

"By the way, Miz Tolland," Martha said nonchalantly, as she flipped through her ledger. "I haven't seen you since your sister died here awhile back. I want to tell you how sorry I am for your loss."

The look of bitterness that crossed Mrs. Tolland's face gave Martha a start. She hadn't particularly noticed the resemblance between the two sisters before, since Nellie was a little woman and her sister was big, but Nellie's sour expression was the mirror image of Louise's. "Thank you," Nellie managed, tightlipped.

"I surely hope they catch the men who did it," Martha ventured, as she prepared to count the money.

For a long moment Nellie said nothing, and Martha counted in silence, convinced that her probing had come to naught. But suddenly Nellie sat up straight in her chair and her cheeks purpled with emotion. "It was that awful husband of hers killed her," she exploded in an enraged whisper.

Martha looked up from her hands, her eyes widening. "Gracious," she exclaimed. "You don't mean it! I thought he was in Missouri at the time."

Nellie had embarrassed herself with her outburst. Her cheeks reddened, and she blinked and flopped back in the chair. "Well," she said, flustered, "I don't reckon he did it himself, but he might as well have, the slimy critter. I'd bet any amount of money that he hired that man to kill poor Louise."

Martha lowered the money to the desktop. Her fingers had suddenly gone numb. "Why, Miz Tolland, what makes you think such a thing?"

"Oh, he's a evil one, all right," Nellie told her. She hitched her shawl up over her shoulder in indignation. "He never did anything but make my sister's life a misery all the years they was married, what with all his tomcatting around. I know for a fact that he was looking to get rid of her, get himself some younger woman."

Martha realized that she could hardly breathe. She swallowed. "For a fact you know this?"

"Louise told me so herself. He never come right out and said so to her face, but he sure spent enough time looking for somebody to take her place."

It seemed to Martha that this was conjecture on Nellie's part, which made her feel a little better. She clucked sympathetically. "Did you tell the sheriff about your suspicions?"

"I surely did, Miss Tucker, but you know he said that was just something called *'specruration'*, and hearsay, and not hardly no proof. But I told him that I knowed that man for years, and I know what he's capable of. I hate him like sin itself for the way he treated Louise, I'll tell you." She edged forward in her seat again. "Why, why, when they was in Missouri, he stepped out on her so much that everybody in Kansas City made jokes about it. Louise like to left him more than once, but he'd make out like he was sorry, and she'd take him back.

"I told her not to stay with a man who took her so lightly, but my sister was a good Christian woman and felt it was her duty to stick with that dog, if she could. He swore up and down to change his ways, though, and they left Kansas City and come here for a fresh start. Louise thought for a long time that things was better. Then that Crocker gal showed up on her front porch saying she was in a family way and expected that Walter would be asking for a divorce directly so they could marry up."

Nellie shook her head. "That's what done it, I think. Louise like to went mad. Thing is, it wouldn't have been so bad if she didn't love the snake so much. Couldn't stand the shame, knew he wouldn't change, and didn't really want to leave him, to boot."

Martha was listening to this diatribe with as much skepticism as she could muster. Nellie would naturally place as much of the blame on Walter as she could. Martha wished she could think of some way to ask Mrs. Tolland about her husband Ned's rumored affair with Louise, but she didn't dare. All this venom gave Martha a cold feeling around her heart, and for a moment she was torn between probing further and changing the subject.

"I heard that your sister Alice likes that devil," Mrs. Tolland said, making the decision for her.

Martha was seized with a sudden dislike for the bitter little woman. She was not happy to hear Alice's name bandied about, especially in this context. Her eyes narrowed, and she stabbed her pen into the inkwell. "You heard that, did you?" she said coolly. "Can't say I know anything about that."

Nellie leaned her elbow on the edge of the desk and peered at Martha slyly. "Well, if there's anything to the rumor, you'd better warn your sister. I will say that Alice is just the type he'd go for; pretty, innocent, and young. Good family, too. Oh, yes, he'd love to get his hands on someone like your sister, I guarantee…"

"Well, Miz Tolland," Martha interrupted her with forced cordiality, "here's your receipt, all nice and proper. You can tell your husband that I entered his payment in the book. It looks like this loan is almost discharged, only two payments left."

Mrs. Tolland swallowed her invective, distracted by the turn of the conversation. "Ned will be pleased to hear that," she said.

⌁⌁⌁

"This surely don't make me feel any better about things," Alafair said to Martha, after listening to the whole story in silence.

After bicycling home from work that afternoon, Martha had found her mother in the vegetable garden behind the house. Alafair was dressed in her weeding garb, a poke bonnet and an apron smock over an old brown skirt and a long-sleeved calico shirt. Her hands were covered by two old socks with holes cut out for her fingers and thumbs, and she stood with one hand on her hip and the other on the hoe handle as she listened to Martha's tale of the unpleasant Mrs. Tolland. Shaw's bitch hunting hound, Buttercup, trotted up to greet Martha, and after putting a wet nose to Martha's hand, returned to sniffing up and down the rows of okra seedlings. Grace observed the proceedings from a blanket-lined clothes basket at the side of the garden, her black eyes peeking over the rim, her dolly in her lap, noisily gumming her fist. Martha leaned over and picked her sister up as Alafair watched them from the tunnel of her bonnet.

"I thought you might be interested in what Miz Tolland had to say, Mama," Martha told her, "but after talking to her for a bit, I don't know how much faith I'd put in her story. It seemed to me that she enjoyed telling me her bad opinion of Walter way too much. I wouldn't put it past her to make things up so he'd look bad."

Alafair shook her head, but she agreed with Martha's assessment. "Well, maybe a sour disposition runs in that family, though if Walter really did do his poor wife that way, I don't blame her for being sour. However, it is just one more bad opinion of Walter in a pile of bad opinions. There's no middle ground in folks' feelings about the Kelleys, is there? Their neighbor, Miz Grant, was more than eager to talk down about Louise and make Walter out to be half-way to a saint."

Martha shrugged. "You know, I was talking to Aunt Josie about it when I went to her house for dinner, and she told me that she had heard from Cousin Hattie that Ned Tolland had been sweet on Louise Kelley at one time."

Alafair chuckled. "That Hattie knows something about everybody," she observed.

"That's what comes of running the mercantile."

"I reckon. Still, I've wondered before if Ned Tolland had improper feelings for Louise—did Josie say when this was?"

"Not long ago, I gather. Back about the time that the Tollands' boy Eddie was born, Aunt Josie said, and he's about four years old, now. Seems there was a right old brouhaha about it. Nellie tossed Ned out in the road and everything. I guess they worked it out, though, to judge by the way they act toward one another now."

"Gossip," Alafair snorted. "Can't tell what's true and what's just made up. Even so," she added, blithely dismissing her own caveat, "if Louise and Ned were misbehaving, it could be that Nellie isn't quite as heartbroke at her sister's death as she's letting on."

Martha was momentarily distracted by the drool on the front of her crisp white blouse. "I declare, Grace, you're as slobbery as a newborn calf," she said, wiping herself off with the corner of Grace's flour sack smock. Grace cooed at her, unrepentant. Martha wiped the baby's face with the tail of the smock and turned her attention back to Alafair. As the eldest of ten siblings, Martha was hardly put off by infant fluids.

"It seemed to me that Nellie was saving all her anger for Walter," she told her mother. "She didn't appear to have any to spare for Louise. Are you thinking that Nellie might have had something to do with her own sister's murder? Maybe she's making Walter out to be worse than he is, so the sheriff won't be inclined to look in her direction."

Alafair took a desultory swipe with her hoe at a weed among the okra plants. "Oh, I doubt it. But I wonder why she's so certain that Walter hired somebody to do in Louise? Is it just that she dislikes him so much that she's convinced herself he must have done it, or does she have some better reason for thinking so?"

"Surely she'd have told Cousin Scott long before now if she had some real evidence that Walter hired a killer."

"Surely," Alafair agreed. She began chopping at the weeds with a vengeance now, and Martha stepped back to avoid the bits of flying dirt. "Still…" Alafair added absently. "I'd like to know what Nellie Tolland thinks she knows about her sister's murder."

Chapter Eleven

Alafair's large family of children fell into three natural groups. The four oldest girls were all born within four years, by virtue of Phoebe and Alice being twins, and all four were grown women now. Gee Dub and Ruth formed their own little unit. Both were thoughtful and quiet youngsters, keeping afloat in the middle of a sea of brothers and sisters. Charlie was the head of a gang that consisted of himself, Blanche and Sophronia, still children. Grace, however, was a creature all unto herself, destined to be spoiled, Alafair feared, born to be the practice baby for all her elder siblings.

It was Sophronia who was practicing on Grace today, happily playing with her in the middle of Alafair's big bed while Alafair gave Blanche a sewing lesson. Sophronia was sitting with Grace in her lap, her legs stretched straight out in front of her, putting on a puppet show with her feet. She had pulled her stockings half off, letting the toe end drape down the bottom of her foot like long hair. She wiggled her toes to animate whichever foot puppet was speaking at the time. As near as Alafair could tell, one foot was called Cinda and the other Minda, and judging from the throaty chuckles she was hearing, Grace was enjoying the show. Alafair made a mental note to make Sophronia some yellow stockings so she could add some blondes to her foot acting company. Alafair and Blanche were huddled together in front of Alafair's treadle sewing machine, which was sitting by a window in a sunny corner of the bedroom. Blanche had pride of place in the chair, and Alafair bent over the almost-eight-year-old, guiding her hands as she sewed a seam.

"I'm afraid I'm going to sew my finger, Mama," Blanche confessed.

"Just pay attention and you'll be fine," Alafair assured her. "Fronie," she said over her shoulder, "don't let Grace fall off the bed, now. She'll sure get away from you before you know what happened. All right, Blanche, you're doing fine. Now, just push down with your right foot on the top and the left foot on the bottom, and get a smooth rhythm going. Pull the material real gentle. Good! Keep straight now."

A movement on the road from the front gate caught Alafair's eye, and she lifted her head to peer out the window. She smiled when she recognized the little woman on the big horse trotting toward the house.

She picked Blanche's hand up off the machine and straightened. "Here comes Grandma, girls."

"Grandma!" Sophronia cried, and Grace squealed, overjoyed at Sophronia's joy. The girls bounced out of the room and Alafair scooped the baby up from the bed, and all four of them were on the front porch in time to meet Grandma Sally as she dismounted in front of the house.

"Come here, girls," Sally called from the yard, "and let me love your necks."

The girls bounded down the steps and threw their arms around their grandmother's round form. Sally seized each girl's neck in a wrestler's hold and squeezed them to her sides, and all three of them walked up the path and up the porch steps like a knot of arms with six feet.

"Come on in, Grandma," Alafair invited. "I'll declare! It's a treat for you to come visitin' us two times in one month."

"Got some news for you, Alafair," Sally told her, flopping into the porch swing. "Let's set here on the porch a spell. It's a warm day for an old woman to be riding."

Alafair sat down in a rocking chair next to the swing. "Blanche," she said, "there's some tea syrup in the ice box. Pump up some cool well water and make your grandma and me some tea. There's already some ice chipped in the little tin bucket in the top of the ice box. I don't want you messing with the ice pick, now. Fronie, go help your sister with the pump. And watch your hands!" she called to their backs as they flew through the front door.

Sally leaned over and relieved Alafair of the baby, who gleefully gripped her grandmother's index fingers and stood up on the old woman's lap. "Whoo, this child is getting strong," Sally observed. "She'll be walking in no time,"

"I'm afraid so," Alafair said with a smile. "It's been a long time since I had a toddler around here. We've already cleared the house of everything below knee level, but I'm going to have to make a new tether for her. She'll be moving fast enough to get into trouble just about cotton picking time."

"I guess when you gave all your baby things to Hannah, you didn't figure on having to ask for them back," Sally said.

"Grace took me by surprise, for sure," Alafair ceded. "I'm practically forty years old, after all. It's almost embarrassing."

"She didn't live, but I was forty-three when my last one come along," Sally pointed out.

"Mercy, Ma, don't remind me," Alafair chided.

"At least you don't already have five grandchildren. Soon, though, I expect, eh?" Grandma Sally straightened and pulled her bonnet off with one hand and placed it on the swing beside her. Her shrewd black eyes glittered at Alafair as she adjusted the baby in her lap and sat back comfortably. Alafair sat down in a chair and crossed her arms over her chest, prepared for a revelation.

"Me and Peter just got back from over to Okmulgee yesterday," Sally began. "We went over and spent Sunday visiting Charles and Lavinia. Went over on Saturday so we could go to church with them. They been bragging about their new preacher and Peter wanted to get a look at him his own self. There we was at church and who should come in but the Crockers…"

Alafair's eyebrows flew up.

"…old Adam and his wife Margaret and their girl Peggy…"

"The girl at the funeral, Walter Kelley's erstwhile lover," Alafair interjected.

"So they say," Grandma affirmed. "I hear from Lavinia that Peggy's swain Billy Bond has spoke for Peggy to her daddy. He's been away working for a while, but they plan to be married this winter."

"They reconciled, then."

"Must have. Charles and Lavinia barely know the Crockers to speak to them, but they hadn't heard any tales of Peggy ever having been with child."

"That's good to hear."

Sally cocked her head and shrugged. "Maybe. Maybe they just don't know. However, I will tell you that I contrived to talk to Miz Crocker after church. I got to talking about the family and steered around to my son Shaw and his kids. Mentioned in the most casual way I knew how that one of my granddaughters was interested in the widower Walter Kelley whose poor late wife was murdered by a couple of low down dogs. I thought the woman was going to explode all over the wall right then and there, her face got so red. She told me that I'd better warn my granddaughter that Kelley might be a charmer and rich to boot, but he wasn't worth spit. Them was her exact words. I said I was surprised she even knew him, trying to get her to tell me more, don't you know. But if Walter ruined her daughter she wasn't going to be telling a stranger about it, and I don't blame her. But she did say that she had heard tell that the barber was too fond of the fair sex. And, that her soon-to-be son-in-law Billy Bond hates Walter Kelley like death, for what reason she weren't at liberty to say, and that he has swore that if he should ever meet Walter on the road he intends to shoot him straight away."

"Did the daughter look sort of like a little bit of nothing?" Alafair asked.

Sally smiled. "That's a good way of putting it."

"That's her, then, the girl by the fence at Louise's funeral. I keep thinking about this girl, Ma. All these folks keep turning up that hate Walter, but Peggy is the only one I can come up with who has much of a reason to have wanted Louise out of the way. She hardly seemed big enough to stab somebody like that, but stranger things have happened. Nellie Tolland's story is that Peggy went over to Louise's house when Walter was at work and told her there was a baby on the way. She was looking to break them up, I reckon, but since it didn't work, maybe Peggy thought that Walter would want to marry her if Louise was dead. Maybe after she killed Louise, she took Walter's shoes and razor for keepsakes."

"Them's a lot of maybes," Sally pointed out. "How did she get Louise's body to the creek?"

Alafair shook her head. "Well, she would have had to have help."

"If she did have help, it couldn't have been Billy Bond. He wanted her back. He wouldn't have been interested in clearing the way for her to have Walter," Sally said. "I know for a fact that Scott has been out to the Crocker farm and questioned Peggy and her daddy and mama. He's still after that man Louise was seen with on the night she died. He knows more about what happened that night than he's telling us."

Before Alafair could comment, the girls banged out the front screen door, each with a tall wet glass of tea gripped in her two hands. Sophronia handed hers to her grandmother, then proceeded to lean her elbows on Sally's knees and go face to face with Grace. Blanche gave her glass of tea to Alafair, who directed her to drag a chair up from the other side of the porch to serve as an end table. Alafair sipped at her overflowing glass, envisioning the trail of tea droplets and ice chips that she knew must stretch from the kitchen to the front porch. The tea was so sweet that it set her teeth on edge. The tea syrup had already been sweetened, yet Alafair could see from the inch of undissolved sugar in the bottom of her glass that the girls had taken it upon themselves to sweeten it even more. She caught Sally's eye over the rim of her glass.

"Mmmm! Delicious!" Sally exclaimed ostentatiously.

Sophronia stood up straight and bounced on her toes. "Blanche and me tasted it when we made it so it would be extra good."

"And it sure is," Alafair said. "Thank you. Now y'all girls go play in the yard a while so me and Grandma can talk."

Sophronia headed down the steps, but Blanche pouted a little at her mother's elbow. "I want to stay with you and Grandma," she said.

Alafair put her arm around the girl's thin shoulders. "I know, honey, but I need you to go and keep Fronie out of our hair for fifteen minutes or so while Grandma and me talk some business."

Blanche knew she was being dismissed, but she accepted her lot philosophically and followed her sister into the yard.

"I'll tell you what, Ma," Alafair continued, once the girls were out of earshot, "whenever we ask any questions about the death of Louise, instead we hear another tale about how Walter leaves a trail of broken hearts wherever he goes."

"Broken hearts and bitter women," Sally added.

Alafair nodded. "I hope Louise finds justice in this world and rest in the next, but even if Walter Kelley is as innocent as the angels of her murder, he ain't the kind of man I want to see Alice mixed up with."

Sally fell silent for a minute while she pondered this statement, pushing the porch swing lazily back and forth with her heels and absently stroking Grace's head. "What do you plan to do about it?" she asked, at length.

Alafair sighed. "I've already got Alice to promise me not to see Walter for one month. I told her if they really love each other their feelings won't fade in a month, and if they do, better to know now." She paused and smiled. "Do you suppose she'd obey me if I forbade her to see him ever again?"

Sally smiled back. "Maybe."

"You really think so?" Alafair asked wistfully.

"No," Sally admitted. "Listen, honey, I think you've done all you can do to discourage her, short of proving that Walter murdered his wife. That month long break is a good idea. But Alice is a woman grown, and mighty confident to boot. She'll do what she wants. Fortunately, she ain't stupid. Maybe she'll decide for herself that he ain't the one for her. But don't push her too much. You don't want to drive her away from you. If she does go ahead and marry him, she may need you later on."

"Shaw says pretty much the same thing. Don't make it easy, though."

"I expect not."

"When Alice was little, she had the hardest head that ever was, do you remember? She never really argued with me, but if she decided to do something, she'd do it whether I forbade her or not. She'd rather take her punishment than not get her way. Her and Charlie are just alike that way. I remember once when Alice was about four or five, I caught her playing in the ash bucket three times in one day. I sent her outside once and swatted her bottom once, and she just jutted out her bottom lip and went right back to the ashes as soon as my back was turned. I ended up shutting her in the girls' bedroom for an hour. I went around outside after about fifteen minutes to check on her through the window and she was standing there making faces at the door. I nearly laughed myself silly." She paused, picked up her tea glass and wiped the moisture from the bottom with her apron tail. "Don't seem so funny now," she added.

A long silence fell. Sally put Grace down on the porch, and the baby half crawled, half wiggled over to Alafair's shoe. She slapped at the shoe for a moment, then pulled herself into a sitting position using her mother's skirt as an aid. Absorbed in this drama, Sally didn't realize at first that Alafair had asked her a question. She looked up. "What did you say, darlin'?"

"I said, do you think that the departed ever talk to us who are still living?" Alafair repeated.

Sally wasn't expecting the question, but she wasn't surprised. She blinked, considering. "Well, I do," she finally confessed. "What makes you think about this?"

Alafair shrugged. "I never told anybody before," she said, "but a few times in my life I've thought…" She hesitated, unsure of Sally's reaction.

The older woman gauged Alafair's mood and smiled. "A few times in my life, I've thought, too."

"Really?" Alafair asked, relieved. "I've never even told Shaw. I was afraid he'd think I've gone right round the bend."

"No, he wouldn't," Sally assured her. "Or he wouldn't say so if he did, because he's heard me talk about it enough. You know, my ma was a full-blood Cherokee from way up in the hills in the Ozarks. Her mama and daddy's folks ran off into the hills while the army was moving them from the Carolinas to the Indian Territory, way a long time ago, on the Trail of Tears. They aimed to get clean away from white folks. My granddaddy hated white folks. He wouldn't have nothing to do with my ma for years after she married up with my daddy. But the Cherokees don't do things the way white folks do. Most figure that if you marry with a Cherokee, you get to be one yourself, whether you're white or black or Chinese. My grandma ran her own house and never paid Grandpa no mind if she wanted to see my ma. I went and stayed with them a lot. They knew English, but neither of them would deign to speak a lick of it, so we kids had to learn to talk to them in the *Tsa-la-gi*. *'Du-da* never had nothing against us grandkids, and he taught me a lot about the world of the spirits, is what he called it. My daddy, though, was a Christian man, and didn't put no stock in that kind of thinking at all, but I don't see why not."

"So you've actually seen some things?" Alafair wondered. She wasn't sure how else to put it. Seen some ghosts? Had some experiences you can't explain?

But Sally understood her all right.

"Why, for certain, honey. Anybody with an open heart is liable to. Especially if the one gone before is someone you love. I'll tell you, I've felt the presence of Shaw's daddy, Jim, many times over the years. My darlin' Jim was a black-haired boy, with green eyes like a mountain stream. His ways was as sweet as honey. When Jim died, it like to broke my heart. Worried him up in heaven, I think. Every once in a while, now, I hear him knocking at the window late at night. I know it's him, because he always just knocks three times. That was our signal to each other when he was alive. 'It's me,' we were saying. It usually happens when we've had a grief or a worry. I think he just wants to know that we're all right."

Alafair was intrigued, and relieved as well. "You know, I think my boy Bobby helped me get home last year when old Jim Leonard knocked me out down there by the creek. He looked older—about the age he'd be now, if he'd lived—but rosy cheeked and happy. It was a comfort to me to see him."

Sally nodded. "It's a blessing."

Alafair looked off into the yard. "That was the worst thing ever happened in my life, when Bobby got into the coal oil behind the stove and drank it and died like that. For years after that, in my dreams, I could see myself running toward town with his little limp body in my arms, trying to get to the doctor. But you know, since that day by the creek, when I saw him, I haven't had that dream."

She looked over to see her mother-in-law regarding her thoughtfully. "He came to let you know he's happy up in heaven," she told Alafair matter-of-factly, "and that you don't have to fret over him any more."

Alafair smiled. "I think that Louise Kelley is trying to tell me something, too," she said. "I don't know why. I just keep sensing things."

"What things?" Sally urged.

"Ammonia," Alafair said. "Sounds funny, I know. I keep smelling ammonia, even when no one else does. I smelled it real strong when I stopped by to look at her grave, and I smelled it in her house, which is what made me take a look at that rug."

Sally raised her eyebrows and nodded. "She was a troubled soul when she was alive. I don't see why she wouldn't still be troubled now. I expect there is something she wants someone to figure out."

"But why me?" Alafair wondered. "Louise Kelley didn't know me from Adam's off ox."

"Because you're the only one she can get through to, the only one who can sense her, I'm thinking."

The conversation was interrupted when Sophronia and Blanche's childish chatter suddenly increased in volume to angry shrieks. Both mother and grandmother leaped to their feet as the girls' play erupted into a real, rolling on the ground dust-up with fists and bare feet flying. Alafair was between them in a second, holding them apart with a bruising grip on their upper arms, their dirty little toes barely touching the ground.

"Ow, Mama, ow, ow!" Sophronia mewled like a pathetic kitten.

"Stop it, now," Alafair said with perfect calm. She let go, and both girls sagged, aware that they were in trouble, now. "What were y'all fighting about?" Alafair asked them as they stared at the ground. They glanced at each other, but neither had anything to say.

"Blanche?" Alafair said.

Blanche mumbled something unintelligible, and silence fell again.

Alafair placed her hands on her hips. "Well, then. It must have been something pretty important, so I expect I shouldn't interrupt you. But it better be a fair fight. You girls turn around back to back."

Blanche and Sophronia looked up at her, baffled. Alafair made a circle with her index finger in the air. "Turn around, now, like I told you."

The girls did as they were told, already experienced enough at childhood not to expect logic from an adult. Alafair pushed them together back to back and passed her hand over the tops of their heads, measuring. "Blanche may be older, but Fronie's just about as tall, so I guess it's fair enough," she observed. She stepped back. "Y'all go ahead, then."

The girls didn't move, but looked up at their mother, still uncomprehending.

"Go ahead, then," Alafair repeated. "You were so anxious to pound on each other. Go ahead on, whale away."

"I don't want to no more, Mama," Blanche fretted.

"Me neither," Sophronia agreed, barely audible.

"Why not?" Alafair asked. "You were mighty mad a few minutes ago. Aren't you mad at your sister anymore, Fronie?"

"No," Sophronia admitted.

"Why not?"

"I don't remember," Sophronia whispered.

"Blanche?"

"No, ma'am," Blanche managed.

"Y'all go around back and wash up, then. Just look at your pinafores." Before she had finished speaking, the girls were gone in a cloud of dust.

Alafair turned to see Sally on the top step of the porch, laughing. Grace was squirming mightily in Grandma's arms, desperate to get down and join the fun.

"Come on, Grandma," Alafair said as she walked back toward the porch. "Let's go inside a spell and I'll make some tea that we can rightly drink. You can see the new dresses I'm making for the girls while I run a mop over the floor."

"Have you decided what you're going to do about Alice?" Sally asked her.

"Oh, I probably ought to let it be," Alafair admitted. "But I probably won't. Look, here comes Shaw."

Shaw cantered up toward the house from the road on his black mare. The sleeves of his work shirt were rolled up above his elbows, and his boots and levis were dusty from working with the mules. He reined before the gate and leaned over the saddle horn when he saw his mother on the porch with Alafair. He pushed his sweat-stained Stetson back with his thumb. "Howdy, Ma," he greeted, white teeth glinting from under the dark mustache. "What brings you around?"

"Evening, son," Sally responded. "Papa and I visited your brother in Okmulgee Sunday last. I come with all the news from over there."

"They fine?"

"They are," Sally confirmed.

"Well, I've got some news that'll interest you ladies. I just met John Lee on the road, yonder. He just came from town. He tells me that they caught the boy who they think killed Louise Kelley. Seems he was holed up down around Ardmore along with a cousin of his. Scott will be going down on the train to pick both of them up tonight."

Chapter Twelve

Harriet Tucker, known to all as Hattie, mistress of the Boynton Mercantile and wife to Sheriff Scott Tucker, walked down the steps of her two-story white frame house on Oak Street just after seven-thirty in the morning, holding a two-and-a-half-gallon milk pail covered with a dish towel. The milk pail was emitting the delicious odors of breakfast into the morning air, and Hattie had to slap the hand of her fifteen-year-old son Spike as he ran past her out of the house.

"But I'm hungry, Ma!" Spike protested.

"You just et, boy," Hattie said, exasperated. "I swear, next time I'm only having girls. Now get on out of here before you're late for school."

Spike hugged her around the shoulders and was gone down the street before Hattie reached the front gate. Hattie and Scott had four sons, all grown or nearly so. They had named the boys the perfectly respectable and ordinary names of James, John, Charles, and Paul, but there were so many other Tuckers named James, John, Charles, and Paul, that Hattie's brood had ended up being called Slim, Stretch, Butch, and Spike. Hattie was pondering the vagaries of having to fill so many bottomless pits and didn't notice at first that two women in a buggy were eyeing her from across the street. Hattie peered at them a moment before she opened the gate and walked across the dusty road to the side of the two-seat buggy.

"I'll declare, Aunt Sally, Alafair. What brings y'all in to town so early?"

"Morning, Hattie," Sally greeted. "Me and Alafair are on a sneaky errand."

"This sounds interesting," Hattie said. "There is something I can do to help, I'm guessing."

"There is," Alafair admitted. "You know how I've been worried because Alice is interested in that barber Walter Kelley whose wife got killed…"

A look of understanding came into Hattie's eye as she peered up at Alafair. "…whose accused killers are just now lying in Scott's jailhouse."

Alafair nodded. "So they are."

"I'm taking breakfast to those men this very minute."

"We figured you might be," Sally said.

A momentary silence fell as the three women gazed at each other. It was unnecessary for Hattie to ask why Alafair and Sally had intercepted her. The hopeful look on their faces told her everything. She gave Alafair a conspiratorial smile and handed the food up to her without a word.

Alafair reached down to relieve Hattie of the pail. "Thank you so much, girl."

"Don't mention it. I really do need to get on over to the store. But you have to promise to tell me everything."

"We will. And thanks again."

Alafair and Sally sat for a minute watching Hattie walk toward Main Street and the store before Sally took up the reins and headed for the jailhouse. "Do you expect that this is how she learns everything about everybody?" Sally wondered.

～～～

The sheriff was finishing up his last cup of mud-black jailhouse coffee before starting out on his morning rounds when Alafair and Sally came into the office with the breakfast pail. Scott Tucker was stocky, balding, middle aged, and easygoing, all of which combined to make him appear quite harmless. However, in Scott's case, appearances were deceiving. He was reaching for his hat on the coat tree, and his hand paused in midair when he saw who had come in. His deputy, a long, slim youth with red hair, stood up at his desk when the women entered.

"Well, well," Scott said. "If it ain't Aunt Sally and Alafair. What a coincidence that y'all should show up on the morning after I got those boys who might have killed Louise Kelley here in my jail."

"Now, Scott," Sally scolded, "don't be smart. We are just delivering the breakfast from Hattie to whoever you got here in jail this morning. She said she feared that she would be late getting the store open."

"That sure is lucky," Scott observed dryly. He plopped his hat on his head and retrieved his gun belt from his desk drawer. "Ladies, I'm afraid I've got to go right now. Trent here can take the prisoners their food." He nodded toward his deputy. "Now, Trent, my aunt and cousin, here, have got it in their heads that they want to talk to those boys, I'm thinking. But I'm counting on you to keep these ladies away from them, you understand? I wouldn't be happy if something happened to my relations."

"Yes, sir, Sheriff," Trent assured him.

"Scott, I'm not going to…" Alafair began, but Scott cut her off.

"No, I'm sorry, Alafair," he interrupted. "I can't have you in there grilling my prisoners. I'm afraid you'd scare the pants right off 'em." He smiled. "They got their rights, you know."

A momentary silence fell after Scott left, then the two women's gazes shifted from the door to the hapless deputy, still standing deferentially behind his desk. He extended his hand.

"Miz McBride," he said hopefully, "I'll take that pail now."

"Trenton Calder," Sally responded, making no move to give it to him. "How's your mother?"

Trent tried not to smile. "She's fine, Miz McBride. Thank you kindly for asking. But I still ain't going to let you go back there."

Alafair almost laughed. Trent was brave. "It's all right, Ma," she said to her mother-in-law. "Let the poor boy do his job. I don't know what those men back there would tell us, anyway."

Sally shrugged philosophically. "I doubt if they'd confess to us," she agreed.

"I expect not. I doubt if they'd speak to us at all. We'd probably just set that pail down on the floor and skedaddle right out of there without anybody saying a word. I don't see no use to both of us going back there, anyway."

"It ain't going to work, Miz Tucker," Trent warned, "so you might as well just give me that pail before the prisoners starve clean to death. Why would you want to talk to them two snakes, anyway?"

Alafair sat down in one of the straight-backed chairs under the window. "We were curious, Trent," she began, "as to whether Walter Kelley himself was involved in any way with his wife's death."

Trent grunted and dropped his hand to his side. There was no need for Mrs. Tucker to explain any more to him. It was a small town. Everyone was quite aware that Alice Tucker and Walter Kelley were interested in one another. "Have a seat, Miz McBride," Trent invited, nodding toward a second chair next to Alafair.

"These biscuits and gravy are liable to get cold pretty quick," Sally warned.

"I expect we can warm them up on the stove, there," Trent said. Sally took mercy on the deputy, who wouldn't sit until she did, and took a chair. Trent finally sat down.

"I know there's been rumors, ma'am," Trent began, addressing himself to his audience in general, "that Mr. Kelley might have hired some bad sorts to help him get out of an unhappy marriage, but neither Sheriff Tucker, nor the U.S. Marshall, nor the county sheriff over to Muskogee has found the slightest evidence of that. I know Mr. Kelley myself, and I'd be right surprised if such an evil thought ever occurred to him in his life."

"If nobody has ever found the slightest evidence that Mr. Kelley had something to do with it, then do you think that one of them boys in there just killed Louise all on his own for no reason?" Alafair wondered.

"Oh, there was a reason, though not much of one. The prosecutor thinks that Miz Kelley and one or both of those two in there were partying and things got out of hand."

"What things?" Alafair asked. "What do you mean by 'out of hand'?"

Trent blushed to the roots of his hair, which turned his entire head several startling shades of red. "I don't think I should be discussing such sordid things with you ladies. I apologize, Miz McBride, Miz Tucker. It ain't my job to have opinions, anyway. Those men are innocent until proven guilty, and I shouldn't be saying otherwise."

"It's all right, Trent," Alafair soothed the embarrassed young man. "You were just trying to set our minds at ease." She regretted his sudden change of heart, since it was now going to be more difficult to pry information out of him, but she appreciated his delicacy toward them. Why couldn't Alice want someone like Trenton Calder?

Grandma Sally, however, wasn't so easily deterred. "So who was it pointed the finger at these men?" she asked.

"Mr. Dills who owns the road house down south of town, where Miz Kelley was last seen alive. Him and a couple other people there seen her leave with one of them late that night."

"So has the murderer confessed?" Sally persisted.

"No, ma'am. He says he left her alive and well right in front of her own house right at about eight o'clock that night. We talked to all the Kelleys' neighbors. The Grants heard a horse and rig later that night, but nobody saw or heard anything else. The other miscreant says he never clapped eyes on Miz Kelley, but Sheriff Tucker found two sets of boot prints down by the creek where she was found." He paused as if pondering his own statement. "Of course, they would say that they didn't do it," he appended.

"So you expect it probably was them," Alafair said.

Trent shrugged. "At least one of them did the deed, and the other helped him dump the body. It's the most likely explanation."

"Who are these desperadoes, anyway?" Alafair asked. "You know, I don't believe I've heard anyone say their names. Are they from around here?"

"Yes, ma'am," the deputy told her. "They're a couple'a old boys from down around Council Hill, Billy Bond and his cousin Jeff Stubblefield."

Alafair slid forward on her chair, suddenly very interested. "Billy Bond? The same Billy Bond that intends to marry Peggy Crocker from Okmulgee?"

Trent eyed her for a moment before he shook his head. "I don't know about Peggy Crocker's marrying plans, Miz Tucker. But there's a passel of Bonds and Crockers both around Council Hill."

Alafair stood up quickly, causing Trent to scramble to his feet. "Well, I think we've wasted enough of the deputy's time, Grandma," she said. "Why don't we leave that breakfast pail with him and get on back home?"

⁓⁓⁓

"Well, that's a handy coincidence," Sally said, as they walked back down Main Street to the Mercantile.

"It's a connection that makes you pause," Alafair agreed.

Hattie came out from behind the counter when they entered the store, her thin freckled face glowing with anticipation. "How'd it go?" she opened.

Alafair shook her head. "Scott was on to us," she said. "He told Trent not to let us back there where the cells are, and Trent obeyed."

Hattie's face fell. "Now, that's too bad."

"What about you, Hattie?" Sally wondered. "Have you learned anything of late about Louise Kelley's murder?"

"Not from Scott, that's sure," Hattie puffed. "He's no good for information at all. It's downright frustrating that he won't tell me anything interesting. His own wife!"

Alafair smiled. Scott knew his own wife too well.

"However," Hattie continued, perking up, "the other day Nadine Fluke let me in on a piece of news that might interest y'all. Susan Grant came into the Post Office…"

Everyone in town knew Mrs. Fluke the postmistress, but it took a moment for Sally to remember who Susan Grant was.

"You mean the girl who lives next door to Walter Kelley and keeps house for him?" she asked.

"She's the one," Hattie affirmed. "Seems that Scott questioned Susan again, without her mother. Susan said her mother and Louise Kelley didn't like one another at all."

"Walter said much the same thing when me and Shaw were over at his place a while ago," Alafair told them. "Miz Grant likes Walter well enough, though. I think she'd like to see Susan and Walter end up together."

One of Hattie's eyebrows quirked. "Nadine seems to think Miz Grant likes Walter even more than that."

"You mean…?"

"If only she could."

"Her husband is gone a lot," Sally observed.

"Miz Grant and Walter? Mercy, she's fifteen years older than him!" A bilious feeling rose in Alafair's throat. This again. Surely no man was that charming.

"That's why Scott thinks it's all palaver and puts no stock in the idea at all," Hattie admitted.

Alafair nodded and looked at the floor, feeling a little bit ashamed for listening so avidly to gossip. It was something to consider, though. She looked up. "What else did Susan say to Nadine?"

Hattie's eyes were agleam. She didn't seem to have Alafair's scruples about passing on secondhand tales. "Susan thinks Walter is a nice man, but has no interest in marrying him. She thinks he's too old for her. And here's something interesting. Susan hinted to Nadine that her daddy takes Louise's part, and thinks Walter treated her bad. So Miz Grant begrudged Louise, and Mr. Grant begrudged Walter."

"I heard that Mr. Grant was mighty sad when Louise died," Alafair said, remembering her wash day conversation with Georgie Welsh.

"What a can of worms!" Sally exclaimed.

Hattie laughed. "Nadine thought Scott gave Susan quite a scare with his questions. Susan told Scott that she never saw a brown stain like the one on that rag rug anywhere else in the house—not on any floor or wall or furniture or bedclothes."

"That rug," Alafair mused. "If this Bond boy killed Louise at the road house and stuffed her body in the creek, how did she manage to bleed on a rug that ended up hidden under a sideboard in her own parlor?"

"Maybe he killed her at her house. He says he brought her home."

Sally shot Alafair a glance. "It seems to me," she said, "that all that blood couldn't get on the rug and not get on the floor as well."

Alafair nodded. "Then Louise may have bled on the rug when she got stabbed, but she may not have been in her house at the time, after all."

Chapter Thirteen

Once out on the sidewalk, Sally slipped her arm through Alafair's and leaned against her confidentially as they walked toward the buggy. "This is quite the mystery, ain't it?" Sally asked cheerfully.

Alafair shook her head, hardly as entertained by the puzzle as her mother-in-law was. "Walter Kelley gets Peggy Crocker in trouble, and then her intended, Billy Bond, threatens to kill Kelley. Then lo and behold, a while later, Kelley's wife ends up murdered by none other than Billy Bond his own self. But why would Billy kill Miz Kelley instead of Walter? She's as much a victim of Walter's bad behavior as Peggy is. He sure wouldn't have wanted to clear the way for Walter to marry again, not with the way his girl felt about him. And if Billy was in the mood to kill somebody, Miz Kelley wouldn't have objected if it was her husband. She'd have probably helped him."

"Maybe he wanted to hurt Walter as bad as Walter had hurt him," Sally speculated. "Maybe it wasn't supposed to be a murder. Maybe things got out of hand, like Trenton said."

"Maybe," Alafair said, but she didn't sound happy about it. "I sure would like to talk to that Billy Bond and hear what his story is."

"I'm sure it'll all come out at the trial."

"By that time, it may be too late for Alice," Alafair protested. "She's determined to have that man, no matter what I say."

Sally nodded. "Let's just think for a minute." She stared off into the middle distance for a long moment, then looked back at Alafair. "Have you ever been back there where the cells are?"

"Yes, once," Alafair told her. "Last year, when John Lee was in jail."

"Do you remember if there were any windows in the cells that look out onto that stable area in the back of the building?"

Alafair tried to conjure the picture in her mind. "If I remember right, there weren't any windows in the cells along the back wall, but there was one window with bars at the end of the hall, off to the side. That would face the alley between the jailhouse and Mr. Spradling's furniture store next door. What are you thinking, Ma? I don't fancy staging a jailbreak."

Sally laughed. "I was more thinking about having a talk with Billy and Jeff through the window."

Alafair was taken aback at first, but it didn't take her long to warm to the idea. "That's a good thought," she admitted. "Let's have a look and see what we're dealing with."

The two women reversed course and casually strolled back past the sheriff's office. They slowed to a dawdle as they crossed the mouth of the narrow alley that opened onto the street between the jailhouse and the furniture store. At first, Alafair could see no window at all. The morning sun illuminated a bright right triangle on the packed earth at the head of the alley, between the brick walls of the two buildings, but sun had yet to penetrate further back, and the nether regions of the alley were vague and shadowy.

"Where is this window?" Sally asked her, echoing Alafair's own thoughts. "I can't hardly see anything back there at all."

"It's about half way down, I think." She squinted into the darkness. "Well, shoot, it must be there. I know I didn't dream it."

"Maybe Scott had it bricked up," Sally offered.

"Maybe," Alafair replied. "Though I don't know why he would." She cast a surreptitious glance down the street and saw no one close enough to be of concern. "Stand guard, Ma. I'll mosey on down there real casual and have a look."

Alafair strolled into the alley while Sally feigned an interest in the maple-wood pie keep in Spradling's shop window. As soon as Alafair stepped out of the sun's glare, her eyes adjusted to the dusky light and the detail of the alley became visible as if by magic. And there it was—a window, in the jailhouse wall—and she wondered how it was that she hadn't seen it all along. The window was rather tall and high off the ground. The bottom of the sill was just above her head. All she could see of the inside from where she stood was a section of the white, stamped-tin ceiling through the stripes of iron bars on the other side of the glass. The window was closed. She reached up with both hands and tried to raise the sash, but it wouldn't budge. The window was probably locked from the inside, but Alafair was unable to get a good purchase on the sash, so she couldn't be sure. She backed off and stood with her hands on her hips for a moment, thoughtfully surveying the problem aperture.

She turned her head to look toward the street. Sally was standing in the brilliant slot of light that framed the entrance to the alley, gazing in Alafair's general direction with a troubled look on her face. It occurred to Alafair that while she could see her mother-in-law in pristine detail, Sally could barely see her standing in the shadows. Useful knowledge for a woman planning clandestine activities.

"Psst, Ma," she hissed. "Come on in here, if there's nobody looking at you."

Sally apparently could hear her with no trouble. She glanced up and down the street, then walked into the alley. She took two or three steps, stopped, and blinked, her pupils dilating. A look of revelation, then amusement came over her face as her eyes adjusted to the low light. "I'll swan," she said. "I didn't see a thing from the street."

Alafair pointed up. "There's the window. Ain't going to do us much good unless you want to sit on my shoulders and shout at them loud enough to be heard through the glass."

Sally's dark almond eyes critically surveyed the offending window. "Is it locked?" she wondered.

"Near as I can tell."

"There's a transom up there."

Alafair blinked at her. "What?"

"A transom," Sally repeated. "Looks like it's open, too, just a little. Those bars on the inside of the window, see, keep it from opening more than a few inches, but I expect it gives them in the cells some air. They probably can hear what's going on out here in the alley, too. In fact, they may be listening to us right now."

Now that Sally had pointed it out to her, Alafair could see the small transom capping the window some four or five feet above their heads. It did, in fact, seem to be open. "Well, then, I hope Trent isn't standing in there listening to us and making plans for our arrest," she said, dropping her voice.

"I expect he would have appeared at the window before now if he was," Sally assured her. "I think that what we have to do now is figure out a way to get up there and see what's going on inside."

But Alafair was ahead of her. She strode toward the far end of the alley and peeked around the wall into the lane behind Spradling's. Empty wooden furniture crates of all sizes sat piled against the wall next to Spradling's service entry. She gestured to Sally to join her, and the two women maneuvered a couple of manageable-sized wooden crates around into the alley and positioned them, smaller upon larger, with a small box on the ground for a step, under the jailhouse window.

They gazed at their handiwork, and then looked at one another in anticipation. There was no question about which of them would do the climbing. Alafair may have been middle-aged and middle-sized at best, but Sally was twenty-five years older and half a head shorter.

"Is this as ridiculous a scheme as I think it is?" Alafair wondered.

"I would say yes," Sally answered.

"Even if them boys can hear us, there's no knowing whether they'll tell us anything, is there?"

"No, there ain't."

"They don't know us from a dog with one eye."

"They don't."

"They'd hardly tell us if they did kill the woman."

"No, they would not."

"Why would they trust me?"

"Why, indeed?"

"So would you give me a hand up, here?" Alafair asked, and Sally moved forward to take her hand and give her a boost as she stepped up on the boxes.

Her perch on top of the sturdy furniture crates was surprisingly firm, but she was up higher than she had anticipated. Most of her body from crown to knees was exposed to whoever on the inside might look her way. She planted her feet apart and steadied herself with her hands on either side of the window frame and pressed her nose to the glass to peer into the interior. It was too late for stealth.

Through the window, Alafair looked down onto the narrow corridor in front of the two cells. She could barely see one booted foot hanging off the end of a cot in the far cell. In the near cell, a tall, unshaven youth stood close to the bars and gazed up at her with an expression of extreme puzzlement. For the space of a breath, the two gazed at one another in mutual astonishment.

"You see them?" Sally asked her.

"I do," Alafair replied. "And one of them sees me, too." She glanced up. The open transom was inches above her head. "Can you hear me?" she asked the prisoner, just a little louder than before.

"I can," he called.

"Keep your voice down," she instructed. "I can hear you fine, and I don't want to alert Trent."

"Who are you?" the youth managed.

"Are you Billy Bond?" she asked.

"I am. What are you doing, ma'am?"

Alafair took a second to scrutinize the captive before she answered. He had obviously been living rough for the past few months. His clothes were a mess, his blond hair stuck out every which way, and he was sporting a scruffy beard. But for all his uncouth appearance, Billy Bond was a good looking young man.

He was tall and slender, broad-shouldered and narrow-hipped. The dark blue eyes that gazed up at her in wonderment had a sad cast to them.

In the far cell, Alafair could see the foot swing off the bunk onto the floor, followed by another foot, then Billy's cousin and jailmate, Jeff Stubblefield, appeared at the bars. He was darker, and quite a bit smaller, but otherwise resembled Billy very much. The look on his face was entirely as perplexed as his cousin's.

Against her will, Alafair was moved to pity by the young men's dishevelment. Why couldn't Scott let them clean up and put on some decent clothes? She sighed and steeled herself to her purpose.

"My name is Miz Tucker," she said. "I want to ask y'all some questions about Louise Kelley."

Billy's expression hardened. "I got nothing to say about that," he said.

"Besides," Jeff added, "why should you care, lady? Who are you?"

"It's a long story," Alafair told them, "and I reckon we don't have much time. You don't know me, it's true, but somebody I care about is involved in this business. I ain't convinced you fellows killed her. Maybe you can tell me something that I can use to help y'all boys get out of there." Even as she spoke the words, Alafair prayed to be forgiven for lying. She had no idea whether Billy had killed Louise or not, but she didn't have time to get the men to trust her through long acquaintance. Self-interest would have to do.

"Who do you think is involved," Jeff insisted, "and why should we help him? We got troubles of our own."

"Shut up, Jeff," Billy said offhandedly. "I don't know what you're playing at, Miz Tucker," he said to Alafair, "but I don't even know no Tuckers to speak to, so I doubt if we can help you. I will tell you this, though. I never killed Louise Kelley, my hand on fifty Bibles."

"Why did you hide out, then?"

"I heard the next day that Louise got found dead. I knew sure as I'm standing here that the Sheriff would come looking for me, and I was right. They got nobody else to blame. I'd never kill Louise for anything. She was the only person standing between that husband of hers and my girl. If I was going to kill anybody, it would have been him, not her. In fact…" He hesitated, peering up at her suspiciously. "Will you really try to help us?" he asked.

"I will if I think you're innocent," Alafair assured him.

Jeff snorted, unconvinced. Billy looked resigned to an unhappy fate, but continued. "It wasn't me looking to kill somebody that night," he said. "It was her. She knew the situation between the barber and my Peggy. She said it wasn't the first time, and she'd had enough of his shenanigans. She drew me aside and tried to give me a hundred dollars to kill her husband for her."

Alafair was so startled by this pronouncement that she nearly fell backwards off the boxes. She felt Sally's hand come up and grab her leg to steady her. She swallowed and leaned back in. "Did you take it?" she wondered.

"No, I did not. I told her I didn't want nothing to do with that. A lot of good it did me."

"Did you tell this to the sheriff?"

"Of course I did, but he don't believe me. I got no witnesses, either."

"What happened after that?"

He shrugged. "I know there's some folks say we got drunk and rode off together. Neither of us was exactly stone cold sober, it's true, but I had my wits about me enough to remember that I took her home on my horse and left her standing on the walk in front of her house, just kind of talking to herself under her breath. I didn't even go inside. She was crying and generally acting crazy the whole way home. She'd holler for God to forgive her and then in the next breath beg me to shoot the barber in the head. I just wanted to get out of there. I met up with Jeff here outside of town later and we camped by Cloud Creek that night. Next morning we started riding toward home and heard in Council Hill that Louise had been found dead."

"Who told you?"

"My ma heard it at the General Store that afternoon."

"Who do you think killed Louise, then?" Alafair asked him.

"I don't have an idea one," he assured her. "I suspect that after I left her, she tried to find somebody else to kill the barber."

Alafair shook her head. "Well, I don't know what I can do for you, young fellow, but I'll try to do something. Maybe one of her neighbors heard you leave that night after you brought her home."

"Anything you can do would be mighty welcome," Billy assured her.

"Don't tell Trent I was here."

"Don't aim to."

Alafair prepared to dismount her perch, but a question occurred to her and she turned back to the window. "Jeff Stubblefield," she called, "why did you go to ground with your cousin? You weren't even there."

Jeff shrugged. "Somebody might have seen me with Billy after he left Miz Kelley. Besides, he's kin." He made this statement as though it explained everything. And to Alafair, it did.

—◦—◦—◦—

"Do you suppose it was Peggy?" Alafair asked Sally, as she snapped the reins over the horse's back and guided the buggy down the road out of town.

Sally pondered a moment. "I can't think of anybody else with a better reason to get rid of Louise."

"Aside from Walter," Alafair said.

"What about the Grants?"

"Miz Grant may not have liked Louise, but that seems like a mighty weak reason for murder. Now, if we were looking for people with a motive to kill Walter, I'd have a bunch of suspects."

"Who knows?" Sally replied. "Peggy looked to me like too little of a slip to have drove a big old knife into somebody's chest.

Nothing surprises me any more, though. Too bad you can't ask Scott what he knows about Billy's story that Louise wanted him to kill her husband for her."

Alafair smiled. "No, I wouldn't like to tell him how I found out about it. As soon as I leave you to home, Ma, I've got to be getting back to the house. I expect I've got one hungry baby waiting for me. Then me and the girls are picking early snap beans and getting them ready to can. I'm going to be overrun with them this year."

As they passed the Boynton Cemetery, Alafair had her eyes on the road, and was startled when Sally grabbed her arm and exclaimed, "Alafair!"

She automatically tugged on the reins and came to a halt. "What is it?" she asked, alarmed.

"Look yonder at who is just coming out."

Alafair blinked at the sloping figure standing alone on the path beside the cemetery gate. "I declare. Ned Tolland," she managed.

Sally scrambled out of the buggy and walked across the road to meet Ned. She was deep in conversation with him by the time Alafair had maneuvered the horse and rig over to their side of the road and stepped down.

Sally took Alafair's arm as she walked up and drew her into the conversation. "Alafair, Ned tells me he was just here paying his respects to his late sister-in-law."

"Yes, I happened upon Ned doing just that a while back. You're a faithful visitor, Ned."

"I like to come regular."

"I suppose you heard that they got the two men they think did it," Alafair told him. "It was Billy Bond and his cousin Jeff Stubblefield. You know, Billy is engaged to that Peggy Crocker girl that you and Nell saw outside the fence at Louise's funeral."

Ned nodded, morose as ever. "Yes, I heard about Billy Bond. I just came by to let Louise know. I got to go home now and tell Nellie. She'll know what to do."

"Do?" Sally repeated. "What should Nellie do?"

"I don't know," Ned told her. "I never expected the sheriff might arrest Billy Bond, him being the betrothed of the gal who was the cause of all this trouble. I reckon Nellie will be as surprised as me. She might have something to say about it."

"What could she say?" Alafair prodded.

A look passed over his face that gave Alafair pause. Was it amusement? Or could it have been irony, or even irritation?

"Nellie usually has something to say about everything," Ned answered.

It occurred to Alafair that perhaps Ned was not as slow-witted as she had thought.

Chapter Fourteen

Alafair's garden was overflowing with spring vegetables this May Day, the day after her escapade at the jailhouse. The lettuce and radishes were just getting past their prime, but the green beans had begun bearing prolifically, as had the carrots, pintos, and butter beans. The tomatoes, melons, and okra plants were growing tall, as well. Alafair and the girls had spent the day before picking, washing, and snapping the first crop of green beans. Now, after breakfast was cleaned up and the menfolk and children away, Alafair, Mary and Martha were in the midst of one of Alafair's least favorite tasks—canning. The jars had already been sterilized in boiling water, and all of last year's rubber sealing rings inspected and replaced if need be. The women had blanched an enormous batch of beans and filled the glass, one-quart jars as full as possible, then loosely screwed on the rubber-sealed lids. Mary placed a layer of cloth on the bottom of a wash boiler, and then they placed in a layer of jars, covered them with another cloth, then another layer of jars.

Alafair filled the boiler with cold water to cover the jars well, then she placed the boiler on the stove and brought the water to a rolling boil. Leaving the girls to clean up and watch the jars and make sure they boiled steadily for the next three hours, Alafair walked back into her bedroom. She paused at the door, wiping her flushed face with the tail of her apron, and stood for a moment watching Alice sew.

The sewing machine was placed under the bedroom window for the best light, so Alice had her back to the door and sewed happily on, unaware of her mother watching her. Her long blond hair, braided with blue-flowered ribbon, was twisted up into a knot at the back of her head. She was singing to herself in time to the pumping of the treadle, engrossed in and enthralled by her task.

"I'll entwine and I'll mingle my raven black hair,
With the roses so red and the lilies so fair.
And my eyes will outshine even stars in the blue..."

She hummed the last line to herself, but Alafair finished it for her in her mind.

Said I, knowing not that my love was untrue.

Sweet Alice, ten years old, full of fun and palaver, running roughshod over her long suffering twin Phoebe, injecting herself uninvited into the affairs of her older sisters, lording it over her younger siblings. Bewitching her father, charming her mother, shamelessly avoiding her just deserts when she misbehaved with a combination of innocence, brass, and wit. Look at her now, eighteen years old, so beautiful, with eyes blue as cornflowers, just as brash, just as witty, just as innocent of the world as she was at ten.

"What're you making, honey?" Alafair asked, and Alice raised her head and swiveled around in her chair to face her mother with a smile.

"Y'all done with the green beans?" Alice countered.

"For now. Just started boiling." Alafair sat down on the bed and smoothed back her unruly hair with both hands. "We got nine quarts with this batch, and there'll be another batch just as big ready to can in a few days."

"I expect I'd better think me up another project I can be working on by then," Alice said brightly.

Alafair blew an unwilling laugh, amused and mildly annoyed at once. "You like to eat green beans well enough," she observed.

"Now, Mama," Alice chided, "you know I'd help you if you didn't already have all the help you need. Now look here what I'm making." She turned back to the machine, cut her thread with her sewing scissors, and lifted her new garment off the table to show Alafair.

Alafair took the skirt into her lap and inspected it with interest. Alice was a gifted seamstress, Alafair acknowledged to herself. Her seams were solid and straight as a ruler. The skirt was inside-out as Alice sewed on it, and Alafair ran her hand over the pearl-colored lining. "This feels like silk!" she exclaimed.

"It is," Alice affirmed. "A real silk lining under a fine worsted."

"Who are you making this for?"

"For myself, this time."

"Mercy, Alice, how did you get enough money for such nice materials?" Alafair asked, dreading to hear the answer.

"I been saving it up for months, Ma. Word of my tailoring skills is getting around," she said proudly. "I've had several jobs sewing dress-up clothes for folks in town ever since I fixed Aunt Josie's wool suit for her. Guess she's been bragging on me."

"I declare," Alafair managed. "If I'd have known that sewing paid so much, I'd have give up being a housewife a long time ago." She turned the skirt right side out. The wool was fine and silky smooth, dove gray with a subtle darker gray vertical stripe. The skirt was narrow and form fitting. It would make the tall Alice look statuesque. Alafair held the skirt out in front of her by the waistband. The diameter of the hem was barely bigger than the waist. "Gracious, Alice, what kind of skirt is this?"

Alice laughed. "It's called a 'hobble skirt,' Ma. It's been all the rage back east for the last couple of years, according to the *Ladies' Home Journal*. I've been wanting to make myself one for ages. Look how the hemline rises here in front, and this false seam goes all the way up to the waist. Looks like a wrap-around, but it isn't."

"'Hobble' is right," Alafair observed. "How do you walk in it?"

"It ain't for walking, Mama, it's for standing around looking pretty," Alice told her with a wink.

The long skirt nearly reached the ankles in the back, but Alafair eyed the way the hem rose into a little 'v' in the front. It would expose part of the wearer's stockinged shins with every mincing step. Alafair hoped that Alice's Grandpa Gunn never saw the girl in it. He would fall over dead of shock. Alafair wasn't too sure about Shaw's reaction, either, come to think on it. But all she said was, "I hope you never have to run away from hungry lions while you're wearing this."

"Wait 'til you see the jacket I'm going to make with it, Ma," Alice told her, excited. "It's short, with three pearl buttons, nipped in at the waist, and has a peplum."

"Where are you going to wear such a fancy suit, sugar?" Alafair wondered.

Alice shrugged. "A girl needs a few nice things. Never can tell. I'll put it in my hope chest."

"Ah," Alafair breathed. She handed the skirt back to Alice. "How are you making it through your month break from Walter Kelley?"

Alice blinked at her for a second, taken aback by the direction the conversation had suddenly skewed. Her expression became guarded. "It's hard," she said.

Alafair leaned forward and placed her hands on her knees, looking sincere and businesslike. Alice automatically drew back in her chair. The expression on her mother's face boded no good.

"Alice, I've been hearing things about Walter in the past few weeks," Alafair began gingerly. "At first, I just asked Scott, and some others who might know something, what they thought about the murder of Walter's wife. I was only interested in Walter because you're interested in him, and that whole situation looked to me like something that might hurt you. And I can't have that. So I hope you'll understand why I've been snooping around, even if you don't much like it."

Alafair paused to allow Alice to comment if she wanted, and after a hesitation, Alice said, "I know you mean to protect me, Mama. And I expect you're finding out what kind of a person Louise was, and that Walter had nothing to do with her killing."

Alafair nodded. "From what I hear, Louise wasn't nothing to write home about, it's true. And it seems she got herself into a situation that got her killed, one way or the other. I guess that there's just no evidence that Walter had Louise murdered. But, honey, I'm also finding out that there was blame enough to go around in that marriage. From what I'm hearing, Walter Kelley is the kind of man who means well, but glides through life without a thought to spare for anyone else…"

"That ain't true," Alice interrupted, calm, but firm.

"Sugar, I'm afraid if you marry that man, you'll be unhappy."

"I know you don't like him, Mama," Alice said, "but you don't know him. I'm not Louise. I'll make him happy. He won't have a reason to look elsewhere if he's with me."

"Oh, honey," Alafair sighed. "It isn't so easy for a leopard to change his spots."

"Ma, I know that was a bad situation with Louise getting killed and all, and you don't like to see any of us kids mixed up with anything that doesn't look just right. But you've got to trust me, Ma. Walter is everything I want. He's fun and handsome and well off, and he really cares for me. I know in my heart that we'll be happy." She leaned forward and took her mother's hand and shook it gently, making her point. "We're doing what you asked, me and Walter. We're keeping apart this month just so you'll see that we're not fooling. But when this month is up, I expect we'll be getting married."

"Has he already asked you," Alafair said, surprised, "without talking to Daddy or anything?"

"No, he hasn't asked me, yet. But he told me he'll be talking to Daddy directly. Daddy likes Walter, Mama. Why don't you?"

Alafair sat up straight on the bed. "I don't dislike him. I just don't like him for you. And I know Daddy likes him, but Daddy doesn't like what he heard about Walter getting that poor girl from Council Hill in a bad way. That's what he told me, anyway."

"You didn't tell Daddy about that, did you?" Alice asked, alarmed.

"He already knew about it, Alice. It ain't exactly a secret."

Alice fell silent. She studied her mother's face for a long moment. "Are you forbidding me to marry Walter?" she asked finally.

"I would if I could," Alafair admitted. "I think he'll hurt you. I can't speak for Daddy. But I'm asking you as sincere as I know how to take this last week or so and think about it as hard as you can. Will you do that for me?"

Alice's face was still as marble. She was gazing at Alafair thoughtfully from under her eyebrows, her blue eyes inscrutable. It was an expression Alafair knew well.

"I hear what you're saying, Mama," Alice answered at length.

"You'll think hard?"

"Yes, Ma, I'll think real hard."

Alafair stood up. "Thank you, hon. That's all I ask." She could hear Grace beginning to squall in the kitchen, so she turned to leave. As she walked out of the bedroom, she heard the rattle of the sewing machine start up again, and Alice humming as she sewed.

～～～

On the same morning that Alice was creating her trousseau, her intended, Walter Kelley, was sitting on a bench on the sidewalk in front of his barber shop, thinking that it was a mighty fine thing to be alive. Just one year earlier, he had been enduring a miserable marriage to a woman who would neither forgive him nor leave him. And here he was now, on a fine spring day, his life as abloom as the dogwoods that graced the residential streets in town. His business was doing so well that he expected he'd have to hire on another barber directly. Nearly everyone in town treated him like a king since his bereavement. And on top of it all, he was head over heels for the prettiest, wittiest, most understanding girl in the county, who, wonder of wonders, seemed taken with him as well.

A trill of female laughter, melodious as bird song, floated on the air and into his reverie. He turned his head to see three young women in pastel dresses and flowered hats gliding down the sidewalk in his direction. He smiled at the sheer loveliness of it all.

All three women looked familiar to him, but he could only call to mind one name. He stood as they neared.

"Good morning, Miss Lollie June. Ladies. Thank goodness it's spring, is all I've got to say, because y'all look as pretty as a flock of bluebirds in them frocks."

The girls giggled, and Lollie June answered. "Why, ain't you the sweetest thing, Walter!"

Walter clapped his hand over his heart. "It's nothing but the plain truth."

Lollie June's ironic smile indicated that she thought his praise a bit overblown, but she enjoyed it nonetheless. "Walter, you remember my friends, Edria Harvey and Maxine Cecil."

He took each delicate hand in turn and nodded a greeting. "I don't believe we've been formally introduced. I'm glad to meet you, ladies. Where are y'all off to on this lovely day?"

"We're doing a bit of shopping," answered the small and buxom Edria.

"And we ought to be on our way," interjected the third one, in a tone of voice that caused Walter to look at her more closely. Maxine, that was her name. She was tall, rawboned, and dark, and while her expression wasn't exactly unfriendly, she did look wary.

He smiled his most charming smile. "Well, don't let me keep you, ladies. I'm doing nothing more useful than holding down this here bench between customers."

"I do declare, Maxine," Lollie June admonished, "you're always in a hurry. But I expect we'd better get on. By the way, Walter, do you have plans for dinner next Sunday? I noticed that you've been coming to church with us Methodists for the last couple of Sundays, then leaving all by your lonesome afterwards. My mother told me that if I ever got the chance, I should invite you along to Sunday dinner with us, and look here how we meet by accident like this! I reckon it's meant to be."

Walter grinned, delighted that the deliciously attractive Lollie June Griffith had been thinking about him. "How very kind you are, to notice my solitary ways and take pity on me. It's true that the last few Sundays I've been on my own. I sure would appreciate a home-cooked meal, Miss Lollie June. Please be kind enough to thank your mother for me and tell her that I'd be delighted to join you for dinner after church next Sunday."

"That pleases me no end, Walter, and I'm sure my mother will say the same. Well, then, you know where we live, over there on Franklin. Let's say one o'clock. That'll give you time to go home for a bit and freshen up, and me and Mama can get the food on the table by then."

"One o'clock it is. And let me say again how grateful I am for the invitation."

After a flurry of courtly good-byes, the girls resumed their walk toward the O R Clothing Company, chatting away, heads together as they receded down the sidewalk. Walter sat back down and watched them thoughtfully until they disappeared into the store.

He had been awfully bored and lonely since Alice had been unavailable, so he was happy with the prospect of a pleasant Sunday afternoon in the company of a pretty girl and her doting mother. But there was something about that tall, dark haired girl giving him the skunk-eye that made him pause.

Maxine, he thought. Maxine Cecil. He had seen her before, but that was no wonder. Yet, something niggling at the back of his mind told him they had actually met, and not too long ago.

Easter, that was it. He had seen her at the McBride farm at Easter dinner. She was Alice's cousin.

The remembrance caused his heart to skip a beat. Dang it all, this was the trouble with being sweet on a girl with as many relations as Adam and Eve. His alarm faded quickly, however. Alice would surely hear about his dinner invitation, but Alice was about as different from Louise as an ox was from a hat. Alice understood him. He sat back on the bench, thinking that it was a mighty fine thing to be alive.

Chapter Fifteen

To pass the time profitably while waiting for the jars of green beans to seal, Alafair sat for a while in the kitchen next to the back door, churning butter, worrying about Alice. She had already skimmed the cream off of the milk, which had been separating for several hours in a five-gallon milk can next to the stove. She had poured the cream into the tall, narrow crock that sat between her knees, and she pumped the dasher rhythmically with her hands. The repetitive motion was hypnotic, and Alafair found herself gazing dreamily out the open back door, where she could see a few of her children playing in the yard. Mary was in the garden, and Martha was moving around the kitchen, making noodles. The clinks and clanks of her chore accompanied the drowsy progression of the afternoon.

Alafair could see Gee Dub coming up to the house from the stable, where he had been helping Shaw with the horses. He's probably hungry, she thought. Gee Dub was accosted by Charlie, Sophronia and Blanche as he came into the yard. He good-naturedly allowed himself to be diverted into a game. Alafair was aware of the sound of the rolling pin as Martha began to roll the noodle dough out on the cabinet.

Alafair couldn't hear what the children were saying, but she watched Gee Dub pantomime instructions to Charlie, who took up a position standing with his back to his brother, his arms down stiffly at his side, like a soldier at attention.

The dasher pumped up and down. Alafair's arms were tiring. Her eyes wandered away from the yard and toward Martha, who was cutting long, thick noodles from the flattened slab of dough. After she had cut the dough into strips, Martha lifted each noodle off the cabinet, one by one, and hung them like pieces of Christmas tinsel over the dish towel draped across her forearm; then she began to scrape and clean the countertop with her free hand.

Alafair looked back out into the yard to see Gee Dub put his hand under each of Charlie's ears and lift him bodily off the ground by his head. Blanche and Sophronia were clamoring for a turn. Alafair stood, irritated and amused at once, walked across the back porch and leaned out the screen door.

"Gee Dub, stop that," she called. "You'll do somebody an injury."

The young kids groaned, disappointed that their game was interrupted, but Gee Dub was unbothered. "Okay, Mama," he said, and came up the steps into the house.

Alafair sat back down in her chair and lifted the lid of the churn to check the progress of her butter. "Are you after something to eat?" she asked Gee Dub.

"Yeah," he admitted. "Daddy said he couldn't concentrate for my stomach growling." The boy was in the midst of a growth spurt. Sixteen years old, skinny as a wire, but seemingly two inches taller every day. All angles and feet. Shaw had observed that when Gee Dub stood still, he looked like the letter L. He ate more than any two people in the family.

"There's potato patties left over from dinner," Alafair told him. "Make yourself a sandwich."

The idea appealed to him and he moved to the task straight away. "Are we having beef and noodles tonight?" he asked Martha, as he sawed a couple of slices off of a loaf of bread.

Gravity had worked to double the length of the noodles hanging over Martha's arm, and she was peeling them off one by one and laying them back on the counter to cut into manageable size. "I planned on drying these," she told him. "I can make some noodle soup to go with the leftovers from dinner, though, if you want it."

They both glanced at their mother, whose eyebrows peaked with interest. "Sounds good to me," she said.

Gee Dub assembled his potato patties on the bread, with some sliced onion and slathers of mustard, and wandered back outside with his sandwich in his fist.

"He's a bottomless pit," Martha observed, as she separated her noodles.

"He's a growing boy."

"Growing right along," Martha agreed. "He's going to be tall."

"Yes, he is, if you can predict by the size of his feet," Alafair said. "This butter is just about made. Hand me them paddles, hon." She removed the lid and dasher and poured off the buttermilk through a sieve into a crock she had ready on the table, leaving big golden lumps of butter in the churn. Alafair spooned the butter onto a stone butter slab.

Martha covered her drying noodles with a dishcloth, then retrieved two wooden paddles from the cabinet. She handed them to Alafair, who used them to shape the butter into a loaf.

"Don't you want your butter mold?" Martha asked.

"No, we'll have this little bit eaten up by tomorrow. No need to be fancy." As she worked the salt into the butter, Alafair glanced up at her daughter. Martha was easy around the kitchen. She was a good cook and housekeeper, neat and organized. She could have run her own house with her eyes closed, Alafair thought. Why, then, does she seem to have no interest in the idea?

Martha had not lacked for beaux in the past few years, and had, in fact, considered at least one marriage proposal. But she had turned him down, and apparently wasn't looking for a replacement fiancé any time soon.

Alafair was proud of Martha's initiative and wasn't bothered by her lack of eagerness to marry, but it did make her ponder. Her daughters were a different type of creature than Alafair and her sisters had been. It was a new century. The way things had been done for time out of mind were coming to an end. The girls had options that had been unavailable to Alafair. It would have been impossible for her to be as independent as Martha, or as forward as Alice. The idea would never have entered her head.

This Twentieth Century was shaping up to be something entirely original in human history, Alafair mused, and it wasn't just that for the first time, people could drive without horses, make light without fire, or even fly. Those were outward things.

A new species of person was being born, one who didn't admit impossibilities. Alafair paused and stared at the butter, suddenly able to see something of the future. Her children were going to be able to think thoughts that had never been thought before. The hair on the back of her neck rose.

How could she prepare them for a world that she couldn't even imagine?

"Ma?" Martha said, and Alafair started. "I reckon you've worked that butter to within an inch of its life."

"I was gathering wool," Alafair confessed. "Mercy, the day is getting away! I've got to get into town for more canning jars before milking time. I'll just wrap this butter and put it in the bucket in the well to cool. If you'll clean the churn for me, I'll go do that, and fetch Mary to go into town with me. Grace will be up from her nap directly. Listen for her, will you? I'll take her with me if she wakes up before I get gone. Phoebe's been in town today, but her and John Lee are coming for supper. Ruth is in the parlor—get her in here to sweep this floor."

Martha held up her hand to stop Alafair in mid-rant. "Yes, Mama," she soothed. "Go get Mary and put your butter in the well. I promise not to let the house fall down for the little while you're gone."

❧

Half an hour later, Alafair rode into town with Mary and Grace to pick up more quart Mason jars from Hattie Tucker's general store. It was a beautiful spring day, with no hint of the storminess that was all too common at this time of year, and the front door of the store was wide open, inviting passersby to come in for a chat; a benevolent snare, Alafair thought, to catch Hattie some company and some good gossip.

The long, narrow room was bordered on three sides by counters, behind which the walls were lined from floor to ceiling with shelves. The wooden floor was swept within an inch of its life, the finish worn white where customers habitually walked and stood. Every step on the well-worn floor produced a homey, comforting creak. The high, white, pressed tin ceiling sported a repeating pattern of squares and curlicues. Three dark brown ceiling fans of molded metal and wood were arrayed in a line down the middle of the room. They were off on a cool day like today, but in the summer they turned lazily, just enough to move the sodden air.

Hattie's store carried an eclectic mix of dry goods and groceries; cloth and sewing supplies, hardware and tools, flour and sugar and canned goods—many of the things that the local farmers couldn't produce for themselves, including the canning supplies that Alafair had come to buy. She was delighted to find Scott inside, sitting in a cane-bottomed chair next to the cracker barrel, visiting his wife during a break in his afternoon rounds.

Hattie was behind the counter, leaning on her elbows, her curly light brown hair askew as usual. "Afternoon, gals," she called to them when they walked in. "Come on over here and let me do some lovin' on that baby."

"Me, first," Scott interposed. "I don't get enough chance to dandle little girls on my knee, either."

Alafair handed Scott the baby, who went to him with alacrity. None of her children had been shy babies. Being held and fussed over by extended family and even strangers had never been anything but a pleasant adventure for any of them.

"What brings you into town this fine afternoon?" Hattie smiled. "I don't often see you twice in one week."

"We're canning snap beans," Alafair told her. "I need more quart jars—had a bunch of them break since last season. A case, maybe. And maybe a half-dozen or so pints. Listen, Hattie," she added, "why don't you and Scott and the boys come for supper this evening after you close up? I'm not fixing anything fancy, but I don't expect you'd go hungry."

Hattie and Scott looked at one another, passing a visual signal, before Hattie nodded at Alafair. "I'm always happy not to have to cook. I'll bring a couple of pies."

After Hattie had disappeared into the storeroom, Alafair turned to Scott, who really was dandling a squealing Grace on one knee. "You taking them boys you have in the jail over to Muskogee today?"

"Not yet," Scott managed, over the baby's laughter. "Their lawyer will be in to see them this afternoon, then we'll probably transfer them sometime Monday. They'll be up for trial in a few weeks, I expect."

"They admit they did it?"

Scott's sharp blue eyes slid her a glance. "What do you think? They're innocent as the day is long, to hear them tell it. They got quite a tale. But it's up to the lawyers and the judges, now."

"Me and Grandma Sally ran into Ned Tolland yesterday morning, Scott," Alafair began. "Remember how I told you I had met him out by the cemetery a while back? Well, we talked to him out there again yesterday. Had a pretty odd conversation…"

Before she could finish her comment, Mary, who was gazing out the store window into the street, said, "Look, Ma, here comes Nellie Tolland, in a big hurry, too."

Nellie burst into the store and paused, blinking while her eyes adjusted to the dim interior. She looked over at Mary. "I hear the sheriff is here," she said without preamble.

"Yes, ma'am," Mary affirmed, nodding toward the cracker barrel, just as Scott said, "Here I am, Miz Tolland."

He handed Grace to Alafair and stood up. "What's the matter?"

Nellie walked over to where Scott was standing, still puffing a bit from her hurried walk from the jailhouse. Alafair could see that Hattie had emerged from the storeroom and was standing at the far end of the counter, her ears practically quivering. Scott wasn't a tall man, but Nellie was so small and dumpling-like that she barely came up to the star pinned on his suit coat. "Your deputy told me you might be here," she began, looking up at him. "My husband has heard that one of the boys you arrested for my sister's murder is Billy Bond. Is that true, Sheriff?"

"Yes, ma'am," Scott said. "Billy Bond and his cousin Jeff Stubblefield."

Nellie bit her bottom lip, distressed. "So it's true," she said to nobody in particular, then looked back up. "Why do you suspect that they killed Louise?"

"Billy was seen leaving the road house with her. Several people seen him, so we know it was him she was with. Then he went to ground. Him and Jeff had been holed up together for months, but we were waiting. We got them the first time they stuck their noses out."

"Mercy, Sheriff, I didn't know that you suspected the Bond boy. I figured you was just looking for a drifter that nobody would ever see again."

"I wasn't," Scott said.

"Well, what makes you think those boys went ahead and killed her, then?"

"Billy admits that he took her home," Scott said, "and there are signs that your sister was killed in her own parlor, then hauled on out and dumped into Cane Creek by two people."

"Yes, signs!" Nellie exclaimed. She looked eager. "What happened to them signs?"

Scott's eyes narrowed. "Why? Do you know something that you haven't told me, Miz Tolland? It's a crime to withhold evidence, now."

Nellie hesitated, still chewing on her bottom lip. She glanced at Alafair blankly, hardly registering her presence, while she considered what to say next. "Why would Billy Bond want to kill Louise?" she reasoned. "His intended and my sister were both ill-used by that man."

"What man?" Scott asked.

"That man," she spat, suddenly livid. "That Walter Kelley. It was him, Sheriff. It was him killed Louise as sure as he plunged that knife into her chest with his own hands!"

Scott grabbed the little woman by the shoulders and forced her to look at him. "Calm down," he ordered. "Miz Tolland, do you know who killed Louise Kelley? You'd better tell me."

"It was him!" Nellie cried, nearly hysterical now. "He was going to do it when he came home that night, I tell you! But he got delayed or something, so he must have arranged the whole thing while he was in Kansas City, I just know it! He paid two ruffians to stab her and leave her laying there in the middle of the floor. There was footprints all around, sheriff, and some of his things. Why didn't you see? He did it, he did it!" She collapsed into sobs. Grace, alarmed at the fury and drama, began to wail. Alafair motioned to Mary, who whisked the baby outside.

Scott took Nellie's chin in his hand and forced her to look at him. "Miz Tolland," he said, "what are you talking about? You know we didn't find your sister's body laying on the floor. There weren't any footprints in her house. You know where we found Louise, now, don't you?"

Alafair and Hattie were rooted to their spots in tingling anticipation. Every hair on Alafair's body was standing on end.

Nellie Tolland stopped howling and gazed at the sheriff for a long moment, wide eyed. She snuffled and wiped her nose on her sleeve before she replied. "Well, it's common knowledge, ain't it?" she managed. "Them Tucker boys found poor Louise hid under some branches in the creek."

"Why did you say 'in the middle of the floor'?" Scott demanded.

"I got mixed up."

"How did Louise get in the creek?"

For the first time, Nellie looked frightened. "I don't know," she whimpered.

"You and Ned own a couple of little jackasses, don't you? I think we should go on out to your farm right now and check their shoes, see if any of them have a triangle nick on the right rear. What do you think?"

"Sheriff, I…" she began, but her breath failed her before she could form the sentence.

"Miz Tolland, did you kill your sister?" Scott demanded.

"No!" Nellie exclaimed, aghast.

"Did your husband?"

"No, no, not Ned! It was that husband of hers, I swear!"

"He couldn't have done it himself," Scott explained patiently, as if to a child. "So, if he paid somebody to do it for him, it had to be Billy and Jeff, and if it wasn't, who was it?"

"I don't know. But it wasn't Billy and Jeff. It was somebody else."

"Why are you so sure it wasn't them?" Scott persisted. Alafair could tell he was exasperated because Nellie wouldn't come to the point.

"I don't want no innocent boys hanged for something they didn't do. I know why Louise met up with those boys that night," Nellie admitted reluctantly. "She was going to ask them something."

Suddenly Scott was all attention again. "Still could have been them."

Alafair guessed what the sheriff was doing. He was trying to get Nellie to admit that her sister had attempted to pay Billy to kill Walter.

Nellie was gazing at the floor, now.

"You don't know anything," he challenged. "You're just trying to implicate Kelley because you hate him. You have no idea why Louise left with Billy."

"I do," she assured him weakly. "She told me. She was going to try and pay him money to punish that man for the way he treated her for ten years."

Alafair saw Hattie's jaw drop.

"To kill him?" Scott asked.

Nellie began to cry again. "No. To beat him up. To scare him. To make him change. I don't know," she sobbed.

But she does know, Alafair thought.

"Miz Tolland, did you or Ned kill Louise?" Scott asked again.

Nellie shook her head without looking at him.

"But you know who did," Scott stated. It wasn't a question.

Only a moment passed before Nellie nodded, not trusting herself to speak.

"I think you better come on back to the office with me and tell me what you know."

Alafair came within a hair's breadth of yelling "No!" The tension of being this close to a revelation and not hearing it was too much to be borne. But Nellie Tolland saved her from making a fool of herself.

"That ain't necessary, Sheriff," Nellie said, calm again. "Louise killed herself. Stabbed herself right in her broken heart. I know because me and Ned found her in her house that night, stabbed and dead. There was a note. She was in misery, you could tell by how she had scribbled that note. I could hardly read it. I finally made out that she had written that she was such a sinner, and evil, she didn't want to live. She said she was going to take a big old knife and run against the wall.

"Louise had come out to our place the day before, for the Fourth of July. She told us that she was meeting Billy Bond the next night, Friday, at the road house. She chose Billy because they both had such a grievance with that man. I had told Louise a hundred times she should divorce him. Just divorce him. She sure had grounds. But she didn't want to. She kept telling me she still loved him. But after that little gal showed up at her door, she finally saw the light. He'd never change.

"She told me she was coming by our place afterwards, to let me know what happened, but she never showed up, and once it got past eight o'clock, I started to worry. So me and Ned finally went into town to check on her. It was real late, maybe nine-thirty on Friday night. The house was dark, and we found her, lying dead on her back right in her own parlor, with that knife in her chest and her arms flung out to her sides. So you see, that awful man may not have stabbed her hisself, but he drove her to it and he should be made to pay. Somebody should make him pay!"

Scott had a hold on the woman's upper arm, as much supporting her as preventing her from running away. He suddenly looked weary. "She stabbed herself," he repeated, as if to clarify. "Held that big old knife against her chest and ran at the wall."

"Yes," Nellie murmured.

"She did this at home. You and Ned found her at home."

"Yes."

"Did you clean up the blood? There must have been blood spattered on the wall. A dent, too, where she ran against it."

Nellie looked up at him. "Well, there wasn't much blood, except on her clothes. I expect she died straight away, and never bled much. There was a little crack in the plaster where she hit the wall, like you said. There was a chair knocked over."

"What happened to the note?" Scott asked.

"I took it with me. Burned it up in my kitchen stove later."

As he listened to Nellie's admission, Scott looked as amazed as Alafair felt. "Well, why in tarnation would you do that? Why would you destroy the evidence, and then stuff your own sister into the creek?"

"No, no, Sheriff, weren't you listening? We didn't put her in the creek. I don't know who did that. When I saw Louise laying there with that look on her face…" She choked back a sob, then continued. "I reckon I hardly saw anything after that. There was blood all over her clothes, I remember that."

"Then how did her body end up in the creek?" he asked.

"I don't know," Nellie told him yet again. "We didn't do it. I cried quite a spell when we found her, before Ned said to me that it was too bad her unhappy life had drove her to this. And he was right, too. All of a sudden, I like to went up in flames. It was like she had decided the only way she could be free of him was for one of them to be dead. I was so angry, Sheriff. I wanted Walter Kelley to pay for it. I went into the bedroom closet and got a pair of that man's shoes, then I dipped my hand right into my poor sister's blood and smeared the soles. Then Ned put the shoes on and made footprints all around, then left them right there in the middle of the floor. Quiet as we could be, 'cause I didn't want the neighbors to hear. I traced a "W" on the floor with her blood, right up near her hand. And I left some of his barber things near her body.

"You were right, Sheriff, I wanted everyone to think that he killed her. I didn't want it to seem possible that Louise done herself in. I took the note, but there was still that place on the wall. I was afraid somebody would figure it out. So we moved the sideboard over to cover the crack in the plaster. I knew Louise's rotten husband was out of town, but he was supposed to be back that very next morning. I expected he'd be the one to find her, and then you'd think he walked right in from the train and killed her. Then he didn't come home that day after all, and Louise's body disappeared right out of her house. I didn't know what to do. After she got found in the creek, I was hoping you'd decide her husband sneaked back into town, murdered her, and then hightailed it back to Kansas City."

She paused and looked at him, but Scott was not inclined to explain his investigation to her. "You destroyed the suicide note, and changed the crime scene in an attempt to incriminate your brother-in-law," he summarized.

Nellie nodded as though this were the most logical thing in the world. "It made me sick to hear somebody had put her in the creek after what we did. But I couldn't let those innocent boys hang for killing her, and me knowing they didn't do it."

"And you left that bloody rug in her parlor?" Scott persisted.

Nellie blinked. "What rug? You mean that rug she was laying on? We found her laying right up next to the kitchen door toward the back. She must have flung herself against the parlor wall and fell back onto the rug. I don't know what happened to it."

Scott glanced over at his wife, perplexed. "You and Ned didn't put her in the creek?" he asked Nellie yet again, apparently unable to believe his ears.

"No, sir. I'd never."

No one seemed to have anything else to say for a long minute, but finally Scott turned Nellie around and ushered her out of the store and down the street to the Sheriff's office. Neither Alafair nor Hattie could manage to move. Mary stepped back into the store with Grace in her arms.

"What on earth happened?" Mary asked, breaking the spell.

Alafair's knees practically buckled. "Lord have mercy," she exclaimed. "I got to sit down!"

"Miz Tolland told Scott that Louise Kelley killed herself," Hattie told Mary excitedly.

"What?"

"It's true, sugar," Alafair affirmed. She sat down in the chair that Scott had vacated and began fanning herself with her handkerchief. "Nellie said that Louise had told her she was going to try to get the Bond boy to kill Walter, or at least to put the fear of God into him. Louise was supposed to go out to their place that night, and when she didn't show up, Nellie and her husband went to looking for her and found Louise in her own house with a knife in her chest. There was a suicide note that said she was going to stab herself for being so low-down. I guess she felt bad for trying to have her husband killed."

Hattie took up the story. "Then, it seems that Nellie and Ned destroyed the note and generally tried to make it look like Louise was murdered. She claims she doesn't know how the body got into the creek where the boys found her."

"Why on earth would she want it to look like her sister was murdered?" Mary asked, aghast. "My goodness!"

"She told Scott that she wanted to make it look like Walter murdered her. Said they took a pair of Walter's shoes, smeared them with Louise's blood, and made footprints on the floor around her body so it would look like he was there. Sounds like she wasn't in her right mind when she thought up that scheme."

"Do you suppose it's the same shoes we found in the road, Mama?"

"I expect so, Mary. Walter told us he was missing a pair. Nellie said she left them in the middle of the floor, but maybe Ned took them later and buried them beside the road."

Walter's shoes and Ned's feet. As she explained to Mary what had transpired, Alafair was thinking of Buttercup snuffling around Walter at Easter, and Crook's interest in Ned's shoes at the cemetery. She wasn't going to doubt the hounds' noses again.

"So who put her in the creek?" Mary asked.

Alafair gave an exaggerated shrug. "Nellie said she didn't know, and I believe her. Somebody found her dead in the house and hid her. Maybe it was Billy and Jeff, fearing they'd be blamed."

Mary put her hand on her forehead as though she was getting dizzy. "But why did she kill herself?" she asked. "Because she felt guilty for trying to get her husband murdered? Heavens! If he was so bad, why not just get a divorce? I don't hold with divorce, but it's sure better than murder or doing yourself in, either one."

Alafair leaped to her feet, startling Mary and Grace, who yipped in surprise. Alafair took the baby from Mary's arms. "Because she couldn't see any way out of her horrible marriage that wouldn't make her even more miserable, I'm thinking," Alafair said. "She probably wanted to make him feel bad, too, but that don't seem to have worked." Alafair's face had paled, and she was quivering with outrage. "I'm telling you, Mary, that man is trouble. I don't care how friendly or handsome or well off he is. Alice can't marry him, she just can't! Maybe she'll listen to your daddy."

With that, she rushed out of the store with Grace in her arms, leaving all her purchases on the counter and her daughter standing in the middle of the floor, stunned.

Mary looked over at Hattie for guidance.

Hattie came out from behind the counter, picked up the boxes of Mason jars, and handed them to her. "Don't worry, honey," Hattie soothed. "You know how your mama is about protecting her kids. She'll calm down by and by."

Chapter Sixteen

By the time they got home, Alafair had settled into a black silence. Even Grace was sensitive to the storm clouds on her mother's horizon, and the baby sat on Mary's lap in quiet wonder all the way home. When they pulled up to the house, Alafair handed the baby to Mary and stalked off toward the fields looking for Shaw, leaving Mary to unload the buggy and take care of the horse as best she could.

Martha and Phoebe had heard them drive up and were at the screen when Mary came up with a box of jars under one arm and Grace on the other. "What's wrong with Mama?" Phoebe asked, as she pushed the door open for her sister and took the jars.

"We heard some news in town," Mary told her. As she walked across the parlor, she could see Alice through the door into her parents' bedroom, still sitting at the sewing machine. "Alice," she called, "come on into the kitchen. I've got something to tell you."

The four sisters sat in silence for a long moment after Mary related the tale of Nellie's confession and Alafair's response to it. Mary and Martha were warily anticipating Alice's reaction, and Phoebe, stunned, had nothing to say. Alice was gazing blankly at the floor.

Unable to keep still any longer, Mary asked, "Well?"

Alice lifted her head to stare off into middle space as she considered her situation, but she didn't answer.

"Sounds like Mama's determined to convince you that Walter is no good," Martha ventured.

Alice's gaze slid back to her sister's face. "Mama can't stop me from marrying him if I've a mind to." Her voice was calm.

Phoebe leaned back against the cabinet and folded her arms across her chest. "Wait a minute now, Alice. Do you really want to choose him over Mama and Daddy? Maybe end up separated from your family?"

"I don't think it would come to that. And if it did, it wouldn't be my doing."

"Alice," Mary admonished, "Mama's not one to make a mountain out of a molehill. She thinks she's got some good reasons for feeling like she does. Have you really studied on what she's been trying to tell you?"

Alice leaped up from her chair and took a few paces around the kitchen, stepping over Grace, who was wriggling around underfoot. "Not y'all, too! I thought my sisters were on my side."

"We are," Martha protested. "Lord knows I want you to have the man you love, but I don't want you to be at such odds with Mama, either."

Alice stopped pacing and placed her fists on her hips. "Well, what does she want from me, then? I've done what she asked me. I've kept apart from Walter all this time and my feelings aren't changed. Don't that prove I know my own mind?"

Phoebe bit her lip. "What if after this month is up, you find Walter's mind has changed?"

"I won't."

"You should be prepared, now. I had dinner with Aunt Josie and Maxine today, and Maxine said that Walter…"

"I don't want to hear any gossip about Walter," Alice interrupted. "That was what drove him and his first wife apart. I won't hear it. I won't believe it."

"Well, I want to hear it," Martha said. "You can just put your fingers in your ears, Alice. What did Maxine say, Phoebe?"

"Calm down, Alice," Phoebe soothed. "It wasn't that bad. Just something you should consider. Maxine told me that her and Edria Harvey and Lollie June Griffith were out shopping this morning and ran across Walter in front of his barber shop. Walter was doing quite a bit of sweet talking with the three of them, and Lollie June invited Walter to Sunday dinner. He accepted. Maxine was surprised, knowing how you two are practically promised to one another."

Alice emitted a disdainful laugh. "That's just his way. He's a man needs company. It don't mean anything."

"Well, I wouldn't like it if my intended acted that way," Mary said.

"I'm not you," Alice blazed. "I trust my man." She turned on Phoebe. "And in future, don't be so eager to pass on to me every ugly rumor you hear. I know Walter a lot better than you."

Phoebe put her hands up to ward off Alice's pique. "All right." She was unruffled. She was used to Alice's outspoken ways. "I just thought you should have all the information you can get before you decide."

"I've decided."

"So I see."

"We just don't want you to be hurt," Mary interjected. "Whatever happens, we're still your family."

Alice nodded, slightly mollified, and the sisters returned to their tasks. As she stirred the soup, though, Alice realized that she was rather dismayed at her mother's renewed opposition to her romance. And, she hated to admit it, but she was more than a little alarmed at Maxine's report.

Her stirring became more vigorous. They just didn't understand. This never would have happened if her parents hadn't imposed this ridiculous separation on her. Walter would never have become bored enough to seek companionship if she had been available to him. She had certainly proved to herself that her feelings for Walter weren't going to change.

I'm not going to lose him, she thought. No matter what.

Shaw was not in the barn. In the large workshop appended to the side of the barn, Alafair found Micah, one of Shaw's hired men, planing a plank for some ongoing repair job. He told her that Shaw, Gee Dub, and the other hired hand, Kurt, had gone out to the back pasture to bring in some of the mules for shoeing. Alafair's righteous indignation about Walter Kelley deflated a bit when she heard that, since the back pasture was a good two miles from the house, and the sun was already sinking toward the horizon.

She headed out of the workshop, but she was still too fired up to go back to the house, and without really meaning to, she found herself walking the path through the corn field that led to Cane Creek. Unlike Bird Creek, which ran through a wooded, overgrown area on the north side of the Tucker property, the banks of Cane Creek were relatively clear, lined only by a few tall elms and cottonwoods and not much brush or undergrowth. Alafair's feet took her directly to the undercut cottonwood whose tangled, half-exposed roots had hidden the body of Louise Kelley.

Alafair stood for a few minutes gazing into the dark water. She crossed her arms over her chest and sighed heavily. "Now what, Louise?" she murmured. "What're all these signs and smells and feelings that you've been sending me, if you just killed yourself? Sweet Lord, how miserable you must have been to want to dash yourself against a wall and plunge a knife into your heart." A shudder passed over her body at the very thought. "Rest now, Louise," she said aloud. "Let it go. There isn't anything I can do to help you."

"Miz Tucker?" said a man's voice behind her.

Alafair turned around, startled and more than a little surprised at herself for not hearing someone walk up on her. "Walter!" she exclaimed. "What on earth are you doing here?"

Walter Kelley was standing a few yards up the hill, gazing down at her with his hands in his pockets and a mildly disconcerted expression on his face. "I just talked to the sheriff," he told her. "I felt the need to come. I've never seen where she was found."

Alafair nodded. It seemed a reasonable explanation, but his presence made her nervous. She suddenly found herself thinking of another chance encounter she had had with a man on a creek bank just the year before. She had ended up with a cracked skull, that time. "How'd you get on the property?" she asked, a little too sharply.

"I cut across from the road," he admitted. "I'm sorry for trespassing, but I was afraid if I went by the house, I'd see Alice, and I promised I wouldn't."

Alafair knew she should be gratified, but she wasn't in a very charitable mood. "So you heard the tale that Louise killed herself," she challenged.

Walter nodded. "So Nellie says. The sheriff told me her story, though I didn't get the feeling that he quite believes it. Sounds to me like a pretty ridiculous thing to do, burn Louise's suicide note and then stomp around the house in my shoes. But then Nellie and Ned never were real clear thinkers."

"Especially when it comes to you," Alafair pointed out, still feeling mean.

A wry look crossed Walter's face. "Especially," he agreed. He walked down toward the creek, and Alafair moved off to the side, giving him a wide berth as he approached the bank. He gazed down into the water. "But I'm wondering who in the world found her lying dead in the house and then went to all the trouble to pick her up—knife still in her heart, mind you—and cart her all the way out here on the back of a donkey to hide her in the creek." He shook his head in befuddlement. "I can't fathom it." He glanced at Alafair. "Maybe Nellie and Ned are lying," he ventured.

"I don't know why," Alafair said.

"Maybe it was them boys that Louise went out with," he persisted. "Maybe the two of them found her and got afraid that exactly what did happen would happen—that they might be accused of killing her, so they hid the body in a panic."

Alafair was about to say something dismissive, but she paused. His theory made sense. In fact, the same thought had crossed her mind. She wished she could arrange another alley interview with Billy Bond and his cousin, but she didn't think she could get away with that twice. "If that's what they did, why didn't they tell the sheriff?" she wondered.

Walter shrugged. "Who'd believe them?"

Alafair pondered this for a minute. "Scott has probably already thought of this and talked to the boys about it, but maybe you'd better mention it to him when you get back to town."

"I will," he said, but he didn't move. He stood where he was, hands in pockets, staring dismally into the creek.

"Why do you care?" Alafair demanded, not caring that she was being unreasonable.

Walter looked up at her, then. He didn't appear surprised by her outburst. He eyed her for a moment while he framed his answer. "I know you don't believe me, Miz Tucker," he said at length, "but I never wanted to be rid of Louise. We got married early. We had known each other since we were kids. My mother thought she'd steady me, and so did I, for that matter. She was a pretty gal, a good cook. Liked everything just so, kept a fine house. I certainly didn't want anything like this to happen. She had cause to be upset with me, I admit it, but I don't know why she hated me so. I did the best I could for her, but it just wasn't ever enough. I'd have give her a divorce if she'd asked for one. Louise had money of her own, that her daddy left her, and I'd have give her as much more as she wanted," he assured her, sad and a bit peevish. "She didn't have no call to try and have me killed."

"You broke her heart," Alafair told him.

He looked away again, back down into the water. "Believe me, if I'd have known she felt so strong about it, I'd never…" The pained expression on his face faded, slowly changed to one of puzzlement. "What's that?" he said.

Alafair didn't understand at first. "What?"

He nodded toward the root tangle at her feet. "What's that?" he repeated. "There, that shiny thing?"

She looked down and saw the silvery glint of the afternoon sun reflecting off of something metallic just under the water, caught in the roots. Before she could venture a guess, Walter crossed in front of her and lay down on his belly on the bank. He stretched out his hand and plucked the object out of the water, then rose to his knees to study it. A sigh escaped him.

"What is it?"

"It's my missing razor," he said.

"Nellie said they left some of your barber things with Louise's body," Alafair told him. "It must have got tangled up with her clothes when whoever it was moved her. Wonder why we didn't see it when we found her?"

"It's got a wooden handle. It probably floated up after a spell and got caught in the roots." He thrust it toward Alafair. "I don't believe I want it any more."

Surprised, she accepted it. Walter stood up and brushed the grass off of his trousers.

"Walter," Alafair said, "do you care for my girl?"

Walter blinked at her before he answered. "I truly do."

"Then leave her alone. She deserves better."

The barber drew back, stung. "Miz Tucker," he said, "I wish you didn't mislike me so."

"So do I," Alafair admitted. "For Alice's sake, I wish you were a better person. Now, I think you'd better get back into town and tell the sheriff your idea about Jeff Stubblefield and Billy Bond."

⌁⌁⌁

"Louise Kelly never killed herself," Scott said. He leaned back from the dinner table and took a swig of his coffee. Through the screen of the open back door, the four people at the table could hear the metallic clinks and good-natured jibing as Scott and Hattie's boys played horseshoes with Shaw and Alafair's children. The days were getting longer, but it would only be a quarter-hour or so before it was too dark to play outside, and children would come trooping back into the house to pop corn on the stove or have another piece of pie. Shaw and Hattie leaned forward in anticipation at Scott's pronouncement. Alafair, still in a black mood after the events of the day, picked apart the remains of her pie with her fork, finding it hard to listen to more speculation about this depressing murder.

She had said nothing to Alice earlier. After meeting Walter on the creek bank, she hadn't seen the point. There was still more than one week to go on Alice's courting moratorium. She had decided to wait and see what fell out after that.

So she had said nothing. That evening had proceeded as normal, but the air between her and Alice had been strained. Alafair knew very well that Mary had told Alice what their mother had said on the trip home, about Walter being trouble, so the tension didn't surprise Alafair. After Scott and Hattie and their boys had arrived for supper, Alice seemed to relax, apparently relieved that no confrontation had materialized. So Alafair had been going about her business ever since, trying very hard not to worry about the future.

"Doc Addison says the knife went in at an angle," Scott was saying, oblivious to Alafair's disenchantment with the topic. "From top to bottom, and not straight on like it would have done if she'd run at the wall. And however it was done, it wasn't at that house. There wasn't any blood, footprints or otherwise. Even the crack in the plaster looked natural to me, and far too low down. Not like Louise crashed against the wall. That knife went into her body hard and she bled hard. There would have been blood everywhere and not just on that rug. In fact, if it wasn't for that rug, I'd doubt that Louise's body had ever been in that house."

"But what about Nellie's story? What about the note?" Shaw asked.

"If there was a note, somebody besides Louise wrote it. Remember how Nellie said it was so scribbled that she could hardly read it?"

Shaw laughed at the grim irony of it. "So the killer wanted to make it look like suicide, and the Tollands turned around and made it look like murder again."

"Yes, if the Tollands are telling the truth."

"Is it possible that they found Louise in her parlor, like they said?" Hattie asked her husband.

"They could have, if she was already dead when somebody put her there. And then somebody else cleaned up good after they took her body away."

"So tell us, Scott," Shaw urged. "What do you think happened to poor Louise?"

Scott paused, enjoying the expressions of fascination on his listeners' faces. He paused and took another swig of his coffee while he considered what and how much he could tell them and keep a good conscience about it. "Well, all I know for sure is that Louise was stabbed with a bone-handled knife and crammed up under some roots in Cane Creek a few hours later by two people, one bigger than the other, if I'm a judge of footprints. They were riding horses and leading a small jackass or jenny with a nicked shoe. I don't know where she was killed and I don't know who did it or why."

"I'm betting you have an opinion, though," Shaw said.

"Might."

"Scott Tucker," Hattie puffed, exasperated. "You're like to drive a body mad. None of us are going to tell anybody what you think. Are we, Alafair?"

"I'm not," Alafair assured him.

Scott laughed. "All right, then. But y'all better not spread it around. If the Tollands found Louise in her parlor, she had to have been killed somewhere other than her house. It wasn't in her yard, either. I had dogs all over the Kelley place after she was found dead, and if she had bled out anywhere around there, they would have found it. Then the killers carried her home and left her in her parlor, after going to some trouble to make it seem that Louise killed herself.

"I expect that Ned and Nellie Tolland found her body in the parlor not long after, when they came to check on her, and believed that she had done herself in. That's when they hatched their knuckleheaded plan to frame Walter, and destroyed all the evidence of suicide. Whereupon, somebody else finds her after the Tollands leave and carts her off to the creek. I'm guessing it was the killer who did that, too. He probably was lurking about when Ned and Nellie came by, and after they left he decided to get rid of the body once and for all. He more than likely cleaned up the house, so it would look like she had never been there at all."

"You believe the Tollands when they say they didn't put her in the creek?" Alafair was interested in spite of herself.

"Neither of their donkeys had a nicked shoe. Of course, it's been months, so they could have been re-shod by now, but it didn't look like it to me."

"Could they have killed her?" Alafair asked. "Nellie and her sister did have their disagreements in the past. Maybe Nellie killed her and Ned helped her to cover it up."

"Could have, but I doubt it. Nellie didn't have to come forward, but she did. The simplest explanation is that Billy Bond did it, even if Louise and him did have a mutual grievance with Walter. It may have been a fight over who knows what. Folks who have been drinking do stupid things. He probably never started out to do any such thing as kill somebody."

"And then him and Jeff hauled her home, then saw what the Tollands did, and decided to get rid of the body for good and all," Shaw reiterated. "What does Bond have to say about all this?"

"Says they never did no such thing, naturally," Scott told him.

"So you're still holding the two youngsters," Hattie said.

"Ned and Nellie, too, for interfering with a murder investigation, and tampering with evidence. Fortunately, I'm not the one who has to decide the truth of it."

"Where do you think Billy Bond got that fancy bone-handled knife to stab Louise with?" Alafair asked. "That's an unlikely thing to take to a road house."

"That knife is a poser," Scott admitted. "I'm betting it was Louise's, though Walter said he'd never seen it. Either she took it to the road house, or somehow or other Bond got hold of it later."

"Maybe it belonged to Miz Grant," Hattie speculated.

"She denies it, and I searched her house pretty good soon after the murder. She didn't have any other cutlery like it, and none of her relations admit to ever having seen her with such a knife. No, I don't think Miz Grant is our killer."

"But you still think Walter is completely innocent of the murder," Alafair said. "Never hired an assassin or anything of the kind?"

"Completely innocent, Alafair. That's what I think."

"Just because you don't like a person, Alafair, it doesn't mean he's a villain for sure," Shaw chided. "I think maybe you've beat that dead horse plenty."

Alafair harumphed and rose to clear the table. She and Hattie left the men to their coffee while they began washing the dishes. Alafair could hear that the kids' games were coming to an end, and they would all be inside in a few minutes.

"What are you thinking?" Hattie asked, as she took a dish from Alafair to dry.

"I don't like it," Alafair told her. "Billy doesn't seem right to have killed Louise in such a mean way, and neither do Nellie and Ned."

"Are you saying that Walter Kelley seems right to have done it?"

Alafair shrugged. "I don't know. Probably not," she admitted ruefully. "I'm afraid Shaw's right about that one. I don't like the man, but I guess that doesn't just naturally make him a wife-killer."

"You think it's somebody else altogether?"

"I don't know, Hattie," Alafair repeated, troubled. "I just don't know. I keep thinking about the knife. It is a kitchen knife, and not the kind of outdoor knife a person like Billy Bond would be toting around. Where did that knife come from?"

"Mercy, Alafair!" Hattie exclaimed. "How much more complicated could this thing get?"

❧❧❧

Alafair lay Grace in her cradle. The baby had fallen asleep after her evening meal, and she looked the picture of innocence, with her sweet cherry cheeks and her rosy bottom lip pooched out.

Alafair brushed her finger along Grace's chin, and the child's long black eyelashes quivered. Alafair smiled and turned to go check on the other children as they readied for bed, but paused when she saw Shaw leaning against the bedroom door, watching her.

"She's finally asleep," she said to him.

But he had something else on his mind. "Before him and Hattie left, Scott told me that you and Ma tried to get in to see the Bond boy at the jailhouse a while back."

Alafair nodded. She didn't see any reason to deny that part of it. After all, Scott didn't know the whole story. "We did. Trent wasn't having it, though."

"You're starting to worry me, Alafair, how you keep picking at this like a scab. What are you trying to do? Are you out to do anything to discredit the barber so Alice will take against him?"

Alafair straightened, taken aback and a little bit insulted that he would see it that way. However, to be fair, she took a moment to consider if there was anything to what he was saying. "I don't know any more, Shaw," she admitted at length. "At first, I only wanted to know for sure that Walter didn't kill his wife, to protect Alice. I'm still wishing she'd cast her affections elsewhere. I want my girls to marry constant men, and I don't think Walter is. But now, I want to find out who did kill Louise."

"And you don't think it was Billy Bond?"

"I'm not convinced, no."

"Why not?"

Alafair swallowed. She wasn't about to tell him about her jailhouse escapade. "It just don't smell right," she said at last.

"And you think you know better than Scott?"

She extended her hands, palms out, in a gesture of bafflement. "What can I say? I feel like…I feel like Louise is trying to tell me something. That there's something everybody is overlooking. I've been thinking that maybe Louise had a regular lover that no one knew about. Maybe this secret lover saw Louise with the Bond boy and killed her in a jealous fit. You know, Georgie Welsh told me she heard that Mr. Grant was all broke up after

Louise died. Could he have had something to do with it? He was at home that night.

"And what about Wanda Grant? As soon as Louise died, Wanda conceived a notion that Walter would be a good husband for her daughter. Could she have conceived that notion before Louise died? Besides, it seems mighty strange to me that with all the goings on at the Kelley house that night, nobody at the Grants' heard a thing. Maybe I should try to go and talk to him..."

"No, Alafair!" Shaw interrupted, and she bit off her sentence, shocked at his tone.

Usually Shaw greeted Alafair's bursts of intuition with a mix of amusement and admiration. She was often right about the unlikeliest things. But something about her bulldog tenacity on this subject filled him with alarm.

"Leave it alone," he continued, firm, but subdued, trying not to disturb the baby. "You're just driving yourself and everybody else to distraction over this, and for no good reason that I can see. Now, just drop it and mind your own business."

He knew as soon as the words left his mouth that he had put it badly, and he was going to have to pay. Alafair fell quiet, and the resentment in her eyes bored hot holes in him as he stood there. For a moment, the only sound Shaw was aware of was the roar of his own blood in his ears. Still...

"I don't want you bothering Mr. Grant, now," he said, more gently.

"I hear you," she replied, curt.

He knew he was going to endure a few days of frosty silence, but he considered Alafair's safety worth it. Her heart is in the right place, God knows, he thought, but whenever one of the kids is concerned, she rushes headlong into situations without thinking about what could happen to her. He could tell there was no point trying to iron it out now. He nodded and left the room.

Alafair sat down in her rocker, indignant at being ordered about, and hurt that he couldn't understand her concern. She started to rock as she mapped out her plan to talk to Grant.

Chapter Seventeen

On Saturday, two days after May Day, Alafair and the younger kids joined Shaw and Gee Dub on their trip into town to buy ice for the ice box. Shaw stopped in the middle of Main Street to drop off Alafair and Grace for an hour of window shopping, and Charlie, Sophronia, and Blanche for a trip to the drugstore for a treat. Alafair stood on the sidewalk with Grace in her arms and watched, amused, as the kids clambered around their father. He dug into his pocket and produced three nickels, leaned down from the driver's seat, and pressed one into each greedy palm. "A licorice whip for me," Sophronia cried.

"Be careful how you spend it, now," Shaw warned. "That's all you're getting."

Alafair grabbed Charlie's arm as he raced past her on the sidewalk. "Watch your sisters," she admonished.

Charlie's blue eyes registered only mild annoyance at the delay before he accepted his charge. "I will, Ma," he assured her, then sped away before the girls could get too far ahead of him.

"This shouldn't take long, hon," Shaw said to Alafair. She nodded, and he eyed her critically for a minute. She seemed to have gotten over in record time his stern warning not to involve herself in risky enterprises. He didn't know whether to be relieved or suspicious. "We'll pick you up right here in an hour or so."

"Go along, then. Me and Grace intend to have a good time."

Gee Dub gave her a lazy wave from the back of the wagon as it rumbled away toward the ice house.

She stood there with the baby in her arms, going nowhere, for quite a while, until the buckboard was completely out of sight. Then Alafair hitched up the baby on her hip and made her way through the horses, wagons, automobiles, and pedestrians to cross Main Street. She walked up the sidewalk to a tall green door which was wedged between the Boynton Mercantile and the O R Clothing Shop. She walked in to a small foyer and up a flight of stairs to the second floor, where she found herself in a long hall with two doors on either side. On her right, the door to the offices of Abner L. Meriwether, Attorney-at-law, stood open.

The frosted glass pane in the door immediately to her left proclaimed in gold leaf that this was the location of the Muskogee Tool Company, Boynton Branch, Office of D.C. Grant. She stood and looked at the closed door for a couple of minutes, suddenly feeling not quite so sure of herself. What if Grant *had* been involved in Louise's murder? Was she going to walk through that office door, never to be seen again? Maybe Shaw was right, and she should mind her own business.

Even as the thought arose, she knew that wasn't going to happen. It wasn't easy for her to arrange opportunities like this one, and she wasn't about to let it pass.

However, she wasn't willing to expose Grace to possible danger. She turned her head and gazed thoughtfully through the open door of Lawyer Meriwether's office.

Alafair could see a young man in shirtsleeves and a red bow tie, sitting at a desk. The wall behind him was lined floor to ceiling with law books. When he felt her eyes on him, the man looked up.

He stood and reached for his suit coat, which was draped over the back of his chair, and began to jam his arms into the sleeves. "Good morning," he greeted, with a pleasant smile. "May I help you?"

She smiled back and stepped through the door. "Morning. Is Mr. Meriwether in today?"

Before the clerk could reply, the door to the inner office swung open and Mr. Abner L. Meriwether himself appeared.

Meriwether was a big, meaty man with a glowing bald head and a giant toothy smile. He was wearing the waistcoat and trousers of a gray three-piece suit. A gold watch chain draped across his ample stomach.

"Why, Miz Tucker, I thought I recognized your voice!" he greeted. "Whatever can I do for you?"

Abner Meriwether had been a friend of Alafair's family for many years, ever since he had been coaxed to leave Texas and move to Indian Territory to act as council for the Cherokee Nation. He handled all the Tucker legal business—tribal deeds, land deals, wills, even the occasional criminal matter, as needed. Alafair was friendly with his wife, and her children played with his children. And she knew he had a soft spot for little babies.

"Good morning, Mr. Meriwether. I have a bit of a favor to ask of you."

Grace gurgled and reached for the clerk's intriguing red tie, and Alafair shifted her to the other arm. The man grinned and offered the baby his index finger in recompense, which she grasped and immediately tried to chew. Mr. Red Bow Tie wriggled his finger under her chin and she chortled. Meriwether laughed, and Alafair breathed a prayer of gratitude that Grace was being so helpfully charming, as opposed to screaming like a banshee.

She plunged ahead before the baby's volatile emotional weather changed. "I have a little business with Mr. Grant at the tool company across the hall. Shouldn't take me but a few minutes, but I'm loathe to take Grace in with me."

Meriwether folded his hands over his girth and smiled. "Yes, it's hard to wrangle a youngster and observe the social graces at the same time," he agreed. "So you were wondering if you could contract for a bit of baby-watching while you conduct your business."

"Well, I thought I'd ask, if y'all ain't too busy right now. It's mighty bold of me, I know, but she's such a squirmer. It'll take me twice as long to deliver my message to Mr. Grant if she's on my arm."

Meriwether turned to Mr. Red Bow Tie. "Well, Bud, how are you coming with that oil rights contract?"

"I'm ready for a break, Mr. Meriwether."

The lawyer turned back toward Alafair and held out his arms. "All right, then, Miz Tucker. If Miss Grace doesn't mind, then I expect we could benefit from her company for a few minutes."

Alafair left Grace sitting on Bud's desk, playing with Meriwether's gold watch and fob. She was secure in the knowledge that Grace was safe, and that someone knew her own whereabouts as well.

She knocked on the door of the Muskogee Tool Company, and entered.

~~~

Mr. Grant looked up at her from his seat behind a large, paper-strewn oak desk which sat right in the middle of the office, facing the door. The Tool Company office was smaller than Mr. Meriwether's, only one room. But it was brighter than Bud's dark, book lined space, due to the tall windows that lined two walls. The windows were all open to admit a pleasant cross-breeze. Shiny hand tools on the shelves to Grant's right served both as bookends and samples for prospective customers.

Like Meriwether and Bud the law clerk, Grant was in his shirtsleeves. He had removed his celluloid collar and unbuttoned the top button of his white shirt. He obviously had not been expecting much walk-in business today.

He blinked at Alafair when she stepped in. There was no look of recognition on his eyes when he smiled at her. He buttoned his shirt, reached for his collar, and stood. "Good morning, ma'am," he said. "What can I do for you?"

Alafair looked him up and down as he arranged his collar around his neck and fastened the studs. Grant wasn't a bad look-ing man; about her age, late thirties, early forties. He wasn't as tall and robust as Shaw, but he was better than medium height and by no means scrawny. He had been shaved close around his ears and the back of his head, while the sandy hair on top was thick and fairly long. He had attempted to comb it straight back from his forehead, but it seemed to want to resist the pomade he had slicked over it, and stood up straight from his crown, like he had had a bad scare. Alafair found herself wondering if Walter Kelley had given him that haircut. Grant's clear blue-gray eyes were gazing at her expectantly as he rolled down his shirtsleeves.

"Mr. Grant," she opened, "I'm Alafair Tucker. You and me met a while back, at Walter Kelley's house, when the sheriff rousted y'all from your supper to see if you knew anything about a bloody rug."

Grant's hand froze in the act of replacing his cufflink. The strangest series of expressions passed over his face. Bafflement, then enlightenment. Dismay. Resignation. The weight of the world. He smiled; a gentle smile, Alafair thought.

"Where are my manners, Miz Tucker," he said. "Yes, I remember you. Please, sit down. I made coffee this morning. I'd be pleased to offer you some, such as it is. It's still hot."

"No, thank you, sir. I don't intend to disturb you long." Alafair walked over to the chair Grant had indicated, but didn't sit, in case she needed to make a quick getaway. Since she remained standing, Grant did likewise.

"Are you here to talk about the murder of Louise Kelley?" he asked her.

Now it was Alafair's turn to be surprised. "How did you know?"

"I know of your interest in the matter, ma'am." A wry look flitted over his face. "And I can't imagine that you're here looking to buy tools."

Alafair had expected to have to dance around the topic for a spell. Well, if he was going to be so direct… "Yes, sir," she admitted. "I have some questions about Miz Kelley's death."

"I don't know what you expect I can tell you that I didn't tell the sheriff, Miz Tucker. It was a most unfortunate thing that happened to that poor woman. I must say that after all this time, I've forgotten much of the little I did remember about that night.

I've tried to put the whole incident out of my mind, if you want to know. It ain't my favorite thing to think about."

"You liked Miz Kelley?"

"I hardly knew Miz Kelley, but she seemed pleasant enough to me."

"Did you like Mr. Kelley, as well?"

"Everybody likes Walter," Grant told her. "And he's a good neighbor."

"Miz Grant is especially fond of him, I hear…"

Grant's expression closed down instantly, and he abruptly moved from behind his desk to stare out the window at the street. He clasped his hands behind his back. "Miz Tucker, I don't know what you…"

"Mr. Grant," she interrupted, "please forgive me. I know you don't have to talk to me. I know it ain't my business to be nosing around like this, asking about such unpleasant things. Certainly everyone with a lick of sense tells me so. But I have reasons to want to know who killed Miz Kelley. I won't bore you with them, but…"

"Yes, I know your reasons, ma'am," he said, without looking at her. "I have similar reasons."

There was an instant of silence before Alafair blurted, "Your daughter?"

Grant looked back at her over his shoulder, but didn't reply.

Alafair sat down. "Are you saying that your daughter is somehow involved, sir?"

Grant looked shocked, as though he hadn't realized how his statement might be interpreted. "No, no," he hastened to assure her. "It's just that my Susan always liked Walter Kelley. My wife is convinced that Susan and Walter are meant for each other. She's been on a mission to get those two together since the day Miz Kelley died."

"Even considering all the talk about the state of his first marriage?"

Grant emitted a humorless chuckle. "Wanda puts all the blame for those troubles square on the shoulders of the late Miz

Kelley. As for Walter, he's rich, he's good-looking, and he lives right next door. As far as Wanda is concerned, there couldn't be a better match for our only child."

Ah, Alafair thought. "And do you share that sentiment?"

Grant walked back to the desk and sank into his chair. He eyed her without saying anything for so long that Alafair began to feel uncomfortable, and reconsider her escape plan.

After an interminable silence, they both spoke at once.

"Mr. Grant..." she said.

"Miz Tucker..." he said.

They blinked at one another, then Grant plunged ahead.

"Miz Tucker, why did you come here? The sheriff has already arrested Louise Kelley's killer."

"I'm not so sure he has, sir," she told him.

"You can't possibly believe I had anything to do with it."

"Oh, no, sir," she lied. "What does seem strange to me, though, is that with as much commotion as was going on at the Kelley house that night, y'all didn't hear nary a thing."

"Why would we? I heard that Louise was killed elsewhere and toted home by her killer at an hour when decent folks are fast asleep."

Alafair hesitated half a second before she brazenly ignored the sheriff's admonition not to talk about what she knew of the murder. "You didn't hear that Miz Kelley's sister, Nellie Tolland, claims that Louise killed herself?"

The expression on Grant's face couldn't have been more shocked if Alafair had pulled a sock full of rocks out of her pocket and hit him over the head with it. He straighted so abruptly that she feared his chair would go flying backwards and dump him on the floor. "She never!" he managed.

Who was "she" and what did she never? Alafair chose to act like he was talking about Nellie and her claim. "She does. She says she and her husband came to check on Louise late that night and found that she had plunged a knife into her own heart. There was a note..."

"A note!"

"Well, according to Miz Tolland, there was. She claims she destroyed it, then tried to make it look like Walter murdered Louise."

Grant slapped the desk with the flat of his hand. "I knew it!" he exclaimed. "I knew somebody had been in there and…"

Time froze for an instant.

The blood rushed to Alafair's head so forcefully that her vision swam. She hadn't really expected to be right.

The look of triumph melted off of Grant's face as it dawned on him what he had said. He dropped his hand into his lap and slowly sat back in the chair. "I've been expecting to have this conversation for months now, Miz Tucker. Of course, I reckoned it would be the sheriff who walked through that door, but it don't matter, really. It's been weighing on me something awful all this long time." He paused and almost smiled at the horrified look on her face before he continued.

"No, Miz Tucker. I didn't kill her, and neither did my wife or daughter. But you were right about our hearing the commotion over at the Kelleys' that night. Well, it wasn't exactly a commotion. But we don't generally hear any noise at all in the street after dark. We did hear Louise come home at around half past eight. Heard hoofbeats on the street, heard her voice. Woke me and Wanda up. Wanda got up and looked out the window and saw Louise standing on the sidewalk in front of her house. Leastways she reckoned it was Louise. It was a woman, and we had heard Louise's voice. There was a man on a horse riding away at a walk. It was too dark for Wanda to get a good look at him. Louise took off walking north. Never did go into her house."

So Billy Bond had been telling the truth about that part, Alafair thought. He dropped Louise off at home and rode away. At least at first. But where had Louise gone?

"We knew Walter was supposed to be out of town until the next day. Wanda said some uncomplimentary things about a woman gallivanting around at all hours of the night while her husband is away. Then we went back to sleep and slept like the dead until about ten o'clock, when we heard a woman crying.

We saw a light in the Kelleys' window, but it looked like a kerosene lantern, not an electric light like Louise would normally have on.

"Still, I reckoned it was just Louise finally coming home. But then we heard somebody come out her back door and drive away in a buggy. It seemed strange. So we decided to go over there and check on Louise to make sure everything was all right."

"Did Susan go too?" Alafair asked.

"My daughter was fast asleep on the other side of the house." Grant was firm. "Susan had nothing to do with that night. Anyway, me and Wanda pulled on some clothes and went into Louise's house through the back door. We nearly perished of shock when we found her laying there dead. Wanda screamed so loud I half expected the whole town to come rushing.

"It was clear that there wasn't nothing we could do for the poor woman. My first thought was to go for the sheriff, of course, but then we got to looking around, and things looked mighty strange, let me tell you. There was three or four bloody footprints around her body, and the shoes that made those prints were sitting on the floor neat as you please. There were barber tools strewn around the room, and the oddest thing was that somebody had written a W on the floor in blood. One look at that knife sticking out of Louise's chest and anybody with half a hold on his wits would know she couldn't have stayed alive long enough to write anything.

"It was clear as day that somebody was trying to make it look like Walter killed her. We knew Walter was due back the next morning. He'd have walked into a trap. If he left Louise as he found her, it would look bad. But if he tried to clean things up, that would look worse. It was near on ten-thirty by this time. We didn't have much time to figure what to do. So we decided to make it look like Louise had never been home at all."

"But why?" Alafair interrupted. "If you had gone for the sheriff right then, Walter would have been in the clear. He was still out of town, and if you could see that somebody was trying to make Walter look guilty, Sheriff Tucker sure would, too."

Grant bit his lip. He looked sad, and more than a little abashed. "In the dead of night, faced with a dead woman, things don't always seem so clear. It was Wanda who wanted to make sure no suspicion at all fell on Walter. She admires him a bunch, you see."

Alafair's eyebrows inched up. Grant's attitude toward Walter was not at all what she expected. All the gossip she had heard from Hattie and Nadine Fluke had led her to believe that Grant didn't care for the man. "So you hauled her off on the back of a donkey and put her in Cane Creek?"

"Oh, no. We don't even own a donkey. We wanted to be quiet, so I wrapped her in an old sheet and put her in a hand cart. I carted her just barely out of town and left her right by the road where she'd be seen at first light, across from Calvin Ross' place. Wanda stayed behind and cleaned that house up so spotless you'd never know anybody had been there that night. I took those bloody shoes with me and buried them in a hole up under the brush on the way back into town. I don't know how Wanda missed that rug. I don't even remember seeing it. Maybe I kicked it back up under the sideboard when I was trying to get Louise's body out of the house."

"You didn't put Louise in the creek?"

"No, I swear it. I left her beside the road just outside of town. Somebody must have come along later and put her in the creek. Though if Louise killed herself, who would want to do that? It must have been pure meanness."

Alafair slumped in her chair and scrubbed at her cheeks with her palms, suddenly so tired that she wished she could just curl up right then and there and take a nap. "Lord have mercy, Mr. Grant," she blurted. "Are y'all crazy? Dogs could have got at her, or a coyote! Besides, didn't it occur to you for a minute that maybe Walter did do it? He could have sneaked back into town early and then left again, telling everyone he was delayed in Kansas City. Maybe Louise really didn't die right away—then she could have tried to write her killer's name in blood. It could have been possible that the killer took off his bloody shoes so he wouldn't leave any more trail than he did, and then left the house in his stocking feet."

"But that's not what happened," Grant protested. "You just said…"

"Yes," Alafair interrupted, "but you didn't know that. You might have been protecting a murderer, for all you know. And your wife wants that man for her girl?"

"He's not a murderer, Miz Tucker. You told me so yourself. He's a good man who don't deserve a moment's suspicion on him."

"How do you know that? How well do you know the man, or his wife either, for that matter?"

Grant smiled at the question. "Well enough, ma'am. I never told anybody this before, but there was some trouble, once, with my business…" He hesitated and looked away. "Some trouble with the books. Walter, he found out. Wanda told him, if you want to know."

The words were costing Grant a lot of effort. His face flushed. But he continued. "He came to me of his own accord and offered to make it good. He gave me money. A lot of money. And he never asked me how I got myself into trouble, nor did he ever ask me to pay him back. I did pay him back, over time. But he saved me from ruin when he didn't have no reason to, and I reckon I owe him something more than money for that." He flicked a glance at Alafair. "So yes, Miz Tucker, I know Walter well enough. And as for Louise, well, Wanda didn't get on with her, but I always felt mighty sorry for her. I know she harried her husband, but I never thought she was a mean person. Just unhappy. She had the saddest eyes. I always thought she really did love him, but they just didn't know how to get on together.

"I felt mighty bad that she got murdered, but I knew as well as Wanda that Walter didn't do it. Of course, if we'd known it was a suicide… But we had no idea what Louise's sister did. Now, she's the one ought to be in jail."

"She is in jail, sir."

Alafair and Grant looked at one another for a moment. She didn't need to tell him that he and his wife were going to be in jail soon, too.

"What are you going to do?" she asked him at length.

"Go to the sheriff, I reckon. Look, Miz Tucker, I know we did a stupid thing. I feel bad about it, though we did have good intentions at the time. I've been expecting it would all come out eventually. I might go to jail for a spell, maybe lose my job, but at least I've got things arranged so that Susan will be all right. Wanda, too, I hope. I'll hate it if she has to spend time in prison, as well." He stood up, resolute, and took his suit coat off its peg on the wall. "Well, best get it over with."

Alafair stood as well. "Lawyer Meriwether is in his office, Mr. Grant. Why don't you and me go over there, and you can talk to him a while, get some advice, before you turn yourself in?"

Chapter Eighteen

Alafair left Grant with Mr. Meriwether, retrieved Grace from Bud's lap, and hurried back down to the street. She felt rather like she had been beaten with a stick. How much more complicated can this thing get, Hattie had asked? She had no idea.

Someone had killed Louise Kelly and tried to make it look like suicide. Then the Tollands make it look like murder again. Then, if Grant was to be believed, he and his wife tried to make it look like Louise had never been home. Had everyone in town taken leave of their senses? And who, please God, had put Louise's body in the creek?

Grace interrupted her mother's reverie by trying to squirm out of her arms and squealing loudly. Alafair returned to the present, cooed at the baby while checking her diaper, and readjusted the child's frock.

It was a pretty day, and a lot of people were in town this Saturday, shopping and strolling. One by one, half a dozen people stopped and spoke to Alafair and chucked the baby under the chin, but after they had passed, Alafair stood in the middle of the sidewalk, pondering Grant's story. It occurred to her that Walter had come off pretty well in Grant's version of events, having performed a selfless act of generosity for his neighbor. And on top of it, Grant hadn't spoken badly of Louise either, which was pretty unusual. Most people who knew the Kelleys seemed to love one and despise the other.

A few doors away, she could see that the barber shop was doing a brisk business. A little further down, several people walked in to Spradling's Furniture. At the end of the street, Alafair could just see the Sheriff's office and jail.

I should visit with Hattie, she thought, or Josie, or Nadine Fluke.

But Billy Bond and his cousin Jeff, as well as the Tollands, were sitting in that jail just a few yards away. Come Monday, they would all be in Muskogee, along with the Grants, and her opportunity would be gone forever. For the people in that jail knew things that Alafair wanted to know.

She imagined herself standing on the boxes at the jailhouse window. "Tell me, Billy," she was saying, "did you think to kill Louise and pin it on Kelley in revenge for what he did to your girl? Tell me, Ned, what kind of woman was the late Louise Kelley? Was it her fault that she died? Was she ever happy with the barber? Was it her nature to be discontent and court trouble? Did your wife Nellie do in her own sister over a liaison between you and her? Did Louise go to Nellie for support after she left Billy, and did Nellie stab her and enlist you in a wild scheme to cover her tracks? What about you, Wanda Grant? Did you dislike Louise even more than you let on? Did you want to clear the way for your daughter? Or was Mr. Grant lying when he told me y'all found her dead? Was he Louise's secret lover? Was it your bone-handled knife in Louise's chest, Wanda? And whose bloodied rug ended up stuffed under Louise's sideboard?"

Dare I, Alafair wondered?

"Ba!" Grace exclaimed, and tried to crawl up over Alafair's shoulder.

Alafair laughed and readjusted the baby in her arms. Bah, indeed. And how would she manage another window interview with all those people in the street and a wiggly six-month-old to wrangle? Yet, she stepped off the curb and crossed the street. She was walking toward the alley when the door to the Sheriff's office opened and a little-bit-of-nothing girl in a nondescript outfit walked out onto the street.

Alafair stopped in her tracks.

"Peggy Crocker!" she called, and the girl turned and looked at her.

"Yes, ma'am?" Peggy managed. Her pale brown eyes widened in mild curiosity.

Alafair walked up to her gingerly, fearing that if she made a sudden move, Peggy would bolt and run like a startled deer. "My name is Miz Tucker," Alafair opened. "Have you been visiting Billy?"

"Yes, ma'am," Peggy replied. "Do you know Billy?"

"We have spoken," Alafair told her. "It's hard for me to believe that Billy did such an awful, mean thing as kill some woman."

"Oh, he never," Peggy assured her. She fell silent and gazed at Alafair patiently, waiting to either hear more or be dismissed.

Alafair studied the girl for a moment, just a little surprised. This was the girl who supposedly had a torrid affair with Walter Kelley, then brazenly went to Louise and informed her that she was carrying her husband's child? Peggy wasn't that pretty, and she didn't seem to be a sparkling conversationalist. She did have the natural attractiveness that comes with youth and innocence, though. Such a girl might think that someone as well favored as Walter left golden footprints when he walked. Not an affair. Led astray, more likely.

Peggy's gaze had left Alafair and was now fastened on Grace. Alafair remembered that Peggy was rumored to have lost an illicit child a few months back, and by the wistful expression on her face, Alafair could believe it. Grace, for her part, was looking back, sizing up her new admirer.

Alafair recognized an opening when she saw one. "This is Grace," she introduced. "We're heading over to Williams' Drug Store to meet up with my other kids and have a soda. Why don't you come along with us? I'll be glad to buy you whatever you want."

Peggy was clearly tempted, but she shook her head. "Oh, thank you, ma'am, but I got to get going. My daddy will be along to get me, directly. He said he don't want me wandering around town."

"You could hold the baby," Alafair said.

Peggy blinked. "Well, maybe for just a minute," she decided.

As the two women walked down the sidewalk, Alafair made innocuous conversation about the weather, asked after the health of Peggy's family, told her a few things about her own family. By the time they reached the drug store, Alafair had sized Peggy Crocker up one side and down the other.

This child, she thought, is as ignorant of the ways of the world as she can possibly be. She would believe anything Walter Kelley or Billy Bond or any other person a year older or an inch taller told her. She was trusting enough to answer any question Alafair put to her without a second thought.

When they entered the drug store, Alafair immediately scanned for her children. Charlie was lounging against a wall next to the book rack with a peppermint stick in one hand and a dime novel in the other—Zane Gray, Alafair noted. The thought occurred to her that Mr. Williams probably didn't appreciate having a sticky-handed boy thumbing through his books and magazines. Blanche and Sophronia were seated at the counter licking ferociously at fast-melting ice cream cones. Alafair led Peggy to one of the two small tables around the corner from the counter and ordered two ice cream sodas from the boy behind the counter. She stood Grace up on the table and held her under the arms while the infant bounced up and down and waved her arms about.

"This baby has enough energy for two youngsters," she said to Peggy.

"Do you suppose I could hold her, now?" Peggy ventured.

"I expect." Alafair walked the baby toward Peggy, who lifted her off the table and into her lap. Grace was amenable, especially after Peggy made a silly face.

"She sure is a cute one," Peggy said. "I can't wait to have one of my own."

"You and Billy are planning on marrying soon, aren't you? I imagine you'll have your own baby to play with pretty quick."

Peggy sobered. "If he don't get hanged for murder, first," she said.

"But you said you know he didn't do it," Alafair noted.

"I do know it," Peggy agreed, "but I don't reckon that my good word is enough for the sheriff. The sheriff says that Billy threatened to kill Mr. Kelley. I don't see how that means he killed Miz Kelley."

"Maybe he wanted to hurt Mr. Kelley, Peggy," Alafair said. She hesitated, feeling bad, but plunged ahead anyway. She didn't expect she'd have another chance. "I saw you at Miz Kelley's funeral, hanging back outside the fence, watching the barber. Do you suppose Billy was jealous?"

Peggy reddened and lowered her eyes. She lifted Grace off her lap and back onto the table before she answered. "Yes, ma'am, I know he was jealous of Mr. Kelley. Turns out he didn't have no reason to be, though. Besides, I don't care how jealous Billy was or what he said, he surely ain't the murdering kind. He was trying to help her that awful night, that's what he told me, and I believe him. Billy's a good boy, a faithful boy, even when I didn't deserve for him to be."

Alafair unconsciously shook her head, suddenly feeling protective of this trusting girl. Peggy seemed to take it for granted that this strange woman who had picked her up on the street and was plying her with ice cream and questions not only knew her whole story but only had her best interest at heart. If she were my daughter, Alafair thought, I'd be tempted to never let her out of my sight.

"Could it be that Mr. Kelley hired somebody to kill his wife, honey?" she asked gingerly.

Peggy turned redder and ducked her head even lower. She kissed the baby's hand, then shook her head. "No, ma'am," she said, finally. "Not over me, he sure didn't. He's a good man, with sweet ways, and not a killer any more than Billy."

"Did you love him, sweetheart?"

She smiled. "I thought so. He was so nice to me, and talked with such pretty words that I reckoned he loved me, too."

"Did you take it upon yourself to tell Miz Kelley about it?"

Peggy looked ashamed. "Yes, ma'am. I wisht I hadn't done that. I thought she didn't love him, so I expected she'd like to know she didn't have to stay with him anymore. But when I told her, she turned so white she like to fainted. I knew right then that she still cared mightily for him. Then I felt bad.

"When I told Walter what happened, he was riled. But then he explained it to me real kind, how we wasn't right for one another. He was right, I reckon. Him and me, we just made a mistake, and I was sad for awhile, but that's all over now. Billy's the one who loves me." The baby's flailing fist struck Peggy in the cheek, and she gently pushed Grace's arm down and glanced at Alafair from under her lashes.

Alafair reached over and squeezed the girl's arm. "I'm sorry, honey," she said. "Have some of your soda now and try not to worry. There ain't any of this your fault, and I'm sure everything will work out fine."

Peggy smiled and sucked on her soda straw, apparently comforted by Alafair's pronouncement.

Alafair, however, wasn't feeling very happy at all. Peggy had not said anything to enhance Alafair's opinion of Walter, though she had to admit that she no longer suspected that he was behind the murder. Not long ago, she had told Billy Bond that she would try to help him, but she hadn't. Billy, she feared, was going to pay the price for Louise's death. The only thing she felt sure of now was that Peggy Crocker may have been the catalyst for a murder, but she certainly had nothing to do with it herself.

Alafair absently spooned some ice cream into her mouth. Blanche and Sophronia had finished their cones and were skipping over. Alafair sighed. She had done everything she could think of to find out what had happened to Louise, but it was out of her hands, now. It seemed like everybody involved could have done it, but nobody did do it. No, there would be no more surreptitious jailhouse talks with Billy Bond. She resigned herself to the fact that she might never be sure she knew the truth about the tragic end of Louise Kelley.

Chapter Nineteen

On the Sunday of the second full week of May, Alafair and Shaw packed part of their brood into the buckboard as they left church for a trip to the pastor's house for dinner. Mary and Ruth had decided to go home with Phoebe and John Lee for dinner at their little house, and Grandma and Grandpapa took the boys and the baby home with them, leaving only Martha, Alice, Blanche, and Sophronia to accompany their parents. As Shaw was about to climb up into the driver's seat, Alice changed her mind and decided to go to Phoebe's as well, and hurried away to catch John Lee before he pulled his rickety wagon out of the yard. Alafair watched her as she disappeared around the Masonic Hall. Walter Kelley had not been to the Christian Church for the past couple of weeks. Alafair had heard that he was attending the Methodist service lately.

The Bellowses lived in a two-story clapboard house just outside of town on the road to Okmulgee, directly across from Calvin Ross' dairy farm. It was a big house for just the two of them, but the last pastor who lived there had had a large family, and Mrs. Bellows liked to entertain. Mrs. Bellows met them in the yard as they drove up. Mr. Bellows was still at the Masonic Hall, where the Christian Church met, for a while, until all the flock had been sent on its way.

She had just had time to show them around her carefully decorated and meticulously kept house when the pastor rode up on his little roan mare. Shaw went with Mr. Bellows to stable the horse while Alafair and Martha helped Sister Norma Bellows with the final touches on the dinner, most of which had been cooked by the efficient Sugar Welsh while Sister Norma was in church, and was now warming in the oven. The little girls were given the task of sitting in starchy discomfort in the parlor, trying all the while not to make noise or a mess.

All was in readiness when the men returned to the house, and the group arranged themselves around the table with the host at the head and the hostess at the foot. Alafair was at the middle of the north side of the table with Sophronia to her right and Blanche to her left. Shaw and Martha faced her on the south side of the table. The meal began with a lengthy and rambling prayer from Mr. Bellows, who Alafair had not realized was so aptly named until that moment. Sophronia became squirmier by the minute as the prayer went on, but the preacher simply raised his volume and continued undisturbed until the end. As Mr. Bellows intoned the "amen," the weary listeners stirred and stretched, except for Blanche, whose forehead remained pressed into the white table-cloth as she napped. Alafair gave the child a nudge, and she started up guiltily and busied herself with her cutlery.

"We're so glad to have you here at last," Sister Norma began, as she started the mashed potatoes around. "My husband and I have been here for over a year now, and we still haven't finished with our plan to invite every member of our flock to our home for dinner. Ulises thinks it's important that the pastor of a flock knows the spiritual needs of every one of his sheep."

Alafair caught Shaw's eye across the table and smiled. Neither one of them enjoyed the biblical sheep analogy very much. "I admire what you've done to the house," she said to Sister Norma. "Miz Blackwell, the wife of the minister who was here before you, had too many little ones to be able to keep it up so nice."

Sister Norma was pleased by the compliment. "Thank you. We've just finished repapering the parlor. It's so much brighter now, don't you agree? And I know I shouldn't have done it, but I busted loose and bought me a new settee a few months ago. That old one we had before had seen better days."

"Norma's mother left her a goodly inheritance, but she never spends money on herself," the pastor said. "I flat out had to insist she do one nice thing for herself. After all, God says 'love your neighbor as yourself.' That don't mean much if you don't love yourself a little, and do yourself a kindness now and then, don't you think, Brother Shaw?"

"I know that y'all came here to this church from over near Oklahoma City," Shaw countered. "Edmond, wasn't it?"

"Edmond, in the old Oklahoma Territory, yes," Brother Ulises acknowledged. "My wife and I were there for five years or so, and loved it. Had us a little farm that did pretty well, and the church there is very strong, very active. But we felt that we had fought the good fight there in Edmond. Many sinners were saved, praise the Lord. I believe you were serving on the board that recommended offering the pulpit to us, Brother Shaw."

Shaw nodded. "Yes, sir. The board liked your enthusiasm and thought you'd fit into this growing community," he said. Alafair had no comment. She knew that Shaw himself had favored another candidate.

"We're overjoyed to be here," Brother Ulises assured him. "So many people moving into this area, so many lost and troubled souls. So much good work we can do."

"Amen," Sister Norma added, and all the Tuckers contributed a raggedy "amen."

Sugar Welsh had provided Sister Norma with quite a feast to serve her guests. The table was covered with dishes of potatoes, mashed and fried, fresh sliced tomatoes and onions, boiled peas with baby onions, applesauce, green beans with bacon, canned tomatoes with macaroni, brown beans with ham hock, a platter of white bread, biscuits and cornbread, and two roast chickens with cornbread stuffing and giblet gravy. Alafair found herself wondering how the Bellowses could afford such a spread, especially if they entertained a different church family every week. The church supplied the house and a small salary, but hardly enough to keep body and soul together. Most ministers took their Sunday meals with members of their congregations, and not the other way around. Alafair knew that the Bellowses owned some property near town, enough to raise a few calves. Their little farm in Edmond must have done very well indeed.

"I don't believe your entire family is with you today," Sister Norma said, interrupting Alafair's thought.

Shaw explained while Alafair wiped applesauce off of Sophronia's pinafore. "Yes, ma'am," he said. "Our boys and the baby are with my mother. Mary, Alice, and Ruth are taking dinner with our newly married daughter Phoebe and her husband John Lee Day. Phoebe loves playing the hostess, and we didn't want to spring the whole bunch on you all at once."

Mr. Bellows laughed. "Are any other of your children married or soon to be?"

"No," Alafair told him. "She's the only one. All the others of marriageable age are too particular as of yet." She smiled at Martha, who responded with an ironic smirk.

"I understand you work at the bank," Sister Norma said to Martha.

Martha blinked at her, surprised at being included in the conversation. "I do," she said.

"I'm surprised such a gentle young lady such as yourself would expose herself to the indelicate world of business," Sister Norma commented. Her tone was perfectly pleasant, but Alafair inferred a slur on her parenting, and bristled. Shaw shot her a warning look, so she plastered a smile on her face and said nothing.

Martha, more used to criticism about her job, was just opening her mouth for some innocuous reply, when she was interrupted by the minister.

"Now, Norma," he chided, "I would think that young Sister Martha here has discovered the perfect place to find herself a husband of means."

Martha snapped her mouth shut. She flipped her napkin out with a crack and laid it across her lap.

"Why, of course, Ulis," Sister Norma agreed. "More peas, Sister Alafair?"

Shaw did most of the visiting with the Bellowses after that.
They discussed the state of the world and the prospects for the
new president, Mr. Wilson, as well as local news, which was
pretty much dominated these days by the shocking charges of
tampering with the dead and interfering with an investigation
which had just been brought against poor Mr. Grant. Alafair
had no opinion that she wished to share about any of it. She did
admire the dinner, though. She made a mental note to pass on
her compliments to Sugar Welsh. And, howsoever thoughtless
with her comments Norma Bellows was, she was a very good
hostess and set a beautiful table. After they had eaten and the
men and children had retired, Alafair and Martha stayed behind
to help Sister Norma clear the table.

"You have some lovely things," Alafair admitted, as she picked
up the china plates to take them into the kitchen.

"Why, thank you," Sister Norma said. "I received many of
them from my mother. She had so many wonderful things,
such good taste. She gave us this silverware on the day we were
married over twenty-five years ago."

"It's beautiful," Alafair said. "So is this wonderful china. It
looks to be old, I think."

Sister Norma expanded with pleasure. "It is. I'm told it's
near to one hundred years old. It was left to us in her will by
a member of our congregation when we were pastoring up in
Wichita ten, twelve years ago, before we went to Edmond. It was
her thank-you to Ulis for helping her to find Jesus."

"I'm honored you'd use it for us," Alafair said, "what with
our little ruffians."

Sister Norma laughed as she dumped scraps into the slop
bucket. "Oh, we've fed many a child who was not nearly as
well-behaved as yours. Never lost a plate."

Sister Norma stepped out to draw wash water from the spigot
by the back door, leaving Alafair and Martha in the kitchen,
stacking dishes beside the sink. Looking for something to dry

dishes with, Alafair opened the bottom drawer under the counter, which was where she kept dish towels in her own kitchen. Instead of towels, she found a fine wooden cutlery box. The box's sliding lid was slightly open. She started to close the drawer and move on to the next, when it suddenly registered on her what she had seen. She jerked the drawer out further and pushed the lid of the box all the way open. Lying neatly in the felt-lined wooden cutlery case was a beautiful set of bone-handled carving knives, all incised with seascapes, lined up side by side in order of size. Except for a conspicuous space on the left, where the largest knife of all was missing.

"Martha!" Alafair hissed.

Martha appeared at her mother's shoulder, alarmed at her tone. The two women stared into the drawer for a second, then looked up at each other.

"What does it mean?" Martha whispered.

"I don't know, honey," Alafair admitted. "I didn't actually see the bone-handled knife that killed Louise. Does this look like the same set?"

"It's exactly the same, Ma. I wasn't close enough to see the engraving very well, but the way the handle curves up into that little knob on the end is exactly the same. How did Louise Kelley get ahold of it from the preacher's house?"

"I don't know," Alafair repeated. "Walter told us that the preacher and his wife were over to their house a lot. I'm guessing Louise was over here a lot as well."

"You think she stole it from Miz Bellows' kitchen?"

"I don't know," Alafair said for a third time. She closed the drawer and glanced toward the open back door. "I do think we ought to tell the sheriff, though."

Martha's brown eyes widened. "You don't think the Bellowses had anything to do with it?"

"Oh, surely not. I expect Louise stole it, like you thought."

"Do you think we should ask Miz Bellows how long she's been missing the knife?" Martha's cheeks were turning red from excitement. "She may not even know it's gone!"

"I think we'd better let Scott do the asking," she told Martha.

"Scott never did let Billy Bond out of jail," Martha observed. "He does think Louise killed herself, doesn't he?"

"That's the story Nellie Tolland tells," Alafair said. "But I expect it's not official."

Sister Norma returned with two pails of water and the speculation ceased immediately. Alafair chatted amiably as she and Martha washed and dried the dishes and the unsuspecting Norma Bellows put everything away. Martha flitted about like a nervous bird and said nothing, so obviously worked up that Alafair feared Sister Norma would become curious and start asking questions. However, the preacher's wife was so intent on singing her husband's praises to her guests that Alafair finally came to the conclusion that Martha could faint dead away from excitement and Sister Norma would hardly notice.

As soon as she could, Alafair dismissed Martha to the parlor. Sister Norma hauled out the rinse water to throw on the flowers by the back door, and Alafair wiped down the cabinets with a wet cloth. It was silly to get too excited over finding a new little bit of information about the death of poor Louise. Maybe Louise really had killed herself, after all, and someone—perhaps Billy Bond—had found her dead and returned her home. Perhaps Louise had stolen the knife from Sister Norma's kitchen instead of using one of her own to do herself in.

Alafair hung the dishcloth on the bar over the sink. If she killed herself somewhere other than her own front room, Louise must have planned the deed in advance. Did she mean to implicate the preacher?

This was all just idle guesswork, Alafair scolded herself. Best leave it to Scott. She lifted the borrowed apron over her head, and instantly her nostrils were assailed with the acrid smell of ammonia. Her heart took a bounce. No, it can't be, she told herself firmly. She hung the apron on its hook and walked smartly out of the kitchen, through the dining area and into the parlor. Martha looked up at her from her seat in the corner, a question on her face that Alafair ignored resolutely. Shaw was on the settee facing Mr. Bellows in a wingback armchair, discussing scripture.

"Where's the girls?" Alafair asked.

"They're playing in the front yard," Shaw informed her. "I done told them that you'd be mad if they dirtied up their Sunday frocks." He smiled at her and patted the settee beside him, inviting her to sit down.

"Join us, Sister Alafair," the pastor said. "We were just discussing the sixth chapter of Galatians. Verse two says that we should bear one another's burdens, and so fulfill the law of Christ, and yet, as Brother Shaw points out, verse five says that every man shall bear his own burden."

Alafair sat down and smoothed her skirt. "My father often spoke on that scripture," she said. "He likes verse six—*let him that is taught in the word communicate unto him that teacheth in all good things.*"

Mr. Bellows' eyes lit up. "Is your father a preacher, Sister Alafair?"

She nodded. "Yes, he's retired these days, but he still preaches now and then at two or three little churches there around Lone Elm, Arkansas."

"Campbellite?"

"No, Freewill Baptist."

"Ah," Mr. Bellows breathed. "I'd like to debate the Word with him, sometime."

Alafair smiled. "He'd love it," she assured the minister. "My favorite verse from Galatians sixth chapter, though, is verse nine—*And let us not be weary in well doing, for in due season we shall reap, if we faint not.*"

Mr. Bellows' finger punctuated the air. "Yes, but let us not forget what it says in verse eight, Sister; *for he that soweth to his flesh shall of the flesh reap corruption; but he that soweth to the Spirit shall of the Spirit reap life everlasting.*"

As soon as the words were out of the man's mouth, Alafair was nearly bowled over by the smell of ammonia. She stifled a gasp and sat back in her seat. The smell seemed suddenly to blow up into her face from the floor, and her eyes were drawn down to the intricate handmade rug on the floor just to their right. It was a pristine white, with a tiny pink floral pattern. Alafair's first thought was that anyone with a white rug on the floor obviously had no children.

"What are you trying to tell me, Louise?" was her second thought.

Her forehead wrinkled as she gazed at that rug, lying at an odd angle on the floor to the left of the settee. Not under or before any piece of furniture, not by a door, just there, to the left of the settee. She looked back up at the preacher.

"Why, I believe that's verse eleven, Brother Ulises," she said.

Brother Ulises' eyes widened with surprise at being contradicted, and about scripture, of all things. "I fear you are mistaken, Sister. Verse eight is, *for he that soweth to his flesh,* which is well known."

"I don't think so, Preacher," Alafair insisted. "My daddy loved that verse especially, and I specifically remember him saying, 'and verse eleven, *for he that soweth...*"

Brother Ulises sputtered, struggling between indignation at being questioned and delight at having before him an ignorant soul to enlighten. He jumped to his feet. "Excuse me a minute, Brother and Sisters, while I fetch my Bible from the bedside table." He rushed out of the room. The instant his back disappeared up the stairs, Alafair fell to her knees and skittered along the floor, passing in front of an astonished Shaw, to the white, flowered rug lying at an odd angle by the settee.

"Alafair, what in the cow eyes are you doing?" Shaw managed.

"Galatians six, verse eleven," Alafair said, lifting one corner of the rug and flinging it back, *"ye see how large a letter I have written unto you with mine own hand."*

Under the white rug, the pine floor was marred with a great, obscene blotch of rusty brown, surrounded by a patch of flooring bleached by ammonia where it had been scrubbed in a vain attempt to remove the stain. But whoever had tried to clean it had waited too long, and the pine boards would never come clean again.

Suddenly, Shaw was on his knees beside Alafair, and Martha had flown out of her chair in the corner and was leaning over her parents in order to see.

"Lord'a mercy!" Shaw breathed. "How did you know?"

"I smelled the ammonia. Somebody must have tried to clean this floor with ammonia."

"You've got a nose like a hound," Shaw told her, impressed. "I don't smell anything."

"Louise must have stabbed herself right here in this spot!" Martha exclaimed.

"Well, Scott thought she didn't stab herself, and I'm beginning to think he was right," Shaw said. "Else how did she get from here to her own front room? Somebody carried her, because she didn't walk, that's for sure."

"Maybe this isn't her blood," Martha speculated.

"Maybe," Alafair said, doubtful. "But what with Miz Bellows' knife sticking out of her chest and the fact that there was no blood on the floor at Louise's own home, but just the rug, I'm thinking…"

"That she died right here and somebody wrapped her up in that rug and carried her home in it, then laid her, and the rug, down on her own floor. And then went to make it look like she did herself in," Shaw finished for her.

"After which the Tollands found her body and decided to make Walter out to be a killer, right before Mr. Grant carted her out to the road," Martha added in an excited undertone. "They kicked that rug up under the sideboard in all the hubbub, while they were wrapping her in a blanket and straightening the parlor. And if Mr. Grant is telling the truth, somebody else picked Louise up and put her in the creek."

"Poor Louise." Alafair lowered her voice to a whisper. "No wonder she can't rest."

Shaw turned to Martha. "Darlin'," he said under his breath, "go outside and get the girls into the wagon. Me and Mama will be out there as soon as we can."

"I'm afraid y'all ain't going anywhere," Mr. Bellows said, from behind them.

Shaw leaped to his feet and planted himself between Bellows and his wife and daughter. "Preacher," he managed, "what the..."

Mr. Bellows was standing at the foot of the stairs, armed with his Bible in one hand and an old Union Army Colt .45 in the other.

"Y'all just stay still, now," the preacher ordered, "while I think on what to do next." He shook his head ruefully. "I knew we should have refinished that floor."

Martha started to stand, but Alafair grabbed her arm and jerked her back down. Alafair thought about the little girls outside and bit her lip anxiously.

"Did you kill Louise Kelley?" Shaw asked the pastor, straight out.

Bellows didn't answer that, but a humorless smile bent his lips. His features had hardened, Alafair observed, and the bombastic and rather silly preacher who had left the room a moment ago was no longer.

"Imagine my disappointment, Brother Shaw," Bellows said ironically. "I return Miz Kelley to her house, arrange her artfully in the parlor, and scribble a suicide note for her husband to find. Then, just as I am safely leaving, I see that sister of hers and her husband show up and fiddle around with my carefully laid tableau. After they leave, before I can rectify the situation, the neighbors troop across the yard, raise a ruckus, and then, for God knows what reason, they carry the body practically to the front of our house and leave her in the road. What else could I do but get rid of her once and for all before the sun came up? I figured I'd picked a spot where she'd never be found, a perfectly secure hiding place in the creek. And then what happens? Your boys find her there not half a day later and alert the sheriff! Yes, sir, God is playing fine little jokes on us."

"You're caught now, Ulises," Shaw said reasonably. "Too many of us know, now."

"Oh, I don't know, Brother Shaw," Bellows replied. "What's a couple more murders, more or less?"

Shaw's gaze shifted to a spot over Bellows' shoulder. "Don't do it!" he exclaimed to the empty air. It was an old trick, but it worked. Startled, Bellows' eyes shifted.

And then all hell broke loose.

Faster than anyone in the room could think, Shaw reached down and grabbed the pink-flowered rug and flung it at the preacher's head. By the time Alafair had blinked, Shaw and the enshrouded Ulises Bellows were rolling around on the floor. Bellows fired wildly, once into the ceiling and once into the front window, which shattered noisily. Shaw grabbed Bellows' gun hand and hammered it against the floor until the .45 went flying across the room. When her thought processes began to function, Alafair realized that she had thrown herself over Martha's huddled form, and that Sister Norma was standing in the door to the kitchen, screeching her husband's name. The gun spun to a stop in the middle of the room, and both women locked eyes on it at the same time.

Alafair launched herself into the air over her daughter and landed with her hand on the grip of the gun just as Sister Norma slid into her and grabbed her wrist. The two women grappled for less than a minute before Martha Tucker rose to her feet, seized a ceramic vase full of wildflowers from the side table, and cracked the unsuspecting Norma Bellows over the head with it. The preacher's wife made a little mewling noise, and slid quietly to the floor. Alafair leaped to her feet, ready to come to Shaw's aid, but it was unnecessary. He had already subdued Mr. Bellows, whose head and upper body were still wrapped in the rug. Shaw was sitting across the man's belly, holding his arms down on the floor, watching the exploits of his wife and daughter with wide eyes. Silence fell like a stone as they all tried to catch their breath.

Finally, Mr. Bellows made a muffled protest, and Shaw looked down at him. "You'd better hold still, now, Preacher," he warned, "or I'll fetch my girl up on you."

Sheriff Scott Tucker stood in the middle of the Bellows' parlor with his hands on his hips, and gazed thoughtfully at the rusty stain on the floor. His deputy, Trenton Calder, stood on one side of him, and his cousin Shaw Tucker stood on the other. The room was a mess. Alafair and Martha stood just inside the front door, behind the men. The little girls were in town with Hattie. A silent and sullen Mr. Bellows and his woozy wife sat side by side on the couch, in handcuffs.

Scott puffed out a noncommittal sound. Or it might have been a laugh. "When Martha come flying into town with her skirt hitched up to her knees and her hair waving in the breeze, I knew something momentous had happened." He drew out the word "momentous," making it seem even bigger than it was. "But you, Pastor, of all people!" He paused and shook his head. "Who'd have believed it? Why did you kill the poor woman, that's what I'm wondering?"

Sister Norma moaned and dropped her aching head into her hands. Bellows awkwardly placed one of his cuffed hands on her knee.

"I didn't kill her, Sheriff," Mr. Bellows vowed, "Jesus as my witness. I was trying to save her. I spent weeks trying to get that woman to renounce her sinful ways and accept Jesus into her heart. I never worked so hard for a soul in my life. But she couldn't change, or wouldn't. Be a submissive and faithful wife, I counseled. She said she'd divorce her husband for shaming her, then turned around and said she loved him and could never leave him. Said she wished he was dead. The Devil was in her. Possessed, I say. She died right here, in this room, in a frenzy of guilt, while I was ministering to her.

"Yes, she came here that night, I admit it. It was late. I was asleep. But I heard her knocking, and let her in. She was a soul in need, Sheriff. She said the awfullest thing—she'd tried to have her husband killed, and would I pray with her. She was wild with shame and grief. She took one of Norma's knives, and before I knew what was happening…" He shuddered, seemingly overcome with the horror of it.

"You're trying to tell me that she did herself in, like Miz Tolland thought," Scott said. His flat tone conveyed his skepticism. "If that's your story, then going to so much trouble to hide her body, then threatening to murder folks when they find a stain on your floor don't make much sense, does it?"

Norma Bellows dropped her hands into her lap and leaned forward anxiously. Her face was alarmingly red. "Sheriff, she was possessed, like Ulises said," she shrilled. "It was the Devil! The Devil done her in! Demons! I saw them in her eyes."

"Shut up, Norma," Bellows hissed.

Scott hushed him with a gesture. "Hang on, now, Pastor. Go on, Miz Bellows. It was demons, you say…"

"They had her," Sister Norma assured him. "I saw her. I wasn't to home when she first got here. I came home late from attending Miz Click at childbirth, and walked into this room to see Louise going after Ulises…"

"Norma! Norma!" Bellows interrupted.

"Pastor," Scott warned, "if you don't be quiet, I'm going to have Trent gag you." He turned back to Sister Norma. "Was Louise trying to hurt your husband?" he asked her.

"The Devil is strong," she told Scott. She was trembling, but she looked more excited than fearful. "I could feel his evil presence when I walked into the house. That's when I saw them here together, Louise and Ulis, right on that old settee, grappling. You don't understand what Satan can do to a man, Sheriff, 'til you see it with your own eyes. I ran back into the kitchen and grabbed that big knife. Louise jumped up and I saw the Evil One in her eyes. I struck her away from Ulis and I plunged that knife in as hard as I could. It was horrible, blood everywhere. Devil's blood, all over my settee, all over the floor, evil blood that would not be cleansed. I poured ammonia on the demon stain, but all my scrubbing only bleached the boards around it." She shook her head.

"I loved that bone knife. I wanted to pull it out, but Ulis said to leave it, that we should take her home, because folks would get the wrong idea if she was found here. I was more than willing to get that demon carcass out of here, too." She smiled at her husband, who looked so pale that Alafair feared he might faint.

"He was right about everything, of course," Sister Norma continued. "We wrapped her in the rug and Ulis took her away. He left it with her body at her house. Then—then! Satan lifted her broken body right up from where we took it and put it down in front of our house!"

Scott nodded. To Alafair's amazement, he was listening to Norma's horrifying story calmly, as though it were the most logical thing in the world. "And then what did you do?" he asked her.

"We had to carry it far from here on the back of our jenny and sink it under some roots in Cane Creek!"

Ulises groaned, and Sister Norma glanced at him, barely distracted. "Satan had her in his grasp, all right," she continued. "It was too late for her, but if I hadn't acted when I did, he'd have had Ulis, too, and right quick. I saved him, Sheriff. I saved him. You don't know."

A dead silence fell. Sister Norma, having explained to her satisfaction, was nodding. Ulises slumped onto the arm of the settee. Everyone else in the room was speechless.

"Hmph," Scott grunted, at length. He looked over his shoulder at Trent. "Deputy, take these folks on over to the jailhouse and lock them up. Then give Lawyer Meriweather a holler. I'll be along directly."

Trent hustled the couple toward the door. Bellows paused as he passed Scott. "She didn't know what she was doing, Sheriff," he said.

"A jury will decide that, Pastor," Scott informed him.

⌁⌁⌁

"Well," Scott mused, after Trent and his charges were gone. "I never did buy that story that Louise committed suicide in her own parlor. Nobody could kill herself like that and not leave blood all over the place. But I was still thinking Billy Bond done it." The sheriff's gaze wandered off into space, and he absently pulled a piece of sassafras candy out of his pocket. He popped it in his mouth as he pondered. "But who could have guessed what really happened?" He shook his head. "So much flimflam…" His gaze shifted to Shaw's face and his blue eyes crinkled. "I been misled, misdirected, bamboozled, and downright hornswoggled."

"I'm inclined to blame the preacher," Alafair stated.

"You would," Shaw said.

"Louise was sad and weak," Alafair continued, ignoring her husband, "and he took advantage of her."

"What about Miz Bellows, Ma?" Martha asked. "Sounds like she did the stabbing."

Alafair shook her head. "Shock must have drove her crazy, is all I can think. She'd sooner believe the Devil was after her husband than that he was a weak man giving in to temptation. At least the pastor tried to protect her just now."

"They said that they are the ones who put Louise in the creek," Scott interjected, "and the jenny with the nicked shoe in their barn pretty much proves it." He gave them a dry smile. "Imagine the look on the preacher's face when the Grants put Louise's body on the road right outside his house just a couple of hours after he had gone to all the trouble to take her home."

"Louise was hauled around something awful after her death," Martha observed.

"That woman was pretty hard done by." Alafair shook her head. "Hard done by."

"What amazes me," Shaw mused, "is why they didn't just brazen it out. So we found that they have knives like the one that killed Louise. She might have stolen it from them. This here stain on the floor could have got there any number of ways. We were just speculating when the pastor overheard us. Why didn't they try to come up with a story? They could have at least thrown us off the scent long enough to make an escape after we went home. Did the preacher think he was going to get away with shooting us all, or what?"

Scott crossed his arms over his chest. "I suspect he didn't think at all, but just panicked. Why did they leave their own kitchen knife sticking out of Louise's chest? It wasn't a well-planned killing from beginning to end. In fact, there wasn't a clear head to be found anywhere that night."

"And yet they almost got away with it," Shaw pointed out. "Thank goodness for Alafair's nose, is all I can say."

Alafair smiled at this. She couldn't smell the ghostly ammonia any more. Now that Louise's killer had been caught, she expected she never would again.

"Who would have suspected them?" Scott said. "I questioned the preacher, but I questioned everybody I thought might know Miz Kelley. It's going to be impossible for him to brazen it out, now."

"A man of God," Alafair said, shaking her head sadly, "using his church's trust and belief in him to lead poor misguided souls astray."

"Is your faith shaken, Ma?" Martha asked her.

Alafair looked at her, surprised that she might think so. "No, hon. Nothing folks do surprises me much any more, and preachers ain't no better than the rest of us. And everybody gets justice in the end, like it says in Galatians, chapter six, verse seven; *be not deceived; God is not mocked; for whatsoever a man soweth, that shall he also reap.*"

Shaw laughed. "Why, honey, looks like you win the scripture quoting contest after all."

Chapter Twenty

It was nearly supper time before Alafair got home, after the time spent collecting the girls from Hattie's, and Grace and the boys from Grandma's, and recounting the afternoon's events to their astonished relatives. Shaw and the boys drove the wagon to the barn, and Alafair sent the little girls to their room to change clothes while she nursed Grace. Martha volunteered to change the baby, so Alafair gratefully sat down in her rocking chair in the front room and removed her shoes before she went into the kitchen to rummage up something for supper. She found Mary and Ruth already laying the table.

"Hey, Mama," Ruth greeted her. "Martha says we missed a bunch of excitement. We started cooking when we heard y'all drive through the gate. Mary already made up a pot of rice."

"Thank you," Alafair sighed. "It's been quite the day. I'm glad y'all girls are home. I expected to have to send Charlie-boy over to Phoebe's to fetch you."

"We've been home a while," Ruth told her. "I wanted to play my piano, and Mary came with me." She gave her mother a sly smile. "Her and Kurt sat on the porch a spell."

Mary shot her little sister a sour look, but after what she had been through earlier, Alafair felt curiously unmoved by Mary's tryst. She tied her apron around her waist and picked up her big wooden spoon to stir the rice. "Where's Alice? She stay at Phoebe's?" she asked.

Mary turned around from the cabinet to look at Alafair. Her forehead wrinkled. "Alice?" she said.

Something—the way Mary looked at her, the tone of her voice, the way the breeze blew in from the window—caused Alafair's heart to skip a beat. She froze with her wooden spoon poised in the air.

"I thought Alice went to the preacher's for dinner with you," Mary finished, baffled, but innocent and unconcerned. "When she didn't come home with you, I expected she stayed at Aunt Josie's."

Alafair didn't reply. She turned on her heel and walked out of the kitchen, through the parlor, and right out the front door, leaving her daughters staring after her, openmouthed. She was down the porch steps and half way to the road when her brain finally re-engaged.

She's a grown woman, Alafair thought, not slowing down at all. She's old enough to make her own decisions, however bad. It's not my place to save her from herself.

She reached the road and turned toward town, walking faster and faster all the while. Her arms were pumping like pistons, and she was still clutching the wooden spoon in her fist.

She's all grown up, Alafair repeated to herself. He wouldn't be the one I'd pick for her, but it's her choice, after all. If she doesn't care that people will talk about her, that's her lookout. There's nothing I can do about it.

By then Alafair was half way to town, her bare feet skimming the dirt road as she walked faster and faster. The look on her face was grim and angry, but two or three tears ran unheeded down her face.

The sun was just sinking below the horizon when she reached the town limits. She stalked down Main Street and turned up Third to Elm before she grabbed her skirt in her free hand and broke into a run. She took the steps up Walter Kelley's front porch in two bounds and flung open the door.

She was in the bedroom before they had time to react, and there she caught them, all in a state of breathless disarray. Walter jumped out of the bed, clutching the sheet to his middle, and Alice struggled to sit up.

"Mama!" Alice gasped.

But Alafair didn't hear her. Nor did she pause, as everything before her eyes went red.

By the time Alafair got home, riding on a blaze mare that she had borrowed from her sister-in-law Josie Cecil, it was dark. Shaw was standing in the middle of the road, pacing up and down with his hands on his hips. He walked up to her when she reined in and seized the horse's bridle. Husband and wife gazed at one another in silence for a moment.

"Y'all eat?" Alafair asked, at length.

"Yes," Shaw said.

"Kids in bed?"

"Little ones are," Shaw told her.

"Did Mary tell you?"

"Yes."

"So you know where I've been."

Shaw nodded. "I figured it out."

Alafair looked off into the distance, then back down at the ashen-faced man standing at her stirrup. "They'll be here directly," she said to him.

"I don't want to see them," Shaw said.

"He's going to ask you for her hand," Alafair continued, as though he hadn't spoken.

"It don't seem that they much cared for my permission before now."

"Shaw…" Alafair began, but he cut her off.

"No, Alafair," he said. "I don't know what you told them, but as far as I'm concerned, they can suit themselves. But I ain't giving them my blessing, that's for sure. They lied to us and snuck around behind our backs like a couple of thieves."

Alafair blinked at him. He didn't even know the half of it, and she had promised Alice that she had no intention of telling him.

She swung down off the horse and landed six inches from his face. She put her hands on his shoulders. "Please, Shaw, please," she breathed. "I know they done bad, but don't turn them away. I'm mad, too, but we can forgive them, can't we?"

Shaw looked down at her, surprised at the urgency of her plea. "But, Alafair, they…"

"Shaw," she interrupted, struggling not to cry, "please. She's my baby. I don't care what she did. I don't want to lose her."

Shaw put his arms around her and sighed a deep sigh.

⌒⌒⌒

Walter and Alice drove up to the house not fifteen minutes later in his Ford touring car. Shaw was sitting on the porch swing with a coal-oil lantern beside him, alone. He did not get up. The young people eyed the father uncertainly for a while, before Walter slowly stepped out of the automobile and walked to the foot of the steps like a man going to his own hanging. Alice climbed out behind him.

"I come to talk to you about Alice, Mr. Tucker," Walter opened.

Shaw ignored him. "Alice, go into the house," he said.

Alice surveyed her father's face anxiously for any sign that Alafair had told him how she had found them in a compromising position. She was relieved to see that Shaw appeared angry and disappointed, but not murderous. He didn't know. "Daddy," she managed, "it's all my fault. Please don't blame Walter."

"Go into the house, Alice," Shaw repeated. "I'll talk to you later."

Alice obeyed reluctantly, walking up the steps and passing Shaw gingerly as she went inside. Shaw's hazel eyes followed his daughter until she disappeared through the screen. His expression was unreadable. He looked back at Walter, still standing in the yard below the porch.

"By all rights, I ought to forbid you to ever see Alice again," he began.

"Yes, sir," Walter said glumly.

"You're a liar and a cheat."

"Yes, sir," Walter agreed.

"I don't blame Alice," Shaw informed him. "She's just a young girl and innocent about the world." His voice raised a little as he warmed to his subject. "But you're a man, and if nothing else, your word ought to be worth something. Which it ain't."

"Yes, sir," Walter jumped in. "I should never have agreed to see Alice before the month was up, I know it. I'm a weak man. I'm like a bee drawn to the sweetest flower in the world. I love Alice, Mr. Tucker. I want to marry her. I'll take real good care of her, and I swear I'll never willingly give her cause to be unhappy."

Shaw eyed the man in the shadows quietly for a second. "Did the sheriff come by and tell you who it was done in your wife?" he asked.

"Why, yes, he come by this evening."

"Was Alice there?"

Walter swallowed. "Yes, she was, but the sheriff didn't see her."

Shaw grunted. "Miz Tucker thinks I ought to let you all go on and get married. She doesn't want for Alice to be divided from the family. So for my wife's sake, I'm going to let this happen without a fuss. But I'm telling you that I was never so disappointed in anyone in my life. It's going to be a tall job for me to ever trust you again."

"I'll see to it that you never again have cause to doubt me, Mr. Tucker," Walter told him. His voice had brightened considerably.

"Well, come on up here, then," Shaw ordered, "and look me in the eye."

Walter walked up the steps and into the golden circle of light cast by the coal-oil lamp on the little table by the swing, and for the first time Shaw could see his face clearly.

"What in the world happened to you?" Shaw exclaimed.

Walter looked back at him out of a hugely swollen and rapidly purpling eye. A long, raw cut ran straight as a plumb line across his forehead. He unconsciously raised his hand to his wounds.

"Wooden spoon," he said balefully. He touched the crown of his head. "You should feel the goose egg under my hair."

Shaw burst into laughter. "I'll swear," he managed, "I do have some fearsome women."

Walter gave him a sheepish grin, and Shaw struggled to contain himself. "Well," Shaw managed at last, "I guess I'd better not ask you to come in, then." He shook his head, serious again. "I'm still mighty angry, don't be fooled. Go on home, now. I'll come into town tomorrow and we'll get this straightened out. Don't try to contact Alice until I say, not if you ever want her to be a part of this family again."

"Yes, sir, Mr. Tucker," Walter acquiesced meekly.

Shaw stood on the porch and watched Walter as he drove away, suddenly feeling much happier.

⌒⌒⌒

Alice Tucker married Walter Kelley on a May morning, in her parents' parlor, with her parents and siblings present, along with her grandparents, several aunts and uncles, many of her girlfriends, and a dozen or so cousins. She was married by her great-uncle, George Tucker, lay preacher and mayor of Boynton. Alice wore her dove- and slate-gray suit with the hobble skirt and peplum jacket, and a sweeping picture hat with three long, jet black feathers in the band across the front. After the ceremony, the family sat down to a wedding feast of slow-roasted beef, brown sugar glazed ham, and a couple of baked chickens with cornbread dressing. There were ten pies: two each of cherry, peach, apple, pecan, one gooseberry, one chess, as well as one fine white frosted sheet cake.

After dinner, the newlyweds drove away in the groom's Ford with their luggage strapped in the back, on their way into town to catch the three o'clock to Muskogee, where they would take the train all the way to St. Louis for a week-long wedding trip.

The men and boys and younger children went outside to sit in chairs under the elms beside the house and smoke and talk or to play, while the women cleaned up the feast. As the afternoon progressed, the weather began to deteriorate. The towering white clouds darkened and lowered, and the wind freshened and changed directions. When the branches on the elms began to whip in the wind and fat raindrops splatter the dust, some families gathered themselves up and headed home. By the time rain began to fall in earnest, only Alafair and Shaw, their children, including Phoebe and her husband John Lee, Shaw's young brother Bill McBride, and Grandma and Grandpapa were left to gather in the front room. Alafair and Martha lit some kerosene lamps as the storm clouds dimmed the daylight.

Alafair sat down in an empty chair close by the bedroom door, where she could watch her family undisturbed and rest her tired feet. For a few minutes, she observed Phoebe's husband, John Lee Day, as he sat beside his wife and gazed at her, his liquid eyes full of adoration. John Lee fit into the family like a hand into a glove. It was hard for Alafair to think of him any differently than she did Gee Dub or Charlie, and even Shaw treated him like one of his sons. John Lee had no blood relations in the vicinity any more. He was theirs and they were his. Alafair loved John Lee, because he loved Phoebe.

It would never be that way with Walter Kelley, Alafair feared. Maybe after years of making Alice blissfully happy, she prayed.

"You're looking mighty thoughtful," Grandma Sally said, as she slid into an empty chair next to Alafair.

Alafair started out of her reverie and laughed. "Oh, I was just thinking about my new son-in-law."

"Alice looked like she was about to take right off into the air with happiness."

"I expect," Alafair begrudged.

Sally's mouth quirked at Alafair's response. "However, you and Shaw looked like you was about to bust into flames."

Alafair emitted a breathy laugh and sat back in her chair, stretching her legs out before her. She sighed. "She lied to us, Ma," she said at length.

Sally's eyebrows raised. "Did she, now?"

Alafair shook her head sadly. "Led us 'round the garden path. In fact, we were pretty much hornswoggled, like Scott enjoys saying. They promised me and Shaw that they'd stay apart for a month, but they only lasted out a couple or three weeks."

"Hmph," Sally commented.

Alafair hesitated, then gave her mother-in-law a sidelong glance. "It was worse than that," she said, under her breath.

A knowing look crossed Sally's face, but she didn't say anything.

"I'm so disappointed in her, Ma," Alafair admitted. "This wedding was harder than all get out for me and Shaw. I could hardly look at her. And she was so happy she didn't even notice."

"But you gave them a nice wedding. Why didn't you and Shaw disown her? Why didn't you throw her out on her behind and let her fend for herself?"

Alafair blinked at her, surprised. "Shaw doesn't know the whole story, and if he did, he'd blame Walter. And as for me, well, she's my girl."

Sally smiled. "There you go."

"I hope you don't think badly of Alice, now, Ma," Alafair said anxiously.

"No, honey," Grandma assured her. "There's nothing new under the sun."

"And you won't tell Shaw?"

"I won't."

"Alice can't see nothing bad in Walter, and I can't see nothing good," Alafair mused. "Ain't it funny how people fool themselves? Just like that mess with Louise Kelley. Talk about hornswoggled! Nellie Tolland blamed Walter for Louise's pretend suicide, so she thought it was justice to make it look like he murdered her. Then, because he had done them a kindness once, Mr. and Miz Grant just knew for a fact that the man they wanted for their daughter would never kill his wife, no matter how it looked. They thought it was all right to fix it to seem he couldn't have possibly done it. And Miz Bellows! She'd rather see the Devil attacking her saint of a husband than believe the evidence of her own eyes—that he was a cheater. Poor old Louise was just a canvas that they all painted their own truth on."

"Sometimes I think everybody makes up the world they live in. We're all so sure of how things are, that we have to try and twist the world around to fit our idea of it. And I guess I'm as bad as anybody."

She paused for a moment, thinking, then flicked a glance at Sally. "Any of your kids ever disappoint you?"

"Every one of my kids has broke my heart," Sally assured her. "And every one has brought me the greatest joy in life."

Alafair nodded. "You know, I was just remembering when Alice was, oh, about six," she mused. "She had this rubber-headed doll. Called him Harvey. I didn't realize that Harvey's bedroom was in the stove. She put him to bed one night real snug all tucked in with his little blanket, and the next morning I fired up the stove all happy and unknowing and melted poor old Harvey's little head all over my nice clean oven. Alice was heartbroken. I'd killed Harvey, don't you know. 'It's so cruel, Mama,' she hollered. 'It's just cruel as knives!' That's the way I feel right now—like a knife in the heart, like the knife that killed the unfortunate Louise Kelley. It's just cruel as knives."

Thunder rumbled in the distance, and then closer, and the rain intensified, pounding noisily on the tin roof.

"Looks like a frog-strangler," Bill observed.

Sophronia appeared at Alafair's side and pushed herself up into the circle of her mother's arm. "I don't like the thunder, Mama," she fretted.

Charlie turned around in his seat and gave his sister a disdainful look. "Thunder can't hurt you, silly. It's the lightning that'll fry you."

"Stop teasing the girls, Charlie-boy," Alafair admonished. Lightning flashed again, and the thunder followed quickly, loud and ominous. The branches of the trailing rose bush next to the house lashed against the window. Blanche got up from her seat on the rug and snuggled herself into the space between her mother and grandmother.

"It's gotten about as dark as nightfall," Mary said nervously.

Shaw put his arm around Ruth, who had pressed herself into his side. "Ruthie, why don't you play us a tune on the piano?" he said. "In fact, Papa, didn't I see that you brought your pipe case into the house earlier?"

"I did, son," Grandpapa Peter affirmed. "And I agree that this here is an excellent time to be playing some music. Gee Dub, my boy, you been practicing on your daddy's old guitar?"

"I have, sir," Gee Dub said.

"Well, go fetch it, then, and if you can find that mandolin y'all used to have, your uncle Bill has been known to pick a tune. Sally, do you have your little flute?"

"It's a wedding, Peter. I brung my little flute in my bag,"

"Bring all the instruments you can find, son," Shaw said to Gee Dub.

Grandpapa removed his uillean pipe from its case, lay it across his lap, and pumped the bag with his arm. Ruth seated herself at the piano. The pipe began to come to life, the drone whining low against the backdrop of the wind and the drum of the rain.

Charlie jumped to his feet. He wanted to play something, too, so John Lee took him out to the kitchen, where they retrieved some spoons and pans for themselves and the little girls, to keep time.

Five minutes later the makeshift orchestra was seated and ready in the parlor as the weather darkened and the gale pounded around them. Grandpapa Peter started out with a long drone, then his fingers moved surely on the chanter, all eyes on him, until his musicians recognized the strains of *Old Torn Petticoat*. Uncle Bill McBride picked up the tune on his mandolin, Grandma Sally on her flute. Ruth and Gee Dub jumped in with their chords, and Martha and Shaw on their fiddles entered on the chorus. Once all the instruments were engaged, the percussion section, who outnumbered the rest of the orchestra, began their stirring, syncopated beat, rattle, pat, jangle, and blow. The thunder boomed. The rain crashed, and the branches scratched at the window as though they were frantic to get into the house. Grace, patting her hands to the music with Mary's help, laughed and burbled. John Lee Day, not yet a fully indoctrinated Campbellite, leaped to his feet and pounded a dance on the wooden floor.

It was black as night outside, now, and the kerosene lamps cast an eerie yellow glow around the room. The storm raged and the music grew louder, as they beat back the Devil.

A blinding bolt of lightning split the darkness, striking a hackberry tree twenty yards from the house, rending it top to bottom. The thunderclap shook the house, followed by a crack as half the tree smashed to the ground. The front door flew open and crashed against the wall. The lamps guttered and blew out, leaving the house in darkness. Two or three girls shrieked, the baby howled, and some boys hollered. The music ceased abruptly, except for the pipe, which breathed out a nasal tone before it died.

And then it was silent. The storm seemed to hold its breath for a moment, as did all the people in that room. Even the wind had stopped.

Out of the silence came three raps at the window—loud, slow, and clear.

Ruth screamed and threw herself into her father's arms. Sophronia and Blanche buried their faces in Alafair's lap, whimpering, and Charlie burrowed between her skirt and her chair like a rabbit going to ground. Nobody else breathed.

Except for Peter McBride. He cast a long glance at Sally before he spoke. "*Sha*, now, young'uns!" he exclaimed. "It's only your Grandpa Jim Tucker, wanting to know if we're all right." He stood up, clutching his bagpipe to his side. "Don't fret yourself, Jim," he called. "Your family is fine."

The rain began to fall again, softly and straight down. Alafair stood up and retrieved some matches from beside the stove, and with children trailing on her arms and legs, went around and relit the lamps. Everyone was breathing now, safe again, all together. All except Alice, Alafair thought. She suddenly felt a deep kinship with Jim Tucker, who had such love for his family that he reached out from the other side to know that they were safe. Then and there she made a plea to Shaw's father, whom she had never known, to keep an eye on Alice.

Alafair's Recipes

FISH

Oklahoma creeks and farm ponds are home to catfish, perch, and crappy (a type of perch, pronounced "croppy," and not "crappy" at all). All of these varieties of fish have tender white flesh and are very bony, requiring the utmost care to eat.

CLEANING FISH

Wash and scrape the scales. Cut off the head, slice down the belly from stem to stern, and pull out the innards. Butterfly the fish and peel out the backbone and as many of the larger bones as possible. Rinse the fish again. Fish guts make very good fertilizer for the garden. You can keep the cats and dogs out of the garden better if the viscera are well composted before using.

FRYING FISH

Large fish may be cut into fillets, small fish may be halved or fried whole. Dip the cleaned fish in cornmeal—or in egg, then flour—or nothing at all if you are a purist. Put enough drippings or lard in the bottom of an iron skillet to float the fish. Heat the fat, but don't let it smoke. Fry the fish slowly, flesh side down, turning when lightly browned.

You can reuse fat in which fish has been fried, but it will be fishy-tasting, so don't combine it with other meat-drippings.

MASHED POTATOES

The queen of vegetables, the ultimate comfort food, infinite use for the leftovers.

Boil peeled and quartered potatoes in salted water to cover until very soft. Drain off most of the water and mash the potatoes with a potato masher. Save the potato water to use for soup, or drink it with a little salt, like tea. It's very nutritious.

Add hot milk (How much? It depends on how tender you like your potatoes. Add about a quarter cup at a time, mash awhile, and see how it looks) and butter, and beat until fluffy.

Place into a serving dish, make a small well in the top of the mound of potatoes, and place therein a dollop of butter to melt.

POTATO PATTIES

There are as many ways to make potato patties as there are potatoes in the world. This is Alafair's usual workaday recipe.

2 cups leftover mashed potatoes
1 cup bread crumbs
Flour for dredging

In a bowl, thoroughly mix crumbs and potatoes with your hands. Form the patties with hands to desired size (3" in diameter, 1/2" thick, is a handy size and holds together well). Dredge the patty in flour and fry in about 1/2" of hot fat. When one side is crispy brown, flip and fry the other side. Drain on a towel-covered plate. Variation: mix 1/4 cup of finely chopped onion in with the potatoes and bread crumbs before dredging.

POTATO PATTY SANDWICHES

Slather mustard on a piece of bread. Arrange several rings of sliced red onion on the bread, then one or two cold potato patties. Top with another slice of mustardy bread. Squash the top piece of bread down with hand until ingredients cohere. Especially good on whole wheat or rye bread.

NOODLES

1 beaten egg   2 tbs. milk
1/2 tsp. salt   1 cup flour

Combine egg, salt, milk; add enough flour to make a stiff dough. Roll a rectangle of dough very thin on a floured surface and let it sit for about 20 minutes. Slice noodles to desired length with a sharp knife, separate them and let them dry for a couple of hours. Drop into boiling soup or broth or boiling salted water and cook 10-15 minutes.

For the over-arm method of stretching your noodles, place a clean dishtowel over your forearm. Slice your noodles about an inch wide, 1/2 inch thick, and a foot or so long. Peel the noodles up and arrange along your forearm rather like tinsel hanging over the bough of a Christmas tree. Go about your business (carefully) for a few minutes until gravity has stretched the noodles to twice their original length. When you remove them from your arm, you may either cut them into shorter segments or use them like linguini. One can also stretch one's noodles by hanging them over a rack, but that isn't nearly as interesting.

BUTTER

Strain the milk that comes right out of the cow through a cheesecloth into a clean milk can. Let the milk stand in a cool place until the cream separates and rises to the top. Skim off the cream into a separate container. The milk that is left in the can is what would nowadays be called "skim milk." Alafair would have called it "bluejohn".

Pour a mixture of three parts cream to one part whole milk into a butter churn which has been scalded with boiling water and then rinsed with cool water. Churn fast at first, then more slowly as the butter forms. How long this takes varies with the weather. When the butter has formed, spoon out the bits with a perforated ladle and plunge into cold water. The butter will float off the ladle. Collect the butter from the water and place it on a work surface. Sprinkle with a little salt (1 tbs. to 1 lb. of butter). Press and knead with wooden spoons or shapers to drain off extra liquid and work in the salt. Form the butter into a loaf and place in a cool location to harden. Butter can be pressed into molds to make fancy or festive shapes.

SUGAR TIT
(ADA Very Much Disapproved)

Place about 1 tbs. of sugar in a mound toward one corner of a clean cotton dish towel. Fold the corner of the towel up over the sugar and tie the corner into a large knot with the sugar inside. Leave the rest of the towel loose. You should now have something that looks like a comet with a small head and a very long tail. Give the knotted towel to the baby to suck. The sugar will liquefy in the baby's saliva and give the knot a sweet taste. Chewing the hard knot will massage and soothe sore gums, and the bulk of the dishcloth will keep the child from swallowing the knot. How it is that a child who sucked sugar tits during infancy ever avoided decay long enough to sprout any teeth at all is a question for the ages.

OATMEAL

Soak one cup of oats in a quart of water overnight. Boil for about 30 minutes in the morning. Without soaking, oats would require a couple of hours of steady cooking to make it digestible. Alafair would not have had access to instant oatmeal.

Serve with cream and sugar and a dollop of butter, or in the Highland way, add a pinch of salt and eat while standing by the fire. Why this must be eaten standing up is unknown. Perhaps if one's digestive tract were not perfectly straight, oatmeal in this semisolid, gelatinous state might be in danger of getting caught on something before it reached the stomach.

WILTED LETTUCE

1 bunch of leaf lettuce
6 thinly sliced radishes

4 slices of bacon
2 chopped green onions

Shred lettuce into a warmed serving bowl. Toss with radishes and onions, season with salt and pepper to taste.

Fry the bacon until crisp and crumble over salad. Pour the hot bacon grease over the lettuce. Toss to coat. Serve right away.

PHOEBE'S FAVORITE CHESS PIE

The chess pie that one finds in restaurants these days, if one finds it at all, often resembles a lemon custard. Alafair's chess pie was plain, gritty, straightforward, and inexplicably delicious.

1 cup sugar
3 heaping tbs. cornmeal
1 egg
1/2 cup of butter

1/2 cup sweet milk
1 tsp. vanilla
pinch of salt

Mix sugar and meal. Add beaten egg and butter and mix well. Add milk and vanilla. Pour into uncooked pie shell. Bake slowly at 300 degrees until firm.

TEA SYRUP

Like your iced tea sweet? This will do it for you. The idea behind tea syrup, which is an ultra-sweet tea concentrate, is that one can make iced tea without having to steep the leaves in boiling water and then cool it down every time she wants a glass, or even a pitcher. Here are a couple of recipes:

6 cups of water
1 cup of tea leaves
4 cups of sugar

Bring the water to a rolling boil, then add the tea leaves. Remove from heat and let it set for 15 minutes. Pour the hot tea through a strainer into the sugar and stir until the sugar is dissolved. Store the syrup in a bottle or other handy glass container. Use one cup of the syrup to about one quart of cold water to make a pitcher of tea. This will keep in the ice box for up to two weeks.

Simply must use tea bags? Here is a recipe using tea bags that will yield a smaller amount of syrup.

3 cups of water
10 tea bags
3 cups of sugar

Boil all ingredients together in a large pot for 10 minutes. Cool down and pour into a bottle. Keep refrigerated. Mix four or five parts water to one part syrup, depending on how strong you like it.

Place Names

Boynton (BOYN-ton) — located in eastern Oklahoma, in Muskogee County, 60 miles southeast of Tulsa. Named for E.W. Boynton, chief engineer on the Shawnee, Oklahoma, and Missouri Coal and Railway line, which ran through the town.

Checotah (shuh-KO-tuh) — named for Samuel Checote, Chief of the Creek Nation, this town is located in McIntosh County, about fifteen miles south of Muskogee.

Council Hill — A former Creek meeting place, now a town situated some ten miles south of Boynton, in Muskogee County.

Lone Elm (lone ELL-um) — a tiny spot in the hills near Mulberry, which is just east of Fort Smith, in extreme northwestern Arkansas. The name of the town comes from a freestanding elm tree. The locals, however, who included Alafair's birth family, the Gunns, would never have called the tree an "elm." The Ozark pronunciation is "ELL-um." Just like it is in parts of Ireland. Lone Elm was a major stage coach station on the Old Wire Road, which ran from Memphis to Santa Fe. Contingents of the Cherokee Nation passed through Lone Elm on the Trail of Tears in 1838 and 1839, and often stopped to refill their water tanks on the Little Mulberry Creek.

Muskogee (mus-KO-ghee) — located about 15 miles northeast of Boynton. County seat of Muskogee County and location of the Federal courthouse. Named for the Muscogee (Creek) Indian Nation.

Okmulgee (ok-MUL-ghee) — located about 15 miles west of Boynton. County seat of Okmulgee County, and capital of the Creek Nation.

Tahlequah (TAL-eh-kwah) — located some 50 miles northeast of Boynton. County seat of Cherokee County and capital of the Cherokee Nation of Oklahoma.